The Love of Her Life

THE CALLAGHANS & MCFADDENS: BOOK 3

Kimberly Rae Jordan

THREE**STRAND**
PRESS

A CORD OF THREE STRANDS IS NOT EASILY BROKEN.

Kimberly Rae Jordan
PO Box 40083 Lagimodiere PO
Winnipeg, Mb R2C 4P3
Canada
www.kimberlyraejordan.com

Publisher's Note: This is a work of fiction. Names, characters, places, and incidents are a product of the author's imagination. Locales and public names are sometimes used for atmospheric purposes. Any resemblance to actual people, living or dead, or to businesses, companies, events, institutions, or locales is completely coincidental.

Book Layout © 2014 BookDesignTemplates.com

The Love of Her Life/ Kimberly Rae Jordan. -- 1st ed.
978-1-988409-20-7

You will show me the path of life;

In Your presence is fullness of joy;

At Your right hand are pleasures forevermore.

Psalm 16:11

ABE CALLAGHAN WATCHED THE WISPS of clouds slip past the window as the plane glided through them, enjoying the sight of his hometown's snowy landscape as it came into view. No matter where he traveled or what cities he visited, this one on the Canadian prairies would always be his home. Even with its frigid winters and mosquito-filled summer days, Winnipeg still held a special place in his heart. He may have craved adventure and spent more time away from the city than in it—especially of late—but his family lived there so as often as his adventures allowed, Gabe went home.

The plane rumbled as the wheels were lowered, and the drop in altitude continued to make his ears pop. Gabe swallowed hard, shifting in his seat as his thoughts turned to what was to come. Considering his penchant for dangerous adventures, he knew that being afraid of something like a plane taking off and landing was a bit of a contradiction, but there was no adrenalin rush for him when the plane left or returned to earth, only anxiety and nervousness. Neither of which he enjoyed feeling. Give him a cliff edge or deep underwater cave any day of the week.

Even though he hated the landing part of the flight, Gabe couldn't keep from watching as the plane descended toward its destination. Judging from what he saw, the city had already received a snowfall or two, so there was definitely a white Christmas in his future. At least coming from Colorado, the cold and snow wouldn't be too much of a shock for him, although it was going to be colder than what he had experienced in Denver.

As he saw the edge of the runway through the window, Gabe tightened his hand on the armrest and squeezed his eyes shut, saying a quick prayer for safety. After the wheels hit the ground and the plane lumbered down the runway, engines roaring as the brakes slowed it down, he opened his eyes. He let out a long breath, grateful to once again be safely on the ground.

Once the plane began taxiing toward the James Richardson International Airport, Gabe turned his phone back on and immediately found a text from his brother.

Mitch: *Only you would end up on the flight that's two hours late. I should make you take a cab.*

Gabe grinned as he tapped out his reply.

Mom would kill you if you did. Don't be a baby and have a Tim's double-double ready for me.

Mitch: *Demanding much?*

Never. And get me a chocolate glazed donut too.

Mitch: *Stop texting and get off the plane...*

Gabe glanced over to see the aisle packed with people eager to disembark. Being a couple of hours late meant that they had arrived after midnight, and he could understand why the passengers were eager to get off. He, however, didn't feel a strong need to be in the press of people in the aisle, so he waited until most had cleared out before he retrieved his hand carry from the overhead bin and left the plane.

When he finally reached the top of the escalator leading down to the baggage retrieval area, he paused to see where Mitch was waiting. It didn't take long to spot his twin, and as Gabe had requested, he stood there with two disposable cups and a paper bag in his hands. Grinning, he stepped onto the escalator, shifting the strap of his backpack on his shoulder.

As he pushed through the metal gate at the bottom of the stairs, Mitch came toward him, a smile on his face. They'd seen each other in August when their sister, Makayla, had gotten married, and they had Skyped regularly, but Gabe was always glad to see his twin brother in person. He was the older of the two, having been pulled from the womb two minutes before Mitch, and being the great brother he was, Gabe never let Mitch forget it.

"Coffee and donut as requested," Mitch said as they neared each other. "You owe me."

Gabe took his cup and the donut bag then gave Mitch a one arm hug. "Thanks, little brother."

Mitch rolled his eyes. "Ready to go?"

"Actually, I have a checked bag to pick up."

"Really? You usually travel pretty light," Mitch said as they began walking toward the baggage carousel.

"Eh, it's Christmas. I bought some presents," Gabe admitted. He wasn't a big one for buying gifts, but for some reason, he'd decided to pick up a few this year.

"Well, wonders never cease." Mitch took a sip from his cup. "And here I thought I'd need to put *From Mitch and Gabe* on the gifts I bought, like I usually do, and send you a bill for half."

The baggage claim conveyor belt started up with a kick. Gabe glanced around, not surprised to see that he and Mitch were garnering a bit of attention. It wasn't a rare occurrence when the two of them were together. Between their height—and looks, if he was honest—and the fact that they appeared almost identical, they usually had more than a few people watching them.

Mitch, however, seemed oblivious to it. "I told Mom you could stay at my place tonight, so they didn't have to wait up."

"I'm not sleeping on the couch, dude, so I hope you have a king size bed now." Gabe watched as the bags began to circulate around the carousel, keeping an eye out for his own.

"Yeah, no worries. I inherited Grace's old bed when her condo sold. It's a nice big king size bed."

Gabe bent over and grabbed the handle of his suitcase, hefting it off the conveyor belt. Mitch took it from him and pulled the handle up. Wheeling it behind him, Mitch led the way to the exit, weaving among the other passengers who were standing around the baggage claim area.

Bracing himself for the cold, Gabe took a deep breath before walking through the rotating door into the cold wintery night. The snow sparkled a bit like diamonds in the lights that shone overhead. Though he wanted to appreciate the beauty of it, the cold definitely detracted from sparkly snow. Instead, he just focused on following Mitch to his vehicle, taking sips of his coffee as he walked. Gabe was relieved to see the vehicle was running, knowing he'd appreciate the warm interior when he climbed in.

"How long are you sticking around?" Mitch asked as he guided his SUV out of the parkade a few minutes later.

"I had planned to stay until after the new year, but honestly, this cold is making me want to leave tomorrow."

"Just keep drinking Tims. That'll warm you up from the inside out," Mitch said as he lifted his cup to take a quick sip.

Gabe continued to drink his own coffee, watching as familiar scenery slipped by on their way to the apartment block their father owned and where several of their siblings and friends lived. One of the apartments was to have been his, but since he traveled so much, Gabe hadn't felt the need to take up space. It had worked out, though, since his family had recently done an apartment shuffle and the one that would have been his was now inhabited by one of his sister's best friends.

He loved Winnipeg since it signified home for him, but he wasn't sure he'd ever live there permanently since he needed more adventure than the prairie city had to offer. It was okay to come and visit for a short time, but for the types of things he liked to do, he needed mountains or fast flowing rivers, at the very least. Which meant he was more likely to settle down in British Columbia or Alberta on the north side of the border or Colorado on the south side, but he was always happy to come home to visit the family.

This time he had business to attend to as well. If he was going to be able to continue to travel, he needed to touch base with a few of his friends with whom he was in partnerships. New things had come up over the past few weeks that were better dealt with in person than through emails or Skype calls.

The windows of the apartments in the building were all dark when they arrived. In spite of the caffeine in the coffee, Gabe felt exhaustion begin to seep into his body as he followed Mitch through the back door and into his apartment. It didn't take him long to change into a pair of pajama bottoms and a T-shirt. Mitch followed suit, and then he pulled out a blanket for Gabe before they crawled into the large bed that now dominated Mitch's room.

"That should keep you from stealing *my* blanket," Mitch said as he pulled the duvet that had been covering the whole bed over to his side. "I swear, if it's missing when I wake up, you're on the floor."

Gabe chuckled and wished he had the energy to do something about it, but he'd been up since six that morning so getting into any mischief would have to wait. "Your blanket is safe. For tonight."

It didn't take Gabe long to fall asleep, exhaustion finally taking its toll.

"WHERE ARE YOU GOING?"

Maya St. James flinched at the sound of her mother's voice behind her. She paused for a moment, schooling her features into a pleasant expression—or what she *hoped* was a pleasant expression—then turned around to face her mother who was already dressed for the day in a long sleeve fitted dress and pumps. Her face and hair were, as always, impeccably done.

Yuka Zevardi took her role as Maya's mother as seriously as she did her role as wife to one of the richest men in the world. It was a rare occurrence to catch her mother without her hair and makeup done and wearing a designer outfit. Though Maya understood why her mother was that way, she didn't want to live that life herself. Unfortunately, her mother stubbornly refused to accept her choices.

"I'm going to work, Mama." Maya clenched the strap of her purse, the leather edge pressing hard into her palm. "Like I do every day."

"I have told you to quit." Her mom walked toward Maya, her heels clacking on the marble floor. "Why are you still there?"

Maya had tried to avoid her mother each day when she left for work which meant that sometimes she left super early and spent an hour or so at the Tim Hortons near the office until it was time to go to work. The argument was old, and Maya wearied of having it whenever she failed to escape the house early enough.

"I'm not going to quit, Mama." Maya straightened her shoulders and met her mother's dark gaze straight on. "I like what I do, and my employer says I'm doing a good job."

Her mom crossed her arms and settled her weight on one slender hip. "Why are you doing this? You don't need to work, and by working, you're taking a job from someone who might need it more than you do. Are you comfortable with that knowledge?"

Maya frowned at the twinge of guilt she felt at her mother's question. "I don't even know if anyone else applied for the job, but they made the decision to hire me. To give me a chance."

"Why do you insist on working?" Her mom stared at her, her dark gaze intent. "You don't need to."

As Maya tried to keep her irritation from showing, she said, "I need to get out of the house. I can't just sit around in my room doing nothing."

"You could come with me and learn about things like fundraising and charitable organizations," her mom said. "Those are honorable things."

"Mama, I know they are honorable things, and I'm involved with several of them, but what I'm doing is good too. You have something to do that you enjoy, I should be able to have that same privilege. I love my job, and I'm working with good people." Maya lifted her chin. "I'm not going to quit."

Before her mom could respond, her phone rang. She fished the phone out of her pocket and pressed it to her ear. Maya took advantage of her mom's distraction to give a quick wave and escape out the door into the large heated garage where her car was parked. The car she'd bought by herself after much research. It was yet another thing her mother had objected to, but Maya had stood her ground, and surprisingly, her father had sided with her.

She hit the switch to open the large door behind her car. There were three other vehicles in the garage which was a bit ridiculous since it was only her mom and dad who lived with her in the house.

Thankfully, her mother's distraction hadn't made her too late, so Maya was able to go through the drive-thru to get herself a coffee and a toasted bagel with cream cheese. It was a cold day, but Maya didn't mind. She never complained about being out in the weather because there had been a time when she hadn't been able to go outside at all, so she didn't take it for granted now.

When she finally settled behind the receptionist desk at C&M Builders, Maya smiled at the sense of belonging that filled her. She checked her email—the one they'd set up for her when she'd started working in August—and began to jot down notes on what she needed to work on that day.

A short time later, the front door of the office opened, and Maya looked up to see Mitch Callaghan walk in, bringing with him a gust of cold air. He unwound a dark blue scarf from around his neck as he stomped his feet to rid them of snow, then approached her desk, a wide smile on his face. Maya smiled back, but then her smile faded into confusion as she took in the man's appearance. It looked like Mitch had visited a tanning salon, had his hair highlighted and grown out some scruff since the previous day.

"Well, aren't you a beautiful addition to the office," he said with a wide smile, showing off his even white teeth.

"Uh…" Maya frowned, a little uncertain how to take the change in Mitch. In the almost five months she'd been working at C&M Builders, Mitch had never flirted with her. And while she didn't have a lot of experience with the opposite sex, she was pretty sure that flirting was occurring.

"Don't harass her, Gabe."

Gabe?

Maya's gaze bounced between Makayla Collins and the man standing on the other side of the desk. His grin grew even wider as he went to Makayla and wrapped his arms around her.

"I didn't know you were coming into the office today," Makayla said as they stepped apart.

"I called Bennett a little bit ago and got his permission to use the boardroom to meet with Forrest and Tennyson." Gabe swung back her way, his blue eyes vibrant as they stared at her. "So, I'm guessing this is Grace's replacement."

"Well, actually, we don't view her as a replacement as we hope she'll stay with us even when Grace comes back." Makayla gave her a smile. "Maya, this is Gabe, Mitch's twin, in case you couldn't tell. Gabe, this is Maya St. James."

Gabe reached his hand across the desk. When Maya slid her hand into his, Gabe's fingers closed around hers and didn't let go. She could feel the roughness of his skin against her palm. And the warmth and strength of his hand as he held hers.

"It's a great pleasure to meet you, Maya St. James." He continued to hold her hand, his grip firm but gentle. She, no doubt, could have freed her hand if she'd been so inclined. "Where have you been all my life?"

Maya felt her eye brows rise and figured they must be up near her hairline, even as heat flooded her cheeks. She had to admit that she was a bit confused by her reaction to the man, but he didn't seem to be suffering from the same malady. Or was that just the way he was with everyone? It seemed to be at complete odds with Mitch's more reserved personality.

"Uh…it's a pleasure to meet you as well." Maya let go of his hand, needing to break that connection while she tried to figure out how to take this man. He was unlike anyone in the family she'd met so far. Actually, he was unlike anyone she'd ever met. Period.

"Don't mind Gabe, Maya," Makayla said with a disapproving look at the man. "He can be a bit overwhelming, even to those of us who've known him for years."

Before Maya could reply, the front door opened again, and Mitch walked in. She couldn't keep from smiling as he did the very same thing as Gabe had when he'd arrived. After stomping the snow from his boots, Mitch joined the group.

"Good morning, Maya and siblings."

Now that the two men were standing side by side, the differences were clear. Though it was very apparent they were identical with their striking blue eyes and dimples in their cheeks, Mitch's reserved personality showed through in his slower smiles and his quieter nature.

When they'd first met, Maya had thought Mitch was cute, but other than that, she hadn't felt drawn to him as anything more than a co-worker. It was completely different from how she couldn't seem to keep her gaze from going to Gabe. There was just something about him that appealed to her. It was like he radiated life with his sparkling eyes, wide smile and larger than life reactions to things.

Gabe draped an arm around his brother's shoulders. "How's it going, Mitchy?"

Mitch rolled his eyes but didn't shrug off Gabe's arm. "It's going fine. What are you doing here? I thought you were going out to the house."

"I'm here to make use of the boardroom to meet with Tennyson and Forrest. But why didn't you tell me about the lovely new receptionist?" Gabe gave her another smile, and Maya felt her heart skip a beat.

"Didn't you come by the office when you were here in August?" Mitch asked, stepping away from Gabe. "She's been here since just before the wedding."

"I came by the office, but I know I would have remembered meeting her." Gabe put his hands on his hips and frowned. "What I don't understand, though, is why she didn't know about *me*."

Mitch shook his head. "I don't talk about you all the time, Gabe."

"Well, apparently you don't talk about me at *all* to Maya."

The door opened again, stopping their conversation as they turned toward it. Two tall men walked in, and Gabe moved in their direction. "Hey, guys. Good to see you."

"Glad to see you're still in one piece," the tall one with dark blonde curls said, a smile on his face as he held out his hand to Gabe.

"Always." Gabe shook his hand then held it out to the other man.

"None of that." The dark-haired man grinned as he bumped Gabe's hand out of the way and wrapped him in a quick hug. "Good to see you again, man. Even if I did have to get up at the crack of dawn to do it."

"Lazy, dude." Gabe punched his shoulder. "I went to bed at almost one and was up by seven."

"Not all of us are suckers for punishment," the man replied with a grin.

After Makayla and Mitch had said hi, Gabe introduced them to Maya. "These are my friends and business partners, Tennyson Page and Forrest Williams."

After they had all exchanged pleasantries and shaken hands, Gabe turned to Maya once again. "Do you have plans for lunch?"

"Plans for lunch?" Maya wasn't sure she'd heard him correctly.

"Yeah." He tilted his head as one corner of his mouth lifted. "I'd like to take you out for lunch."

Maya felt a burst of excitement, but at the same time, she was nervous. It was a rare thing she went out with anyone but her parents. Since starting with C&M Builders, she had joined the staff on Fridays for lunch sometimes, but she'd never gone out with a guy. Just the two of them.

She glanced over at Makayla for some guidance, but the other woman just gave her a slight smile and a shrug. With equal parts trepidation and eagerness, Maya turned back to Gabe and said, "No, I don't have plans for lunch."

"Perfect," Gabe said, his smile broadening. "Now you do."

"Okay." Maya hoped the smile she gave him in return was as enthusiastic as his.

"See you in a bit." He swung back to the two men as if it was the most natural thing to invite a woman out to lunch then go back to business. "Let's go, guys. I've got plans."

When they'd gone down the hallway to the board room, and Mitch had headed for the back offices, Maya turned to look at Makayla. "Um. Was that okay?"

Makayla tilted her head. "You mean accepting Gabe's invitation for lunch?"

Maya nodded. "I wasn't sure what to say."

"It's fine," Makayla assured her. "But only go if you want to. Don't feel pressured. I know Gabe can be a force to be reckoned with."

Maya thought about it for a second then said, "I do want to go. He seems like a really interesting person."

"Oh, he's interesting all right," Makayla said with a rueful grin. "Just don't fall in love with him. He doesn't live here. And probably never will."

Makayla's words sank in, but somehow it didn't dim the interest Maya had in the man. As a whole, the Callaghan and McFadden family was fascinating to her. Since she was an only child, it was so interesting to see the interactions between the siblings she saw at the office. Even the youngest ones, whom she'd met when they'd stopped by, seemed to get along really well with their older brothers and sisters. So it wasn't a surprise that Gabe Callaghan interested her, but her intrigue of him was more than she'd felt for any of the others.

"Just tell me when you guys are taking off for lunch," Makayla said.

Maya nodded then returned to her work as Makayla went back to her office. Although, how she was supposed to concentrate on work with a lunch date looming, she didn't know.

Chapter Two

*G*ABE LISTENED—SORT OF—as Tennyson gave the run-down on a company they were to start working with in the new year. Usually, he was excited about a new project, but this time around, he found he was distracted by thoughts of the woman at the reception desk. He regretted not having met her when he'd come for the wedding in August. To have lost four months of knowing Maya St. James seemed a shame.

He tried to keep his focus on the discussion as they broke down their responsibilities for the next project. It wasn't a difficult thing to do since they each had skills and interests that allowed them to naturally take on different roles within the projects they were working on. Of course, Forrest liked to discuss it all anyway. Tennyson and Gabe were convinced it was mainly so he could hear his own voice. They tended to let him ramble on and then just followed through with how they usually did things.

When the conversation shifted away from his part of the upcoming project, Gabe found his attention drifting as well. How could it not, when he still was trying to figure out his reaction to the woman with the dark brown eyes, framed by even darker lashes, set in a delicate face? The slight tilt to her eyes, her silky dark hair, and the light tan of her skin spoke of a mixed heritage, and Gabe wanted to find out what that was. And he wanted to learn about her family and all the things that made her who she was.

Something told him that one lunch wasn't going to be enough.

He'd be hard pressed to explain to anyone the way his interest had been piqued from almost the moment he'd laid eyes on her. Seeing her working at the desk immediately told him that she was a good person since his family wouldn't have hired someone who wasn't. A quick glance at her left hand had shown it to be free of rings, so he'd assumed she wasn't engaged or married. But it had been the flare of interest in her eyes that had let him know that there wasn't another man in the picture, and that was what had prompted the lunch invitation.

Was it love at first sight?

Before that day, Gabe would have said no because he hadn't believed it to be possible. However, he couldn't deny that he'd never reacted to anyone at first meeting the way he had to Maya. If there was one thing that Gabe had always done, it was to follow his instincts. And in this particular case, his instinct said to get to know Maya St. James.

"So I guess we're not going for lunch, eh?" Forrest asked when they finished up an hour and a half later.

"Sorry, boys," Gabe said as he got to his feet, gathering up the papers and his laptop. "Maybe next time."

"I absolutely can't believe you're putting a woman ahead of us." Forrest sounded outraged, but Gabe knew he was only joking. "We always do lunch or dinner after our meetings."

"Yeah, but you know how I am. Never letting an opportunity pass me by."

The two guys good-naturedly grumbled their way out of the building, appeased by Gabe's offer to meet up with them for dinner later. Once they were gone, Gabe went back to Maya's desk where she greeted him with a tentative smile.

He leaned a hip against the desk and crossed his arms. "So, what are you in the mood for?"

"I don't know." Maya gave a slight shrug of her slender shoulders. "I'm not really too fussy."

"You're not a vegetarian?" Gabe asked.

"No, not at all."

"How about Montana's? Would that work for you?"

Maya smiled as she nodded. "Sure, that would be great."

"Are you ready to leave now or do you need some time?"

After a glance down at her desk, Maya said, "Maybe give me about five minutes."

"Sounds good. I'm just going to talk to Bennett." Gabe gave her a wide smile before heading down the hallway to find his older brother.

MAYA SAVED THE FILE she'd been working on for Makayla then sat for a moment, trying to calm the nerves that were fluttering in her stomach. She'd been able to ignore them while she was working, but now that lunch time was drawing close, the butterflies were back.

The thing causing her the most anxiety was wondering if the lunch invitation was actually a date. Her inexperience with stuff like this—even at the age of twenty-four—left her feeling confused and uncertain.

Given the way she'd been forced to live her life, Maya had often wondered if this day would ever come. If a man would ever have enough interest in her to want to spend more time with her. To ask her out on a date.

Maya hoped that this *was* a date since Gabe was the first man that she'd really felt this kind of attraction to. Though she wanted to spend more time with him, she was still a bit nervous about it. After all, they'd only just met. Was it normal to feel that way about someone so quickly? Unfortunately, she had no one to ask in the few minutes before they were due to leave.

One very good thing about this being a lunch date—if it was an actual date—was that her mother wouldn't have a chance to interfere. Maya had no doubt that if her mother had been aware of the invitation, she would have found some way to put a stop to it.

"Ready to go, beautiful?"

Heat rushed to Maya's cheeks at Gabe's words. She'd never considered herself beautiful, so to hear that word from a man she'd just met was something of a surprise.

"Um…yes, I'm ready." Maya got up and retrieved her purse from the desk drawer.

"Is this yours?" Gabe asked as he motioned to the coat rack behind her desk. At Maya's nod, he plucked it off the hook and held it for her. She slid her arms into the sleeves, and after he lifted it onto her shoulders, she quickly buttoned it up. "Makayla, we're off!"

Makayla popped her head out of her office. "Okay. Have fun."

"No worries. Fun's my middle name," Gabe called back as he opened the front door.

As Maya walked out of the building with Gabe by her side, she began to consider something else that hadn't occurred to her earlier. Though she'd felt comfortable with all the members of the Callaghan and McFadden family she'd met so far, she had managed to keep conversations fairly surface. They didn't know anything about her past, and she'd given only the most vague information about her family. And she definitely preferred to keep it that way. However, now that she was going to have this time alone with Gabe, he was probably going to be asking her questions she wasn't entirely comfortable answering.

At his vehicle, Gabe opened the passenger side first, offering his hand with a smile to help her climb inside. May hesitated for just a moment before taking his hand, appreciating his strength as she stepped up into the truck. He waited until she was settled in her seat and buckled in before closing the door. Maya took advantage of the few moments alone in the cab of the truck before Gabe climbed behind the wheel to try to settle her nerves by taking a couple of deep breaths.

"Is Winnipeg your hometown?" Gabe asked as he steered his truck out of the parking lot a few moments later.

"Yes. I was born here." She hesitated. "How about you?"

"I was born in Brandon but grew up in a small town not too far from Winnipeg."

"When did you move here?"

Gabe didn't answer right away, and Maya wondered if she'd inadvertently steered the conversation into a touchy area. She'd thought it was a fairly safe question, but now she wondered if it was something negative that had forced them to make the move.

"Dad moved us to Winnipeg when I was around five. I didn't know the reasons at the time," Gabe began, pausing again as he turned onto the highway. "When my parents divorced, my mom didn't ask for any sort of custody of us four boys. Instead, she went on to remarry and have another family. Living in a small town, there were rumors spread and lots of gossip about us which was made worse because our situation was fairly high profile since my mom's dad was a former mayor of the town. Finally, my dad decided we'd be better off in Winnipeg. And we were. Almost right away, we met my step-mom, Emily, and her four kids." Gabe tossed her a quick smile as he pulled into the parking lot of the restaurant. "And the rest is history."

Grace Moore, the woman she was covering for while she was on maternity leave, had given Maya a brief rundown of the blended family—although she'd left out the *Mitch has an identical twin brother* bit of information. She hadn't asked many questions because she hadn't wanted any asked of her. Also, Grace had had other things on her mind with her husband's recent passing and her pregnancy.

"So you've been working for the company just since August?"

"Yes. Right before Ethan and Makayla's wedding. They hired me to help Grace out and then to cover for her once she went on maternity leave."

"Where did you work before this?"

That was one of the questions she didn't want to answer because it would only lead to more questions, but she couldn't bring herself to lie. "This is my first job in the field since finishing my business admin course."

She saw the surprised look Gabe shot her as he turned off the truck's engine.

"Uh, how old are you?" He lifted a hand off the steering wheel. "Wait. That's not a question I'm supposed to ask a woman."

Maya gave a soft chuckle. "I'm twenty-four."

"And this is your first job?"

"Doing this type of work." That wasn't necessarily a lie.

Thankfully, he didn't pursue anything further since they needed to get out of the truck. As they walked on the snow packed parking lot to the sidewalk in front of the restaurant, Gabe placed a hand on her back. When they approached the door, he opened it and held it for her so she could enter the restaurant and escape the cold.

They were seated quickly and left with menus. Even as she glanced over the options, Maya tried to organize her thoughts so that she could hopefully control the conversation and keep it away from the things she didn't want to talk about yet. It was just too bad that most casual conversation between two people just getting to know each other included a lot of what she didn't want to share yet.

Knowing that this wasn't going to be a long meal since she needed to get back to work, when the waitress returned, Maya just ordered a sandwich while Gabe went for a burger and fries. After the waitress collected their menus and left them alone, Gabe leaned forward, his arms resting on the table and his bright blue gaze focused on her.

Before Gabe could pose any questions to her, Maya asked, "Since I haven't met you before, I'm assuming you don't live here."

"No, I don't live in Winnipeg full-time, but when I'm not traveling the globe, I'm either here or in Denver."

"Is the traveling for your job?" Maya wondered what he had been thinking, asking her out when he wasn't even living in Winnipeg. She recalled Makayla's caution about not falling in love with him and knew she needed to take that advice to heart.

"Sort of, but most of my work is related to business interests I have here in Winnipeg. Fortunately, I can do a lot of that work remotely." Gabe reached out and ran his fingers along the sides of his glass of soda. "I travel mostly for adventure."

"Adventure?"

A big smile spread across Gabe's face, his dimples deepening. "Yep. I like Bungee jumping. I like rock climbing. Skydiving. Scuba diving. Anything that gives me a rush."

Maya considered his words, wondering what it would be like to do things like that. She hadn't even considered attempting anything that dangerous. Over the years, just doing what she had to, to get to that point in her life, had been a rush for her.

"So what do you do for fun?"

She'd been so caught up in her head, Maya had forgotten to continue to ask him questions. There was no way to avoid answering him, so she scrambled for a response that would satisfy him and was truthful.

"Well, I'm definitely not into the extreme kind of fun you are," she said with a smile. "I tend to stick close to home."

"And do what?" Gabe prompted, apparently not willing to let her off the hook.

"I like to read. I do some cooking. I enjoy swimming and spending time on the computer."

Gabe arched a brow. "Not at the same time, I hope."

"At the same time?"

"Swimming and spending time on the computer."

Maya laughed. "I do like to multitask but not to that extent."

The waitress appeared with their food, and the conversation ebbed for a bit as Gabe said a prayer of thanks for the meal—after checking that she was okay with that—and they began to eat. Maya was actually surprised at how relaxed she was considering the direction the conversation had taken.

"You said you like reading," Gabe commented between bites of his burgers. "Who is your favorite author?"

"It's really hard to choose just one. I read voraciously." Her love of reading had been somewhat forced on her in her early teens when she'd been stuck inside for months on end. "I like suspense and psychological thrillers. Stuff that's a bit on the frightening side."

"Really? You like being scared?"

"I guess so," Maya admitted. "That's probably how I get *my* adrenaline rush."

"I enjoy thrillers as well. Also stuff by James Patterson and others like him. I spend a lot of time on planes, so I read quite a bit. I also read a lot of non-fiction."

Books seemed to be a safe subject for them, and they stayed on that topic for quite some time. They veered a bit into movies and TV, with Gabe revealing a preference for movies since it meant he didn't have to commit to watching a new episode of a show each week. Maya, on the other hand, preferred TV shows where she could become involved in storylines and characters.

Maya found that she was disappointed when the meal ended and they had to head back to the office. She wondered if this was just a one-time thing. Considering that Gabe would most likely be leaving again soon, it might be better if it was. There was no doubt that he held a fascination for her that she'd never felt for any man before, but if he wasn't going to be around much, that wasn't a good thing for her.

AFTER HELPING MAYA OFF WITH her coat back at the office, Gabe found himself lingering by her desk, unwilling to end their time together, but then the phone rang, grabbing Maya's attention and reminding Gabe she had a job to do. Gabe knew he should let her get back to it, but he wasn't interested in leaving the building just yet. He gave her a broad smile, then headed down the hallway to where the offices were located.

Gabe stuck his head into Tristan's office and spotted him sitting with his back to the door, facing his monitor. "Hey, Tris. How's it going?"

When Tristan didn't respond, Gabe plopped down in one of the chairs next to his brother's desk. He waited for a moment, then gave the desk a kick. That got Tristan's attention, and he spun around in his chair, tugging his earbuds out.

"Hey," Tristan said with a growing smile when he spotted him. "Just a second." He swung back to his monitor and tapped a couple of keys before turning his attention back to Gabe. "So what are you doing here at the office?"

"Had a meeting and then took Maya out for lunch."

Tristan's brows rose. "Took Maya for lunch?"

"Yeah." Gabe paused then asked, "How well do you know her?"

"Not too well. I mean, she seems like a sweet girl. She's friendly and helpful." Tristan tilted his head. "I'm afraid I don't know much about her personally. Makayla's probably the one you should be talking to. Or Grace."

"Grace is a bit busy at the moment," Gabe pointed out. "Maybe I'll have a little chat with Makayla later."

"Why are you so interested in her?" Tristan asked, a quizzical look on his face.

And wasn't that just the question of the hour? Gabe sat for a moment, trying to come up with an explanation. On the one hand, it was no surprise that he'd asked her out. He tended to live life following his instincts and impulses. When he'd walked into the office and seen Maya's friendly smile, he'd known he wanted to get to know her better. Though he'd found it amusing to realize that she'd initially thought he was Mitch. It had been awhile since that had happened.

Still, he wasn't completely sure how to answer Tristan's question. "Her smile just did something to me and made me want to get to know her better. So, I asked her out."

Tristan grinned as he shook his head. "Only you, Gabe."

"You weren't interested in her, were you?"

His brother shook his head. "Not me, but I'm not sure about Mitch."

"Bennett?"

"I think that's a definite no. Benn's hung up on Grace."

"Seriously?" Gabe had suspected—once upon a time—that Bennett had a thing for Grace, but he'd figured that Bennett had gotten over it when she'd married Franklin.

"It seems that way. He'd been spending a lot of time with her and was with Grace when the baby was born, but since then, he's kind of distanced himself from her for some reason." Tristan's brows drew together. "But you know what Bennett's like. He's not really talking to anyone about what's going on."

Gabe nodded, understanding completely how Bennett was. He had never been a guy to confide in people. At one time, his main confidant had been Kenton, but in recent years, there was a noticeable tension between the two of them. Gabe made a note to spend some time with his older step-brother while he was there. Though he wasn't always around when his siblings might need someone to confide in or lean on, if he was there when they needed support or a confidant, he tried to step up.

"So, if you and Bennett aren't interested in Maya that just leaves Mitch."

Tristan shrugged. "Yeah. I don't know how he might feel about her. He hasn't said anything to me."

The fact that Tristan wasn't saying for sure that Mitch *wasn't* interested in Maya made Gabe feel a little unsettled. He had to wonder if his brother might have feelings for her. However, Mitch hadn't mentioned anything about her, and they'd always talked about everything—especially girls that snagged their attention. Surely if Mitch had been interested in Maya, he would have said something.

"I'll have a conversation with him tonight," Gabe said as he got to his feet. He decided he needed to leave the office and head to his parents' house. Until he had a chance to chat with Mitch, he didn't want to think anything more about Maya. Although that might be nearly impossible, he would make a concerted effort.

"Are you planning to hang around this time?" Tristan asked as he swung side to side in his chair.

And yet another question he didn't want to answer. "For now, just until after the new year."

Tristan scowled, a rather unusual expression on his face. "Then why are you even trying to start something up with Maya? If you're just going to leave again, that's not fair to her."

Gabe could hardly deny the truth in Tristan's words. But there was just something about Maya that made him want to get to know her better. To be a part of her life. Honestly, what he was experiencing might seem a bit ridiculous to people watching it unfold, but to him, it felt completely natural. He'd felt the urge to get to know her, so he'd asked her out for lunch.

He still wasn't sure it was love at first sight, but clearly, there was something about her that had drawn him in. Now he wanted to find out what that was. He just had to figure out what he was going to do if Mitch did, in fact, have an interest in Maya.

Chapter Three

I'M GOING TO HEAD OUT NOW."

Maya looked up from the files in her lap at the sound of Gabe's voice. She smiled as he came to a stop in front of her desk. "Thank you again for lunch."

"It was my pleasure." He pulled on his jacket and looped his scarf around his neck. "Would you be interested in doing it again?"

A frisson of excitement shot down her spine, but she also felt a bit like she was at a crossroads. Was she willing to allow her emotions to get more involved with this man who would be leaving again in a few weeks? She couldn't deny that she wanted to get to know him better, but she had no experience in these sorts of things and wasn't sure that she was equipped to handle the type of relationship that he might require considering his frequent travels.

Sure, it might seem like she was getting ahead of herself, thinking about being in a relationship with Gabe. However, the reality was that this could be the start of one, so she needed to be sure it was what she wanted.

Carpe diem, sugar. Carpe diem. That's what you need to do.

Seize the day. That's what her best friend—the one she'd met online but never in person—had drilled into her since the beginning of that year. That's how she'd ended up with a bank account she'd set up on her own, a new car, and a job. Was it possible she might even end up with a relationship?

"I think I would be," Maya said, hoping that seizing the day didn't lead to heartache down the road. But maybe that was something she needed to experience. After all, by the time most people were twenty-four, they'd had at least one heartbreak. Maybe it was just her time.

"Great!" Gabe reached into his jacket and pulled out a card. "This is my cell number. Can you text me, so I have your number?"

Maya took the card. "I'll do that."

Gabe walked backward toward the front door, keeping his gaze on her. "Talk to you later." With a final smile, he turned to push open the door and left the building.

She sat and stared at the door for a moment before looking down at the card in her hand. Should she text him right away? After a brief internal debate, Maya set the card to the side. She needed to focus on work. He'd been enough of a distraction to her day.

When Maya left the office a few hours later, even the fact that it was already dark couldn't dampen her good mood. And when she got home and found out that her mom was heading out to a Christmas party with her dad, her mood improved even more. It meant she had the whole evening without having to worry about her mom coming to her room and trying to talk her out of working—or ever leaving the house.

Maya popped into the kitchen to find Elisse, their cook, standing at the counter with a bowl in front of her.

"Hello, darling," Elisse said when Maya pressed a kiss to her cheek. "It's just you for dinner tonight, so I made lasagna."

"Oh yum," Maya said as she hopped onto a barstool at the island counter. "I'm going to eat in my room tonight, I think."

"Sounds good." Elisse gave her a wink. "I think I'll see if Thomas is interested in joining me."

Maya laughed. "Excellent idea. I think he loves your lasagna as much as I do."

"You're not wrong," Elisse said as she set a tray on the counter then fluffed her silver curls and gave Maya a wink. "And I don't think that's all he loves."

Maya laughed at the older woman's antics, knowing that she was right. Both Elisse and Thomas, their daytime driver, had been previously married but had lost their spouses within a year of each other. Maya had known each of the deceased spouses and knew that they would be happy if Elisse and Thomas found love again with each other.

As Elisse worked to get her meal together, Maya pulled her phone out of her purse along with the card Gabe had given her. She stared at her phone for a moment before tapping his number into a contact screen and then sending a quick message.

Hi, Gabe. This is my number. -M

Gabe: *Finally! I was beginning to wonder if you had lost my card. ;)*

Nope. Sorry. Just wanted to wait until I got home.

Gabe: *You're a good employee!*

I try! :-)

Gabe: *Oops...gotta run. Getting called for dinner and we're not allowed to have phones at the table. Chat later.*

Maya smiled at his words. She'd heard Danica—the youngest daughter of the Callaghans—telling Sierra, Ethan's teenage sister, how she'd missed a text from a guy she liked because she wasn't allowed to have her phone at the table.

She set her phone down on the counter, watching as Elisse put an oval dish with a baked lasagna in it on the tray. Maya knew that the lasagna was made with eggplant instead of noodles, but that was only because her mom and dad weren't home. There was a bowl with a salad and another one with a selection of berries. She so appreciated that Elisse was willing to work with what she wanted to eat even if that happened primarily when her parents weren't dining at home.

"There you go, sweetie," Elisse said as she pushed the tray toward Maya.

"Thanks so much, Elisse. It looks delicious." Maya slipped her phone onto the edge of the tray and carefully picked it up.

Once in her room on the second floor of the west wing of the house, Maya put the tray on her desk then went to change into something more comfortable. It didn't take long to slip out of the pencil skirt and loose blouse she'd been wearing and into a pair of yoga pants and a long sleeve T-shirt.

Maya flipped the switch to bring the gas fireplace to life then turned off all but the lamp on her desk. Circumstances beyond her control had kept her in this room for a good portion of the last decade of her life. One would think she would hate the room, but the opposite was true. Her mother had given her free rein to do what she wanted with the large suite, so Maya had spared no expense creating a haven for herself.

From the large four poster bed to the comfy chairs in the seating area, everything had been chosen with an eye to pleasing her aesthetically or because it was comfortable. The sage green walls were offset with chocolate trim. The curtains and bedding contained both colors while the windows were covered by darkening blinds since there were times she slept late into the day. It didn't happen as frequently now, but at one time, it had been the norm for her.

Once she had everything set up to her satisfaction, including a playlist of music drifting softly in the air, Maya sank down into the chair at her desk and brought up the chat program on her laptop. With a sigh of contentment, she took a bite of the lasagna, savoring the rich tomato flavor mixed with the cheeses she loved so much.

After a moment, she leaned forward and typed out a message in her chat program. *I met a guy!*

It took all of five seconds for the familiar sounds of a Skype call to start up. She'd figured that comment would be the one that would prompt a response out of her best friend. Okay, pretty much her *only* friend. The one who knew almost everything about her life. Almost.

From the moment they'd met in a cancer survivors online group three years ago, they'd had a connection. Close in age, they'd had similar cancer journeys, and even though they had opposite life stories, Lainie Deyes had become a super important person to her.

Though they were very close, Maya had never told Lainie that her family was rich. Very rich. And courtesy of a trust fund her father had set up for her, Maya was rich in her own right. But that wasn't information she tended to share with people since when someone found out about her wealth, it seemed to be a relationship changer.

Plus, when her dad had given her her first laptop and allowed her access—albeit rather limited—to the internet, he had emphasized quite heavily that she needed to keep her identity under wraps. He'd done what he could to protect her, including giving her his mother's maiden name because of his own very distinctive last name, so even as an adult, she'd continued to keep her connection to her father and mother a secret. She knew that Lainie just assumed her parents were Mr. and Mrs. St. James.

Her dad had even gone so far—once she'd reached adulthood—to set up an apartment in a building he owned in her name. She used that for all snail mail correspondence and had given it when applying for the job at C&M Builders. In the current day and age when everyone had access to Google Earth or map apps on their phone, typing her actual address into any of those would have been fairly revealing.

Though she'd balked at all the measures her dad wanted to take, she'd stopped complaining when word came of a kidnapping attempt on the teenage son of an acquaintance of her dad's. He'd let it be known that she could agree to the measures he insisted on, or she could have a full-time body guard. Needless to say, she agreed to everything he'd insisted she do for the sake of her safety. Which had included not revealing everything about herself to her best friend.

It wasn't like she'd lied to her, but that was only because Lainie hadn't asked the right questions. Ones like: *So is your dad in the top 10 of Forbes Richest Men?* Or *Does the square footage of your house rival a mall's?* or even *Does your home come with an indoor* and *outdoor pool, a bowling alley and a movie theatre?*

With a sigh, Maya took a glance behind her to make sure that the laptop wasn't aimed at the room at large. Once she was sure that all that Lainie could see would be the wall behind her with a small painting on it, Maya clicked to accept the call and start up the video.

"A guy?" Lainie shrieked as her image came up on the screen. Her blonde hair created a curly halo around her head, and her blue eyes were huge. "A real, honest-to-God man?"

Maya laughed. "Yes. A real man."

"Oh, my goodness. You have to tell me all about it." Lainie leaned in close to the screen.

"I'm going to eat while I talk because I'm hungry," Maya said as she picked up another forkful of food. "Remember how I told you about Mitch at work?"

"Yeah, you said he was cute, but you didn't seem into him."

"I wasn't. I'm still not, but no one told me he had a twin brother. An identical twin brother who I actually *am* attracted to."

"Really? He looks the same as Mitch, but you're attracted to him when you weren't to Mitch?" Lainie's brow furrowed as she spoke.

"I don't know how to explain it except that Gabe exudes a zest for life that Mitch doesn't seem to have. Or at least not in the same way that Gabe does." Between bites, Maya went on to tell Lainie all about her time with Gabe, answering each of the questions her friend had. Telling someone about it made it real, and Maya felt another burst of excitement.

"I can't believe the guy asked me out the first time we met," Maya admitted as she picked up the bowl of berries then pushed the tray to the side.

Lainie laughed. "I can't believe that you said yes!"

"Well, that's your fault. If this all falls apart, I'm going to blame you."

With a hand pressed to her chest, Lainie leaned back in her chair. "Why me?"

"You were the one who told me to seize the day," Maya reminded her. "So when he asked me out, I seized the moment and said yes."

"Are you going to go out again?" Lainie asked. "It seems like he must have felt the connection as much as you did."

"I think so." Maya pulled her legs up into her chair and crossed them. "He gave me his number, and we texted for a couple of minutes earlier."

"I think that's so cool. What a start to a relationship."

"Well, if that's what this is." Maya looked down and plucked at the material of her pants. "When should I tell him? Maybe he'd reconsider things if he knew."

She didn't have to clarify what she was talking about. Lainie knew exactly what she was referring to. Maya looked up to see her friend's frowning face on the laptop screen.

"Oh, sugar. I don't know."

It was a subject they had discussed a few times, but they'd never been able to figure out the best thing to do. Telling someone you had

had cancer, not once, but twice, wasn't exactly first date chat material. And yet, was it fair to continue to date without giving him all the information?

It was one of those things that weighed on Maya, and for the first time since feeling that connection with Gabe, she questioned if she was doing the right thing. She couldn't guarantee that the cancer wouldn't return. The chances that she might have to deal with it again in her lifetime were higher than for the average person. Was it fair to ask a man to take on that possibility?

"This is probably not going to go anywhere," Maya said, but even as she voiced the thought, her heart rebelled at the idea. "He doesn't live here. How could we have any sort of relationship if he's not even around?"

"Well, if you don't think he'll be around long, maybe you don't have to say anything about it." Lainie tapped a finger to her lips. "At least not for now. If something changes and it seems like you guys might be getting serious, you could tell him then."

"I still can't believe that he wanted to go out with me," Maya said with a grin at the memory.

"Why not?" Lainie asked. "You're cute and so sweet. What's not to like?"

"You're just being nice," Maya said with a laugh as she drew her legs up and wrapped her arms around them.

"I'm not. I just hope that someday I meet a guy that wants to ask me out the first time he lays eyes on me." Lainie glanced away from the camera then said, "I'll be right there." She looked back at Maya and made a face. "I need to go. We can chat later. I'm happy for you, sugar!"

Lainie's image winked out before Maya could say anything. She stared at the screen with a frown and wondered if there was stuff going on in Lainie's life that she wasn't telling Maya. Over the years, Lainie had shared about her family. How her parents had split up and how Lainie felt responsible for it since it happened after her first cancer diagnosis. Also, she had three siblings—one older brother and a younger brother and sister—none of whom she was close to. Maya had hoped that would change for her now that her cancer was in remission, but she wasn't sure that was happening.

With a sigh, Maya leaned forward and closed out the program. She sat for a moment before getting to her feet and picking up the tray. The kitchen was empty when she got there, so she put her dishes in the dishwasher. After filling her water bottle, Maya returned to her room, determined to stay there so she wouldn't run into her mom whenever she got home from her party.

Back at her desk, Maya picked up her phone and glanced at its screen, surprised to see a text message from Gabe.

Gabe: *Are you going to the company Christmas party on Friday?*

Maya dropped down onto her bed and leaned back against her pile of pillows. Remembering her conversation with Lainie, she debated how to respond.

IGNORING THE CHATTER going on around him, Gabe kept checking his phone. While he didn't think Maya was sitting around waiting for a text from him, he hadn't thought it would take fifteen minutes—or longer since he was still waiting—to hear back from her.

The couch next to him shifted, and Gabe looked over to see Mitch settled down beside him. "So, I hear you had lunch with Maya."

Yes. I did." Gabe slid his phone into his pocket so he wouldn't be tempted to keep checking it while he talked to his brother. "Is that going to be an issue for you?"

Mitch stared at him for a moment before he sighed. "No. I think she's nice and all, but it was clear pretty quickly that she didn't have any interest in me. I thought she was sweet—is sweet—but clearly not for me. Kinda sucks to think it was my personality that was lacking since we look the same."

"We look the same? No way, dude," Gabe said as he bumped Mitch's shoulder. "I'm the handsome one."

"Jerk," Mitch muttered as he returned the shoulder bump. "Are you going to ask her out again?"

Gabe nodded. "I'm kinda hoping she'll go with me to the Christmas party. Do you know if she plans to go?"

Mitch shrugged. "I don't know. You might have to ask Makayla about that. She talks to Maya way more than I do."

"She probably won't help me out," Gabe said as he glanced over to where his step-sister stood with her husband. "She already kinda said something about me getting involved with someone when I don't live here full-time."

"That is something to consider. It's not really fair to Maya." Mitch paused. "I mean, are you just wanting to get to know her as a friend? Or is it something more? Something that might end in marriage?"

"Marriage?" Gabe turned to stare at Mitch. "How did we get from going to the Christmas party together to marriage?"

"You know that Dad has always told us that we shouldn't date just for fun. If the person isn't someone we're willing to marry, we shouldn't be dating them."

Gabe fought the urge to roll his eyes. "How else are you supposed to get to know a person if you don't go on dates? I have no idea if I would be willing to marry Maya because I don't know her. Going on dates is my way of remedying that."

Mitch stared at him for a moment before looking away. "I guess, in the end, it's between the two of you. Just know that Makayla wouldn't be the only one upset if you did something that hurt Maya. Don't lead her on. I think that's the most important thing. If taking her out is more about just having some fun while you're here, make sure that she knows that up front. Something tells me, from the little I know of her, that she doesn't just date for the sake of dating." He hesitated, still not looking at Gabe. "But who knows. I could be wrong."

Ugh. Why did Mitch have to drag it all down? He'd always been the more serious of the two of them, and sometimes it drove Gabe absolutely nuts. Why couldn't his twin be less of a stick in the mud? He was always so serious and so focused on doing mundane things. The way Gabe looked at it, he didn't have the time to wait around to get to know Maya by hanging out with her in group settings. For all he knew, she didn't socialize with his family outside of work events.

His phone vibrated in his pocket, and Gabe pulled it out to see that Maya had replied.

Maya: *Yep. I plan to be there.*

Gabe had planned to ask her to go as his date, but Mitch's words kept repeating in his head. Even though they'd frustrated him, he couldn't ignore them.

Excellent! I'm going as well so I'll see you there.

Maya: *I'm really looking forward to it. Makayla has told me a little bit about the plans for the evening, and it sounds like fun.*

There was no doubt it would be a fun evening. His dad spared no expense when it came to the annual Christmas party for C&M Builders employees. The venue would be decked out, and the food would be excellent. In addition to a live band that would play Christmas music all evening, there would also be gifts and recognition of employees. All in all, it was a great time for the forty employees and their dates. Usually some of the company's business contacts attended as well.

So what have you been up to this evening?

Maya: *Had some supper. Chatted with my best friend. Watching some Netflix at the moment. How about you?*

Had a family dinner at my folks' place. Catching up with the siblings. Trying to figure out how Mitch and I are twins when we're actually total opposites. I'm exciting and fun to be around, and he's a stick in the mud.

Maya: *I'm sure you know that Mitch isn't really a stick in the mud. He's been so sweet to me since we first met.*

Great. Now he'd made her defend Mitch. That wasn't exactly what he'd hoped to do. He'd said it in jest, but it seemed she didn't know him well enough yet to realize that.

Well, once you get to know me better, you'll see that I'm definitely the more handsome one.

Maya: *LOL As far as I can tell—aside from a tan and a few high-lights—you guys are identical.*

Yeah, we are. I'm the older one. Has Mitch told you that? Probably not. He doesn't like identifying as the younger brother.

Maya: *I'm an only child, so I have no idea what it's like to have an older or younger sibling. Are you guys close? In spite of one of you being a live-wire and the other a stick in the mud?*

We are, really. But we have certain roles to maintain. I like to tease him and he likes to be teased.

Maya: *Somehow I'm not too sure about the second part. : D*

"Hey there, son. Planning to join the conversation?"

Gabe looked up at his dad who stood next to the love seat where he and Mitch were sitting. "Sorry, Dad. Let me just finish this."

His dad gave him a nod as he settled into the recliner next to where he sat. Makayla was curled up beside Ethan on the couch while Bennett sat in an armchair, his legs stretched out and his fingers laced over his stomach. He was staring into the fireplace, seemingly oblivious to the conversations going on around him.

Sammi—his other step-sister—was there with her boyfriend, Jayden. They'd been dating for a while now, and she seemed smitten. Gabe was going to have to do his duty as older brother and interrogate the dude at some point. But not right then.

He looked back down at his phone and tapped out a message. *Gotta run! Had fun chatting. Look forward to doing it more. Hopefully in person. ;)*

Maya: *Yes, it's been fun. Have a good night.*

Gabe hated having to end the conversation, but he knew that his dad would keep sending frowns in his direction if he continued to focus on his phone instead of his family. Even Dalton—the youngest of all of them—apparently knew better than to be on his phone when his mom and dad gathered them all together.

He stared at the huge tree twinkling in the corner of the family room, its branches dripping with decorations. They'd already decorated it before he'd arrived home because his mom liked having the tree up by December 1st. Christmas was definitely in full swing at the Callaghan-McFadden home.

Gabe smiled as he leaned back in the loveseat, happy he'd decided to come home early for Christmas. Usually, he showed up a couple of days beforehand, but this year, he'd had the extra time and had decided to spend it in Winnipeg with the family. And he'd even shown up with Christmas presents, though now he was giving serious thought to trying to find something for Maya too.

He wouldn't mention that to anyone though. No doubt they'd think he'd lost his mind.

Chapter Four

HERE ARE YOU GOING?"

Maya fought the urge—yet again—to roll her eyes at the question. It seemed to be the only one her mother asked her anymore. At least her mother could truly plead ignorance of the answer—unlike weekday mornings—since it was late Friday afternoon, and Maya was all dressed up to go out. That, in and of itself, was a rare occurrence.

"Where are you going?" her mom repeated, this time in Japanese. As if Maya might not have understood the question in English.

Maya smiled at her, trying to hide her irritation because she really *did* understand why her mom was always asking her where she was going. She just didn't like it. "The company I'm working for is having their Christmas party this evening. I'm going."

Her mom's brows drew together as her gaze traveled from the top of Maya's head to her shoes. "You look beautiful."

A rush of warmth flooded Maya, and her smile became more genuine. "Thanks, Mama. I wasn't sure what to wear to a company party, but I hope this will be okay."

"You've been to your father's parties before," her mother said.

Yeah, she had been, but it had been a few years, and even then, most people hadn't known who she was. Her father had guarded her existence very carefully, and her "date" for those parties had always been Elisse and a bodyguard who monitored anyone who came in contact with her.

At those parties, she and her mom had usually been the best dressed people there. It was a bit of overkill when it came to their outfits, and something Maya had hoped to avoid with the dress she'd chosen for this particular party. And she'd be lying if she said she hadn't wondered about what Gabe would think of any outfit she chose. Surely it was a bad sign that after knowing Gabe for not even a week—and sharing only one meal with him—she was choosing outfits based on what he may or may not like.

"Do you want to have Jeffrey drive you?"

Maya thought about turning down the offer, but the idea of not having to drive on the snowy streets was actually appealing. They had two drivers who were on-call all the time. Thomas for daytime and Jeffrey for evenings. "You and Dad don't need him?"

"No. Your father and I are dining at home tonight, but we'll be out tomorrow night."

"In that case, yes, I'd like to have Jeffrey give me a ride."

Her mom gave a quick nod before heading toward an elegant phone that sat on a narrow antique table in the large foyer. An enormous poinsettia also sat on the table, just one of many decorating their mansion for the Christmas season.

"Hello, Jeffrey. We need you to drive Maya to a Christmas party, please." Her mom paused then said, "Yes, she's ready to leave shortly. Please use the Mercedes."

"Thanks, Mama," Maya said, still sort of amazed that her mom was being so agreeable about her evening plans.

"I hope you have a lovely time," her mom said with a smile that didn't quite reach her eyes.

Though she'd originally planned to wear boots, if Jeffrey was going to drive her, he would drop her off right at the door of the venue. She ran back upstairs to her bedroom to put on the shoes she'd abandoned earlier. Sitting on her bed, she bent over to fasten the ankle strap of the black velvet platform shoes that had a chunky curved heel. They added about four inches to her height which brought her to the lofty height of five foot seven.

After the shoes were secure, Maya got to her feet. She walked over to her mirror to take one more look at the outfit she'd chosen. She'd changed so many times that she'd actually run out of options, which was hard to do since she had an abundance of clothes. The final outfit she'd decided on consisted of a black skater style skirt that ended above the knee, worn over a pair of black tights. The skirt had a wide waist band into which was tucked the fitted deep red blouse she'd chosen. It had a solid red strapless bodice overlaid with matching lace that rested just off her shoulders and extended to her wrists.

She'd managed to do her hair in an updo with loose curls. Thanks to the huge number of beauty tutorials on YouTube, she'd managed to figure out how to do the hairstyle and also her makeup. Watching YouTube videos had been just one of the many ways she'd tried to fill the hours of each day before she'd gotten her nerve up to apply for a job which would require her to leave the house.

Her jewelry consisted of pieces her parents had given her over the years—a matching white gold necklace and earring set with diamonds that hung in delicate teardrops. The diamond bracelet that circled her wrist was a gift from her father on the day they'd received the news that her cancer was once again in remission. And the delicate ring she wore had three stones in it. The center one was her birthstone while the ones on either side represented her parents. The ring had been a gift from them on her eighteenth birthday.

Though all the jewelry was quite simple in design, anyone with an eye for the authenticity of the diamonds would know that the pieces' combined worth was in the thousands of dollars.

After a final spritz of *Nuit De Noel Parfum* by *Caron*, Maya once again left her room and went downstairs to find her long black cape. She was just fastening it when the front door opened, and Jeffrey stepped inside wearing his chauffeur uniform. He smiled at her as he waited by the door. Jeffrey had started working for them four years ago, and Maya knew that he was being trained to take Thomas' job when the older man retired.

"Good evening, Miss Maya," he said as she approached him, pulling on her gloves as she walked.

"Hi, Jeffrey." Though Maya tried to engage in a less formal manner with the staff, some were reluctant to embrace it. She knew that they were probably worried about their jobs if her mother got wind of them being too familiar, so Maya never forced them. "Good night, Mama."

Her mom gave a slight nod of her head, her hands clutched together in front of her. Clearly, she was anything but happy about Maya's evening out, which made Maya wonder what was going on in her mom's head. She didn't think for a minute that her mother had had a change of heart when it came to her life outside the gates of their mansion.

Jeffrey held the rear passenger door open for Maya and waited until she was settled before closing it. Maya looked out the window at the door of her home, a large wreath festively decorating it. Only in the last few years had she come to realize just how ridiculous their lifestyle was. Especially in light of where her father had chosen for them to live. Maybe if they lived in Vancouver or Toronto, their wealth wouldn't have been as noticeable, but in Winnipeg, it was a guarantee that no matter where they went, they would be the wealthiest people there. It was just one more reason she was grateful for the lack of connection between her and her parents in most circles.

"Where am I going, Miss Maya?" Jeffrey's voice interrupted her musings, and she looked to the front of the car and saw that they had reached the end of their very long driveway. He had come to a stop, awaiting further direction.

Maya passed on the information that Makayla had given her to a venue located not that far from their house. She'd been there for a wedding a few years ago, and it had been beautiful. She was excited to see how they'd decorated it for Christmas.

And yes, she was excited to see Gabe. Now that she was out from under the eagle eye of her mom, she could allow the smile she'd been fighting to curve the corners of her lips at the thought of seeing him again.

Jeffrey had Christmas music playing softly over the radio as he drove, so by the time they reached the turn-off for the venue, Maya was in the Christmas spirit and very ready for the evening ahead. As they made the last turn to reach the entrance, she could see how beautifully decorated it was on the outside with lots of twinkling white lights while lighted Christmas trees stood in each of the floor to ceiling windows along the front. The driveway led to the porte cochère of the venue.

After Jeffrey had pulled the car to a stop under the covered portion of the looped driveway, he got out and came around to open the door for her. "Would you prefer me to wait here or do you have a specific time you wish me to return for you?"

Maya took his hand and exited the car. "You can go back home. I'll text you when I'm ready for you to pick me up. It's not too far away."

Jeffrey nodded. "I'll wait for your text."

He accompanied her to the front door and opened it for her before returning to the vehicle and driving away. Maya hoped that no one had seen her arrival, but given the fact that there were a lot of large windows in the foyer, it was likely someone had.

"Good evening, Maya."

She turned to the sound of the voice, her cape swirling out around her. There was no doubt that it was Gabe headed her way. He and Mitch may have been identical, but Maya had no longer had any trouble telling the two of them apart.

His smile grew wider as he came to her side. "I was wondering when you were going to get here. May I take your coat?"

Maya lifted her hands to undo the clasp on the neck then turned to allow Gabe to take it from her shoulders. She slipped off her gloves and reached to shove them into one of the pockets of the cape, clutching her purse in the other. "Thank you."

She didn't miss the way Gabe's gaze traveled over her. It took a similar path as her mother's had earlier, but its impact was completely different. The appreciation in Gabe's gaze for her appearance brought heat to her cheeks and a small smile to her lips.

"Well, let's get this hung up so we can mingle for a bit before going to our seats." He laid a hand lightly on her back as he steered her to where someone was checking coats for the evening. After he had handed it over and given her the ticket which she slipped into her purse, he said, "I made sure that we were seated at the same table."

Maya gave him a quick look. "Is there assigned seating?"

"No, but I asked Sammi to save us seats at their table."

"Sammy?" Maya asked, wracking her brain for the person associated with the name.

"Sammi is one of my younger sisters." Gabe gave her a curious look. "You don't know much about my family, do you?"

"Um…well, I've…I guess I haven't really socialized with them much." Maya gripped her purse. She had been invited to join them on a few different occasions, but she'd declined each time. She'd been afraid of having to reveal too much about herself if she became social with them instead of just maintaining an employee/employer relationship.

"After tonight, you'll have no excuse not to. The family business has needed to expand beyond just family members, but we like the employees to feel as if they're part of our extended family."

Maya had seen that but had resisted being drawn in. She had a feeling that all of that was going to change that night. As they moved through groups of people in the foyer area, she recognized a few faces, but most were unfamiliar to her.

"You look beautiful, by the way," Gabe said as he guided her toward where Mitch stood with a couple of people she didn't know.

"Thank you. It took me far too long to decide what to wear."

"Well, it was definitely worth the effort." Gabe looked down at her and smiled.

Warmth crept through her at his compliment. Aside from the odd compliment given her by her parents or Elisse, Maya wasn't used to people showing their appreciation of her appearance. It was something she found that she enjoyed, knowing that she'd made an effort and someone had appreciated it. Or rather, not just *someone* but Gabe.

The thought made her pause, totally unaware of the conversation going on around her. This man's opinion was coming to mean too much to her too soon. They'd only known each other such a short amount of time. That thought scared her a bit. What if she started to feel more and more drawn to him while the connection was just a bit of fun for him while he was there for the holidays?

Was this her time to fall in love and experience her first heartache? Or was it possible for her to just keep it light? A crush that never developed into anything more?

Finally, a sliver of rational thought intruded on her crazy mind meanderings. Just because it was the first *in real life* crush she'd ever had, she didn't need to be heading them toward marriage already. She'd had celebrity crushes before, but they hardly counted since Chris Hemsworth and David Tennant were both married, and in David's case, a little too old for her. However, now that she was experiencing this stirring of feelings for Gabe Callaghan, she could see that her celebrity crushes had been nothing but admiration for the men who starred in her favorite movies and TV shows.

Okay. So she sort of felt like there was a fork in the road for her. Which, when she thought about it, was kinda deep for a Christmas party, but still it was there. Did she just roll with how this might go with Gabe? Accepting that heartache might be waiting for her? Or did she keep her distance and wait for a man who engaged her emotions but was also able to be present in her life?

"Why don't we go on in?" Gabe suggested, his low voice close to her ear.

She had to take the risk. Her life had been all about someone keeping her safe and protected, but this...she couldn't *not* take the chance. If it was time for her to experience her first heartbreak, then so be it.

Maya smiled at Gabe and allowed him to guide her into the large room that was set up for the dinner. All the tables that ringed the outside of the room were covered in white tablecloths with large green and red centerpieces that included a candle in the middle of each. There were a ton of twinkling white lights draped around the room and hanging from the ceiling. Gas fireplaces were spaced along the walls, and at the far end of the room there looked to be a setup for a string quartet. A huge tree was in the opposite corner, decorated with more twinkling lights and green, red, and gold balls and bows.

Bing Crosby's *White Christmas* drifted through the large open space that somehow managed to feel cozy in spite of its size. Maya found herself humming along as Gabe walked with her to a table near the Christmas tree.

She couldn't stop smiling as she took it all in. Christmas was her absolute favorite time of year. When she'd been younger, Christmas was when her parents had relaxed their protectiveness enough to allow her to be out in public more. She'd been able to attend parties at her friends' houses or Elisse would accompany her to parties put on by her mom and dad at venues away from the house, and just for a little while, she was a young lady enjoying life instead of living in fear of what cancer had done to her and the threat that would always hang over her head.

"This is my sister, Sammi," Gabe said as he gestured to the young woman seated at the table already. "Sammi, this is Maya. She's taken over for Grace while she's off."

"It's nice to meet you, Maya," Sammi said with a friendly smile. "I've heard lots about you, but I don't get into the office much at all these days so we've never had the opportunity to meet."

Maya immediately saw the similarity between the woman and Makayla. They both had dark brown hair as did Bennett. She knew that they were a blended family, so it wasn't surprising that they didn't all look alike. What she found most interesting though was how the step-siblings interacted with each other. As Gabe bent to slide his arm around Sammi's shoulder to give her a hug and drop a kiss on her cheek, Maya could see that there was an easy affection between them.

"Nice to see you again, Jayden," Gabe said as he straightened and looked at the man seated to Sammi's right.

Maya's immediate thought was that he looked like he belonged on a beach in California. He was tanned which was a striking contrast to his light blue eyes. His hair was blonde with even lighter highlights in it. The smile he gave them as Sammi introduced him to Maya was stunning, showing off his even white teeth.

"This is Jayden Murray," Sammi said, turning to smile at the man.

Jayden gave her an affectionate glance before he looked up, holding out his hand to Gabe and then to Maya. "Good to see you again, Gabe, and nice to meet you, Maya."

Gabe pulled out the seat next to Sammi and looked over at Maya with a smile that lifted one corner of his mouth. "Would you like to have a seat?"

Maya settled onto the chair, impressed by Gabe's manners. He took the seat next to her, resting his arm across the back of her chair as he leaned forward to talk to Sammi and Jayden.

Gabe was looking festively handsome himself dressed in black slacks and a white long sleeve shirt under a dark green and red plaid vest. It made Maya smile to see that he didn't have a problem embracing the colors of the holiday. It wasn't every man that would do that. In fact, Jayden was dressed in a long sleeve, light blue shirt with a dark blue tie. Nothing even remotely Christmassy about his attire except for the woman on his arm. Sammi looked elegant in a deep red dress with a wide neckline.

"How's work going?" Gabe asked Sammi. "Are you enjoying your new job?"

Sammi relaxed back in her chair, leaning into Jayden's side, her hands resting in her lap. "Yes. While I did enjoy working at the hospital, I find the stable hours at the nursing home much easier to work with."

"And what do you do, Jayden?"

Maya hadn't really interacted much on a personal level with the Callaghan-McFadden family, so she found it interesting meeting the members of the family who weren't part of the business. She just hoped that they didn't have the same curiosity about her life.

"I'm working part-time as an assistant youth pastor at the church and also helping my dad out at his car dealership."

"Youth pastor and car salesman?" Gabe asked, arching an eyebrow. "That's quite a combination."

Jayden smiled. "I know, right? But you gotta do what you gotta do to make ends meet. I want to be in the ministry, but right now there isn't a full-time position available for me."

"So you guys met at church?"

Sammi nodded. "Yeah, I volunteered as a chaperone for a lock-in for the youth since Sierra and Danae were going. Jayden was there too."

Maya listened as they discussed the church, enjoying the way Gabe's arm on the chair pressed against her back. It made her feel included. Part of the group.

"Are you saving these seats?" Tristan stood at the chair beside Gabe.

"Hey! Nope. It's all yours, bro," Gabe said.

Soon Mitch joined them at the table, and then a few more people appeared that the others obviously knew, but Maya didn't. Bennett and Makayla and Ethan were seated at another table with Steve and Emily Callaghan. The rest of the tables were gradually filling up, and the noise level increased, almost drowning out *Jingle Bells* that was being played over the sound system.

Once the majority of the tables had filled, Steve Callaghan got to his feet and with Bennett at his side, made his way to the microphone at the front of the room.

"Good evening, everyone," Bennett said. "If you haven't found your seat yet, I'd like to invite you to do so now."

Even from this distance, Maya could see the strain on Bennett's face. Though he hadn't been outgoing in the way that Gabe seemed to be, Bennett had always had a ready smile when she'd spoken with him, but lately, his smiles had been few and far between. She didn't know exactly what had transpired, but it seemed that it had something to do with Grace and her new baby.

"Thank you for coming to the C&M Builders' Christmas party. We are grateful for another wonderful year of great projects and growth for our company which makes this our biggest party to date. If this is your first year with us, we hope that it won't be your last." Bennett paused as applause swept the room. When it had died down, he leaned toward the microphone again. "And now I'd like to ask my dad, Steve Callaghan, to say a prayer for our evening."

Maya looked at the older man as he stepped forward and slid an arm around Bennett's shoulders. "Let's pray."

She was part of a family who attended church sporadically, although that hadn't always been the case. At one time, they had attended more regularly, but now it was just at Christmas and Easter.

From conversations she'd heard, Maya knew that the relationship this family had with their church was much different than hers and her parents. It was just one more thing that she was curious about. From the first time she'd heard Bennett pray at one of their staff lunches, she'd been intrigued. And Steve's prayer was much like his son's had been. They weren't the recitation of prayers like she was used to hearing. This seemed much more familiar, as if he had an intimate relationship with the God he was praying to.

Though she had prayed over the years—it was hard to face death and not find oneself praying to whatever deity out there that might be listening—it had never been the way Steve Callaghan prayed. He even included Grace and her baby, Olivia, in the prayer.

It was different. Intriguing. And something she wanted to know more about.

Once the prayer was over, servers began to file into the room, plates balanced on their steady arms. Conversation ebbed and flowed as they worked their way through the courses of the meal. Maya found the food to be as good as any she'd ever had at any other Christmas party.

After they had finished a delicious chocolate mousse dessert, the string quartet took the stage and started to play Christmas music. She smiled as the first song they played was *Deck the Halls*. Because her mom had insisted that she have a well-rounded education, she'd taken music lessons and had learned to play both piano and violin. That had been before cancer had entered their lives and changed her mom's outlook on Maya's life.

Maya pulled her thoughts back from that path, focusing instead on the people who had begun to spill onto the large open floor that was ringed by the tables. She found herself swaying in time to *It's Beginning to Look a Lot Like Christmas*, grinning as she watched couples attempting to dance to the song. Most Christmas music wasn't really intended for the type of dancing people did at parties these days, but several seemed determined to give it a whirl.

When *Silver Bells* began to play, Maya turned to Gabe who had shifted to sit more closely to her, his arm resting across the back of her chair as he leaned back in his.

"Do you dance?"

Gabe's gaze flicked to the dance floor before looking back at her. "No, I don't."

Maya's shoulders drooped, and her disappointment was no doubt clear on her face. Dance lessons had also been a part of her life at one time. She'd learned the fine art of ballroom dancing at a young age, her mom wanting to make sure she wouldn't embarrass herself if she would one day attend functions where dancing might be required.

Sadly, by the time she would have been old enough to attend those parties, dancing had been the last thing on her mind. Maya frowned, clenching her hands together in her lap. Why did the memory of her cancer keep invading her thoughts? Tonight was a magical evening for her—she didn't want it marred by the memories of that horrible time.

A hand covered hers, taking hold of one as her grip loosened. Gabe got to his feet, pulling her along. She looked up to find him smiling down at her.

"Let's give this a try," he said before leading her through the maze of chairs to reach the dance floor.

Releasing her hand, he turned and held out his arms, an expectant look on his face. After a brief hesitation, Maya slid her right hand into his and stepped close enough that his other hand could settle on her upper back, and she could rest her hand on his shoulder.

He held her there for a moment in that position before he began to move, leading her through the steps for a waltz to the slowed down version of *Silver Bells* that the quartet was playing. For someone who'd said he couldn't dance, Gabe was doing a pretty good job of leading her around the perimeter of the dance floor.

"I thought you said you couldn't dance," Maya said, looking up at him in the subdued lighting.

"Oh, I didn't say I *couldn't* dance, I said I *don't* dance—although clearly, I made an exception for you." Gabe's smile widened, and Maya's heart skipped a beat at the expression on his face and at his words. He'd made an exception for her. The words made her feel special. Like she was worth doing something he didn't enjoy. "I was part of a wedding where the bride insisted that all members of the entourage had to learn to waltz. It's just that my family isn't really much into dancing."

"But your dad includes it in the employee party," Maya pointed out.

"I think Dad figures that since he's not providing alcohol, the least he could do is give people the opportunity to dance if they so desire."

"Why no alcohol?" she asked as they paused in the dance before moving again when the next song started up, thankfully still with a waltz beat. She was also thankful that the music was soft enough to allow them to carry on a conversation.

"I think it's because Dad knows of the tendency for people to over-indulge at events like these. It can impact others at the event, plus some people still insist on driving, no matter how much Dad has tried to dis-suade them. It just seemed easier to not offer it. There were a few complaints the first year, but people know now. It's just one evening, and if they need a drink that badly, they can stop somewhere on their way home."

Maya could see the wisdom of that. She'd seen drunkenness at par-ties in the past. Elisse had always made sure she wasn't in the vicinity of it, but that didn't mean that she hadn't seen the drunken men making passes at the women around them. Or the women who'd had one too many glasses of wine flirting like crazy. Her mom had muttered under her breath about it, and Maya found she was looking forward to sharing that tidbit about this party with her mom. Maybe it would give her mom a more positive outlook on the life Maya was trying to forge for herself.

And even better, she couldn't wait to tell her about how she'd danced with Gabe. How he'd held her elegantly, indulging her even though he hadn't really wanted to dance. It was just so perfect. She'd imagined so many times over the years what it would be like to have a boyfriend. To have a guy want to spend time with her. To want to get to know her.

Gabe Callaghan seemed to be offering her the chance to realize that dream. But was it only for a moment?

Chapter Five

*A*LL GABE'S PLANS TO just play the role of friend to Maya had gone out the window when he'd seen her for the first time earlier that evening. The way she'd smiled at him had taken his breath away, and that was it. His good intentions had left the building. He'd never felt this kind of attraction to someone before. Yes, she was beautiful, but there had been something else there. When he'd asked her to lunch, and she'd accepted, Gabe had known he wasn't the only one experiencing that instant connection.

He'd known for sure she was special to him when he'd caved in to dance with her, wanting to do anything to get that disappointed look off her face. It had been a couple of years since he'd danced. After that wedding, he'd resolved to never, ever do it again, and yet, here he was…dancing. The big difference was that he actually wanted to be doing it this time around.

Gabe felt a bit disappointed when the music moved on to a Christmas song that didn't have a rhythm he knew how to dance to. Maya looked disappointed as well when he slid his hand from her back. He kept hold of her hand though as they moved off the floor and went back to their seats.

"Wow, you guys really cut the rug," Jayden said once they were seated.

"Definitely the best dancers out there," Sammi agreed then grinned at Gabe. "I didn't know you could dance like that."

"Well, I was forced to take lessons for a wedding I was part of, but today it definitely helped to have a talented partner. I don't think I danced this well at the wedding."

Sammi turned to Maya. "Where did you learn to dance?"

"My mom wanted me to learn, so I took a ton of lessons when I was younger. I guess it's kind of like riding a bike. It all came back pretty quickly."

"You looked so beautiful out there. I think I'd like to take some ballroom dance lessons," Sammi said with a look at Jayden. "What do you think? That could be our date night."

Jayden gave her a rueful look. "Sorry, doll. That's not gonna happen."

Even though Sammi looked disappointed, she didn't press the issue. Instead, she asked Maya about her dance experience. As their conversation continued, Gabe gradually came to the realization that while there was a lot of talking going on, most of it was Maya asking questions about them. She somehow managed to deflect any questions that were directed at her.

Gabe found that curious, and it made him curious to figure out why she didn't seem to like to talk about herself. Apparently, it was going to take spending a lot more time together in order to get to know her even better. Not surprisingly, Gabe didn't have a problem with that.

When there was a lull in the conversation, Gabe asked, "Have you ever been rock climbing?"

Maya's brow furrowed at the question, and she shook her head. "Like on a mountain?"

"Well, yes, I have done rock climbing on mountains, but in this particular case, given that we have no mountains around here, I go to an indoor place." Gabe smiled at her. "Wanna come along?"

He kind of figured she'd say no, but for sure she wouldn't say yes if he didn't ask her. She stared at him for a moment, her expression still a bit perplexed.

"I've never done anything like that before. Isn't it really dangerous?"

"Nah. Not the indoor places. They have lots of safety gear in place for the people that climb there."

"When were you going to go?"

Gabe fought a grin. At least she hadn't said no. Yet.

"I was thinking of going tomorrow morning." He did smile then and gave her shoulder a gentle nudge. "Come with me. I'll teach you how to do it. It's safe. I promise."

Sammi laughed. "Normally I wouldn't take your word on something being safe, Gabe. That's all pretty relative with you, but yes, Maya, in this case, it is pretty safe."

"You've done it before?" Maya asked.

"Yeah. I've gone a couple of times," Sammi said. "I'll be honest, though, it's more Gabe's thing than mine."

Maya seemed to be taking her time as she considered it, which was the opposite of her nearly immediate acceptance of his lunch invitation.

"We could do lunch afterward." Gabe glanced over in time to see Sammi grin at him, clearly enjoying his attempts to land a date with Maya.

"Okay," she said, her expression relaxing as she finally committed to it. "What time were you thinking of?"

"Why don't you give *me* a time? I'm not on a schedule, so I can adapt to what works for you."

"How about…ten?"

"Ten is good." Gabe would have agreed to any time if it meant she was going to show up.

Though he normally would have been moving around the room, socializing with the people he knew who had worked for the company for several years, Gabe found he didn't want to leave Maya's side. When the party began to wind down around midnight, Maya appeared to notice that people were beginning to get up and leave because she pulled her phone out of her small clutch.

She frowned as she read something on her screen then tapped out a message before slipping the phone back into her purse. "Just my mom checking up on me. I guess I should get going now that I have something to do tomorrow morning."

"Yes. I don't want you too tired to enjoy our time together." Gabe wished that he could offer her a ride home, but since she'd gotten there on her own, he assumed she had her own vehicle.

"I've really enjoyed this evening." Maya got to her feet. "Thank you for making it so memorable."

Gabe smiled down at her as they slowly moved toward the doors that led to the foyer. When they reached the coat check, she claimed her cape which he then took and helped her put on. "Can I pick you up tomorrow?"

"Um…I think it would be best if I just met you there," she said. "Can you text me the address?"

"Sure. I'll do that once I'm done here." He turned when he heard someone call his name. After lifting a hand to acknowledge the person, Gabe turned back to Maya. "I'm looking forward to tomorrow."

"Me, too." She finished closing the clasp of the cape at her throat, then pulled on a pair of gloves. "Thank you again for a lovely evening."

Gabe wanted to at least give her a hug and a kiss on the cheek, but that seemed awfully forward considering they'd just recently met. Instead, he settled for reaching out and squeezing her hand. "Drive safe."

"You too."

He watched her walk toward the doors leading out of the building, then turned as the person who'd called out to him reached his side. When he glanced back to the entrance, Maya was gone. Thankfully, he had the anticipation of seeing her the next day, and that kept a smile on his face as he visited with the man at his side.

"I HAVE WONDERFUL NEWS!"

Maya had barely stepped foot in the foyer of the house when her mother came to greet her. Though it was past midnight and she wore a long flowing night robe, her mother's face was still fully made up. Maya considered sharing about her evening with her mom, but she decided she wanted to savor it a bit by herself first.

"What news?" Maya asked as she undid her cape and draped it over her arm. She slipped off her shoes and dangled them from her fingers as she watched her mother, curious about the excitement on her face.

"Your father has agreed to let us use the jet to go to Paris for Christmas." Her mother beamed as she spoke. "I was thinking we could stay for a couple of weeks. Maybe into the new year."

Maya's shoulders sagged. At one time, she would have been thrilled at her mother's news. The last time she'd been to Paris, she'd been just twelve years old. Over the years, she'd begged to go back, but her mother hadn't wanted her to be so far from their home if she needed medical care. That she was acquiescing now just showed Maya how desperate she was to block Maya from the life she was trying to create for herself.

"I can't go, Mama. I have a job now."

"It's a job you don't need," she said. "Wouldn't you rather go to Paris?"

"No, actually, I wouldn't."

Her mother turned on her heel and headed for the sweeping staircase that led to the second floor, calling back over her shoulder, "I don't believe that. You have wanted to go to Paris forever."

Maya couldn't disagree with her, but at some point, it had become more important for her to find a way to live a meaningful life. A life that gave her a sense of accomplishment. So yes, she would love to go to Paris, but not at the expense of the life she was beginning to lead.

Her mother reached the top of the stairs and turned to the right, her hand trailing along the balcony railing as she headed for the wing where she and her husband had their suite. Maya walked over to a nearby chair—a spindly antique one that wasn't much good for anything but decoration—and dumped her cape, purse, and shoes on it before heading toward the short hallway that led to her father's office.

The door was open halfway, and warm light spilled out. She pushed the door open the rest of the way and walked in, knowing that her dad wouldn't object to her presence. He lifted his head from whatever work he'd been focused on, his light gray eyes watching her as she approached.

Maya sat down in the chair across the desk from him and frowned as she crossed her arms. "Why didn't you say no?"

Her dad leaned back in his chair, his lean frame stretching out as he did. "There are only two people in this world I can never say no to."

She huffed out a sigh. "But, Daddy, she is only doing this so I'll quit my job. If you'd said no, she wouldn't be able to try and manipulate me like this."

There was a softness to Maximilian Zevardi's face that Maya knew few people had ever seen. He was a man known for his ruthlessness in the business world, but he was never that way at home. When it came to her and her mom, he would do absolutely anything for them.

"I couldn't say no to her, sweetheart. I'm sorry."

"I just want to live my life. I mean, really live it. I want a job. An apartment. A boyfriend. And maybe someday, a husband and kids. I'm never going to have any of that if I'm locked up here behind the walls of this mansion. What kind of life is that?"

Her dad sighed. "I know. I really do. But I'm scared of what might happen to your mom—and to me—if anything ever happened to you, and we hadn't done our best to keep you safe."

"You're smothering me. I might as well still be sick because I have no life."

"Sweetheart, don't say that." He paused, the corners of his mouth pulling down into a frown. "You know we were never able to have any other children. Your mom suffered miscarriages both before and after you were born. It seemed unusually cruel to then have you get sick not once, but twice. Your mom wants you to live."

"But on her terms," Maya pointed out. "I'm an adult now. Please, Daddy, help me live like one." She straightened up in her seat. "I think I want to move into my own apartment."

This time her dad's frown turned into a scowl. "I'm not sure that's a good idea."

"So now you're going to prevent me from spreading my wings just like Mama has?"

He sighed. "It's late. Let me talk to your mom tonight and then maybe the three of us can sit down tomorrow and figure out if there's a way for all of us to be happy. To reach a compromise of sorts."

Maya's shoulders slumped. It would be two against one. What kind of compromise could they possibly reach that would make her feel like she actually had a life to live? "Okay. But it will have to be tomorrow afternoon or evening. I'm hanging out with a friend in the morning."

She could tell her dad was dying to ask for more information, but instead, he just nodded. "Let's meet for dinner."

Knowing that was likely as good as it was going to get, Maya got up and went around the desk to give him a hug and a kiss. Then she went back to gather up her things before retreating to her room. As she looked around the place she had turned into her sanctuary—the one place her mom hadn't bothered her—Maya realized she wasn't all that keen to move out. However, if it was the only way she was going to be able to live her life, then it was something she'd do without hesitation.

As she sank down on the edge of her bed, Maya felt the energy of the evening drain away. All she wanted to be able to do was share her excitement with her mom. To tell her about how much fun she'd had. To laugh about how her dance lessons had finally paid off. She wanted to tell her mom about how Gabe made her feel. Her first crush. Maybe even her first love.

But instead, all the excitement had been doused by her mom's attempt to manipulate her. Again. Maya loved her mom and dad so much, and that was the reason she'd taken as long as she had to come out of her shell. She'd taken small steps when, in fact, she could have done something much more extreme. The trust she'd received at twenty-one had given her the financial freedom to do whatever she wanted. She could have bought her own first-class plane ticket to Paris and rented an apartment there for herself.

Instead, she'd kept her aspirations much more realistic. She'd found a way to go to school online because she'd known the battle she'd have faced with her mom if she tried to go to university. But the job, the car, the life she was trying to build was still more than her mom could handle.

Was she going to be forced to choose between her mom and the life she wanted for herself?

Maya flopped back on her bed and closed her eyes, trying to recapture the feeling she'd had when she'd left the party. Hopefully, since she'd stayed up so late, her mom wouldn't be up early so she wouldn't have to deal with her before heading out the next morning. She was determined to meet Gabe in the morning and embrace a new experience.

THE NEXT MORNING, Maya had her iPad set up on her makeup table watching YouTube videos while she got ready for her date—although, was it really a date?—with Gabe. Because she'd been forced to live so much of her life inside, Maya had found early on that the internet was her best connection with the outside world. Whether it was connecting with others around the world or watching the lives others lived through videos, the internet had been her way of escaping the barriers her over-protective mother had put into place between Maya and the world.

So as she put on a bit of makeup, Maya listened to someone describe rock climbing for beginners. She'd started out watching rock climbing videos, but all she could see were the many ways she was going to fail. Finally, she focused on her makeup and just listened as the man explained the basics. She didn't think Gabe would set her up to fail, so she had to believe he'd seen something in her that made him think she could climb rocks.

She really hoped he was right.

When Maya finally pulled into the parking lot of *Rock On*, her nerves were out in full force. *Seize the day.* She had to keep reminding herself that she wanted these types of experiences. She wanted to experience life in a way she never had before.

Maya stared at the large building that looked more like a warehouse than a gym. Gabe had sent her a text just as she was leaving the house to let her know that he was there already and to go on in when she arrived.

"You can do this," she muttered as she pushed open her door and got out of the car. As the cold air hit her, Maya lifted her shoulders and buried her hands deep into the pockets of her jacket. The freezing temperature was a good reason to hurry into the building even though she would have preferred to take her time.

She had thought the place would be crowded given the number of cars in the parking lot, but as Maya walked inside, she found that the space was so massive that there was plenty of room. Rock music thumped in the air, but thankfully it wasn't obnoxiously loud as it wasn't exactly her favorite style of music.

Not sure where to go, Maya came to a stop just inside the door and stared around. There were several walls with colorful hand and foot holds covering them. She stared at some of the walls that were not just vertical like she'd expected but that went past vertical which meant the climber was actually hanging upside down.

There was no way she'd be doing that. No matter how much she might like Gabe. If he encouraged her to give it a try, her answer would be a resounding *no*. There was seizing the day, and there was just foolishness, and for her, hanging upside down clinging onto a rock was foolishness. Especially on her very first day of rock climbing.

"Hi! Can I help you?"

Maya turned to see a young woman standing behind a long desk to her left. After a final glance at the rock walls, she moved toward her.

"Is this your first time here?" the woman asked.

"I guess it's pretty obvious, eh?" Maya said with a smile. "I'm actually supposed to be meeting someone here."

The woman's smile widened. "Gabe?"

"Yes. He said he was here already."

"He is. Let me take you to him." She began to walk the length of the desk, pausing in front of an open door. "Jack, can you watch the desk? I'll be right back." Without seeming to wait for an answer, the woman came around the end of the desk and joined Maya. "My name is Cathy. And you're Maya, right?"

"I am. It's nice to meet you."

Cathy led the way to one of the past-vertical walls Maya had seen. She came to a stop a little ways from the wall and pointed to the man who was about halfway up the wall. "There he is."

"Is he a regular here?" Maya asked as she watched Gabe pause, looking as if he was just hanging from an extended arm with his feet braced against the wall. Suddenly he moved, smoothly extending his other arm to grip a hand hold and move further along the wall. Maya held her breath when he paused again, waiting for his next move.

"Yes. He's actually one of the owners and has helped design several of the walls."

Maya heard the admiration in the woman's voice as she stared up to where Gabe had once again advanced on the wall. Did this woman feel the same way for Gabe that Maya did?

"He's amazing to watch," Cathy said. "He has such a grace to him as he climbs. Like it takes no effort at all."

Maya turned her gaze back to Gabe, watching again as he moved, showing the grace Cathy had mentioned as he swung by his hands for a moment before bringing his feet to the wall and pausing. She decided then that she didn't need to climb. She'd be happy to just watch him. Gabe in motion was truly a thing of beauty.

However, she had a feeling that Gabe wouldn't let her do that. Something told her that he would want to share his passion for the sport with her.

He hooked his safety rope one last time before reaching the top, bringing cheers from the people on the ground. It was then that Maya realized that it hadn't just been her and Cathy who'd been watching his climb. Gabe gave a wave as the person who'd been holding the ropes lowered him to the ground.

Once on the ground, Gabe spoke to the man as he worked himself free of the rope. Cathy headed in their direction, so Maya followed her. Gabe looked up as Cathy approached, his gaze quickly moving past her to Maya.

"You up next, babe?" Cathy said as she joined them, slipping her arm around the waist of the man Gabe had been talking to.

"Nope. I had my turn earlier and failed to reach the top." The man gave a shake of his head. "I design this wall, and he just breezes through it."

"You did a good job, Brent." Gabe slapped him on the shoulder. "Just not good enough."

"I found someone who was looking for you," Cathy said with a wave at Maya.

"So I see," Gabe said as he smiled at Maya. "Good morning. I'm glad you could make it."

"Hi." Maya felt warmth spread through her at the smile that seemed to be just for her. "I'm feeling a little intimidated, I have to admit. Are you sure you wouldn't rather just go for breakfast?"

Brent and Cathy both laughed before Brent said, "Sorry to tell you, once Gabe gets someone in those doors, he doesn't let them out unless they at least attempt to climb a wall. But don't worry, you're in the best hands with him."

"Well, on that note," Gabe said, rubbing his hands together, "let's get you ready to climb."

As they walked toward the front of the building, Maya said, "Are there bunny walls?"

"Bunny walls?" Gabe asked, a note of humor in his voice.

"You know. Like bunny slopes for skiing."

"Ah, yes. There are beginner walls. Don't worry. I'd never throw you on a tough wall to start. I want you to enjoy this after all. If you don't, you might not come back with me, and that would be a shame."

"I'd come back to watch *you* climb any day of the week. You looked amazing up there."

Gabe shot her a grin. "You thought I looked amazing?"

Maya laughed. "Like you don't know."

"Usually people put their stuff in a locker, but you can just put your things in the office with mine." Gabe guided her behind the desk to the open door. "Hey, Jack."

"Yo, dude." Jack gave them a nod as they walked past. "Dudette."

Maya leaned toward Gabe and softly said, "Dudette?"

Gabe chuckled. "Yeah. Jack likes to pretend he's a surfer or something."

"Or maybe he just has a bad memory and can't remember anyone's name." This came from a large man sitting behind a desk. While Gabe was tall and on the lanky side, this man was tall and well built.

"Hey, Hunter. This is Maya. I invited her to come try out some climbing." Gabe helped Maya out of her jacket.

"Good to meet you, Maya." The man got up and held out his hand. "Welcome to *Rock On.*"

"Thank you." Her hand was swallowed up in the man's. He gave a firm, but not finger breaking, shake before releasing her hand.

"Let's find you a pair of shoes," Gabe said.

"I wasn't sure what to wear, so I hope this is okay." Maya motioned to the stretch skinny jeans she wore with a long sleeve T-shirt. Her mom probably would have had a fit that she was leaving the house dressed that way, but it seemed the most appropriate for what the day held.

Gabe gave her a quick look over before nodding. "That's just fine."

Cathy appeared in the doorway of the office. "What size shoe do you wear?"

After Maya told her and then slipped on the shoes Cathy returned with, it wasn't long before Gabe took her to a wall that—thankfully—looked a little less intimidating than the one he'd been climbing. As he ran through the basics, she recognized several terms that she'd heard on the videos earlier. Though she was sure he could do it all in his sleep, Gabe took his time to explain everything to her. From the reason why his shoes were shaped a bit differently from hers to the different types of buckles on the harness she would be wearing.

Though getting the harness on her and the rope attached required Gabe to be in her personal space, she appreciated the fact that his hands didn't brush against any parts of her body that they shouldn't. He was all business as he got her ready.

For her part, Maya definitely enjoyed having Gabe that close. She found herself appreciating the scent of whatever cologne or aftershave he was wearing. His hair fell forward over his forehead as he bent to show her the figure eight knot he'd made by feeding the rope through the two loops on the harness.

"And that's strong enough to hold me up if I fall?" Maya asked, still not convinced this was the best idea she'd ever agreed to.

He looked up at her as he gave the rope a tug, the skin by the corners of his eyes crinkling as he smiled. "Yeah. You don't have to worry about that. If these will hold me, they'll definitely hold you."

Chapter Six

NCE GABE DECLARED HER READY TO GO, Maya turned to look at the wall he'd brought her to. She knew it wasn't a difficult wall, but it was still rather imposing. *Seize the day.* She was going to trust that Gabe wouldn't have her doing anything that would be potentially life threatening.

As he walked her closer to the wall, Gabe continued to give her instructions. "Try to keep your arms extended. Keep the weight on your shoulders, so your arms don't get overtired."

Maya remembered hearing something about that in one of the videos she'd watched.

"These beginner walls have fairly straightforward routes to the top, so you should be able to find a path without too much trouble." He guided her toward a starting position. "And don't worry if you don't make it to the top your first time. This is more to just get you informed and comfortable with the equipment and the wall. Next time you'll be able to concentrate on just the climb."

Maya looked over at him and arched a brow. "Next time?"

"Oh yes. There will be a next time," Gabe said with a confident grin. "You'll be back for more."

Reaching out to grasp the first handhold, Maya glanced over her shoulder. "You seem pretty confident about that."

"You'll see." He took a couple of steps back, the rope he would use to spot her in his hands.

Taking a deep breath, Maya turned her attention to the wall and began to tentatively move up. Though she could see the next places her hands and feet needed to go to, she tried to move carefully. It wasn't a race, and in her mind's eye, she could see the woman she'd watched on YouTube climbing with graceful, smooth movements, much like Gabe had shown earlier.

She wanted to reach the top, to show Gabe that she could do it, but midway up, her arms and legs began to tremble with the strain. She paused, holding onto the grips, trying to keep from slipping off them.

"You okay, Maya?"

Maya resisted the urge to look down at Gabe. Instead, she looked up, trying to gauge how far she needed to go in order to reach the top.

She took a deep breath and let it out, realizing that there was no way her body was going to get her to her destination. Her head dropped forward.

"You've done great, Maya." Gabe's voice was full of encouragement. "For your first time, you've gotten really far. If you're done, just push back from the wall. I've got you."

Maya knew she had to let go, but she didn't want to. It was so important to her that Gabe know she could do this, but there was just no way she was going to be able to. With a sigh, she pushed away from the wall and let go. Her stomach clenched as she swung in the air before landing on the ground.

Immediately, she was captured in a hug, her arms held tight to her side.

"You did great!" Gabe released her and stepped back, his hands coming to rest on her upper arms. He massaged the muscles there. "How are you feeling?"

She looked up at him as she clenched and unclenched her hands. "I wanted to get to the top."

"I know. That's how I felt the first time I tried climbing, but I didn't make it either."

"Really?" Maya gave him a skeptical look. "I find that rather hard to believe."

"It's the truth. It's taken many years and a lot of practice to get to the point I'm at now." His hands slid further down her arms, continuing to massage them. "But how did you like it?"

"I didn't think I'd like it, but there was something invigorating about having to rely on just my own strength to get up there." She stared down as his strong fingers worked the muscles in her hands. "It was amazing."

"I knew you'd like it," Gabe said. "You seemed like a person who was up for a challenge."

"Well, to be honest, I've never thought about doing something like this," Maya said, feeling a bit bereft as he let go of her hands. "And there just might be a next time."

"I'm glad to hear it." Gabe grinned, his blue eyes twinkling. "You're welcome here at the gym anytime you want. Did you want to try again now?"

"I don't think I can," Maya said with a shake of her head. "My arms feel like they're about ready to fall off, and I don't think I'll be able to walk for the rest of the day if I try again. Maybe you can give me some pointers on exercises that would help me gain strength and do better next time."

"That I can do, but first, let's get you out of this harness." Gabe quickly undid the rope and then the buckle of the harness.

Once she was free, they returned to the office where she switched from the climbing shoes into her boots. She made a note to buy some shoes of her own since she really did want to try it again. But there was no way she'd ever tell her mom what she'd been up to. It was just one more thing she was going to have to keep from her parents even though what she wanted most was to be able to share all these experiences with them.

"Ready to get some lunch?" Gabe asked as he handed her her jacket.

Maya nodded. "I didn't really eat much for breakfast, so I'm definitely ready for some food."

Gabe rapped on the desk where Hunter sat. "I'll be back a bit later."

"Have fun," the other man said with a broad smile.

As they walked toward the exit of the building, Gabe said, "How about we take my truck. I'll bring you back here afterward, if that's okay."

"That's fine."

GABE PULLED INTO the small parking lot of the restaurant he'd decided to take Maya to. He was so pleased with how things had gone at the gym. Knowing that she was a little apprehensive, he had just wanted her to try it once. It was something he loved doing, and for some reason, he'd really wanted her to give it a try. He wanted it to be something they could do together again.

"I've never been here before," Maya said as she walked with him to the entrance.

Gabe wanted to take her hand, but he knew it was probably a little too soon for that. He opened the door and let her precede him into the restaurant. He hadn't been sure where to go, but he'd wanted a place where they could sit and talk in peace and quiet without feeling rushed.

The hostess greeted them with a smile and then led the way to a booth in the back corner. She waited until they'd both slid into their seats before handing them the menus.

"Your waitress will be with you shortly." With a quick smile, she left them alone.

"You've been here before?" Maya asked as she opened the menu.

"Yep. I found this place a couple of years ago. I try to come at least once whenever I'm home."

Maya looked at him for a moment, her dark gaze serious before turning her attention back to the menu. He wondered what she'd been thinking, but couldn't bring himself to ask. It wouldn't have surprised him if it had to do with his frequent travels. Mitch had cornered him again after the Christmas party to ask him what he was thinking when it came to Maya.

Mitch hadn't been the only family member who had noticed his infatuation with the company's new receptionist. Makayla and Bennett had both asked him what he was thinking getting close to her when he'd be leaving again in a few weeks. Unfortunately, he had no answer for them.

He'd never considered settling down in one place. Winnipeg was always the place he came back to, but it hadn't been the place where he stayed since he'd graduated from university. It had been a few timely decisions with Tennyson Page and Forrest Williams that had allowed him the ability to work from anywhere in the world as long as he had an internet connection.

He'd gone on to make some wise investments in the meantime—including the rock climbing gym—which had added to the money that was accumulating in his bank account. Gabe wasn't focused on the things he could buy with that money. He liked the freedom the money gave him to travel the world, chasing the adrenalin rush that gave him a reason to get up each day. There was no physical item he could buy that could ever give him a similar feeling.

Meeting Maya was the first time he'd felt that rush of anticipation for anything but an adventure. He didn't know what it was about her, but he just couldn't ignore it. He had to discover why she made him feel that way. Why, for the first time in his adult life, he was tempted to put the chase on hold for the chance to stay in Winnipeg for longer than just a couple of weeks.

When their waitress appeared to take their order, Gabe motioned for Maya to go first.

"I'll have the BLT salad with Ranch dressing on the side," Maya said. "And a glass of water with lemon."

Gabe always found it interesting to see what people he had just met liked to eat. It gave him some insight into them, or at least he liked to think it did. With Maya, knowing what she liked to eat would make things easier when he chose places to take her out to eat.

The thought made him pause when he realized he was already planning on going out to eat with her again.

"And how about you, sir?" The waitress's question brought him back to the present.

"Oh. I'll have the double cheeseburger with French fries. And water for me as well."

"So. Tell me about yourself," Gabe said when they were alone again.

Maya's brows rose. "What exactly do you want to know? I'm afraid I haven't led a very interesting life."

"Well, you know about my family."

"I think I do. I mean, just when I think I've met you all, another one pops up." She smiled. "Like last night with Sammi. I actually thought you meant a guy when you first mentioned her. Maybe you need to give me a rundown just to make sure I know everyone now."

"Okay. Here's a rundown on the rest of the family—in order of age, not beauty or importance. Kenton is the oldest, and he plays in the NHL. Then there's Bennett, Makayla, Ryan, me and Mitch. Sammi and Tristan are the youngest of the blended family then my dad and Emily had Danica and Dalton."

Maya sat back in the booth, a slightly stunned look on her face. "Wow. That's quite a family. I'm an only child, so I can't begin to imagine having that many siblings. I think my mom would have loved to have more kids, but that wasn't meant to be."

"I enjoy being part of a large family. There's usually someone up for doing something. When we were little, if Mitch didn't want to play with me, I could usually talk Ryan or Sammi into doing something. Of course, most weren't interested in the things I liked to do."

"Like what?" Maya asked.

Gabe grinned as memories flooded his mind. "Well, there was the time I wanted us to jump off the roof of the porch onto the trampoline. I managed to talk Ryan into doing it with me, but when I miscalculated the distance I needed to jump in order to land in the middle of it, I ended up breaking my arm. I also loved to climb trees to see how high up I could get. And then there were the ramps I used to set up so we could jump our bikes. I always went the farthest because I would go the fastest before hitting the ramp. Mom will tell you that I am solely responsible for every gray hair on her head."

"I can't even imagine. My mom was way too protective of me to let me even consider doing anything like that. Of course, I'm not sure I would have wanted to anyway."

"Yeah, the girls never were as eager to join me. In fact, I'm not sure I was ever able to convince Makayla or Sammi to do the more risky stuff."

The waitress returned with their food, interrupting their conversation. Gabe hesitated for a moment then said, "Do you mind if I say grace for the food?"

"Not at all," Maya said then bowed her head.

As Gabe said a prayer of thanks for the food, his dad's words came to mind about dating someone who didn't share his faith. Maybe that was a discussion they needed to have along with all the other getting-to-know-each-other questions.

"This looks delicious," Maya said as she picked up her fork.

"I haven't had a bad dish yet in all the time I've been coming here." Gabe reached for the ketchup. "Do your parents live here in Winnipeg?"

Maya nodded, her fork pausing on its way to her mouth. "Yeah. My dad is from here. My mom's parents came to Winnipeg from Japan, and my mom was born here. My mom worked for my dad, and that's how they met."

That explained the exotic look Maya had with the combination of Asian features blended with Caucasian ones. Her brown eyes were round but still had a slight tilt to them that made them beautiful to him. Her dark hair and lightly tanned skin were definitely from her mom, but Gabe wondered if the one dimple she sported came from her dad.

"What does your dad do?"

Maya took the time to chew her bite of food before answering him. Gabe got the feeling that she was chewing a bit more than she needed to, and he wondered why she wasn't eager to answer the question.

"He's in business. To be honest, I don't know exactly what he does. He travels a lot."

"Does your mom still work for him?"

Maya shook her head. "She quit after they got married. My dad's business was doing well enough at that point that she didn't need to work, so she could stay home with me."

"You didn't want to work for your dad?"

"Absolutely not. I'm sure my mom wishes I would have gone to him for a job, but I needed to stand on my own." She paused. "It's bad enough I'm still living at home."

Gabe grinned. "Well, technically, I still live at home too. I mean, I used to have an apartment in the building my dad owns, but after doing some shuffling around, someone else needed the apartment, so I gave it up. Now when I'm here, I stay with my folks."

"Is that where Grace moved to?" Maya asked.

"Yep. After her husband died, she decided to move out of their condo and back into the building where Makayla, Bennett, and Mitch live."

"It's neat how you all get along well enough that you want to live close together."

Gabe sighed. "We don't all get along that well. Bennett and Kenton have some issues. They used to be best friends, but now whenever they're in the same room, the tension is so thick you could cut it with a knife."

"What happened?"

"No one knows for sure, but I personally think it has something to do with Grace."

Maya's eyes widened. "Grace? Really?"

"Yeah. She and Bennett have a history going back to when they were all teens, and I think Kenton got mixed up in it somehow." Gabe swirled a fry through the ketchup. "It's probably a good thing Kenton plays down in LA even though my dad keeps hoping he'll get traded to the Jets."

"Will Kenton be home for Christmas?"

"Not likely. The team doesn't get much—if any—time off at Christmas. Most times, Kenton is the only one not home. Ryan lives in Minneapolis, so he'll be home. Do you have other family you get together with at Christmas?"

"Not really. My dad is estranged from his family, unfortunately, and my mom's parents have both passed away. They were older when they had her, and she was an only child too. I think that's one of the reasons she wanted more children." Maya paused and took a drink of water. "My mom wants to go away for Christmas, but I told her that with my new job, I can't."

"I'm sure Bennett would give you time off if you asked. Family is always important to us so he'd be fine with you spending that time with yours."

Maya shook her head. "No. I'd rather not ask. I want to stay here for Christmas."

"I can't say I'm disappointed to hear that," Gabe said and gave her a wink. "I'd like to spend some more time with you over the holidays."

The dimple made a brief appearance in Maya's cheek as she gave him a shy smile. "I'd like that too."

As the meal progressed, Gabe shared a bit about his latest travels which had been among his less exciting trips. They hadn't involved the high level of adventure he usually went after. His next few trips would include more heart-pumping adventures, especially the trip he'd committed to with three of his friends in March. They were going to be jumping out of a helicopter to do some extreme skiing and snowboarding.

They talked a bit about a new movie that had come out recently, and Gade didn't hesitate to offer to take her to see it.

"When were you thinking?" Maya asked as she pushed her plate to the side.

"Maybe some night this week?" Gabe suggested.

"Sure. I'd like that. Just call or text me. Or will you be in the office?"

Gabe finished his last bite of burger then took a drink of water. "To be honest, I don't spend much time in the office, but I'm willing to make an exception this time around. I might come in and borrow the boardroom to do some work of my own."

Maya smiled, the dimple in her cheek deepening. "Your brother might decide to charge you rent for office space."

Gabe started to laugh. "He can always try."

They declined dessert though the selections the waitress presented looked tempting, then Gabe took care of the bill even though Maya had offered to split it.

"I asked you out. This is my treat." Gabe couldn't imagine a situation in which he'd accept his date paying for one of their meals. He was just a bit old-fashioned in that regard, he supposed.

"Well, thank you. The food was delicious." She got to her feet as he did and smiled at him. "And the company was wonderful as well."

As they walked to the car, Gabe found himself considering the poise with which Maya conducted herself. The way she always put him at ease, keeping the conversation flowing even though she did tend to keep the focus off herself. At some point, he was going to get her to answer the questions that kept coming to mind the more time he spent with her.

When they got back to the gym, Gabe didn't turn off the car right away. He found that he didn't want their time to end. Knowing that he would be leaving in a couple of weeks, he wanted to cram in as much time together as he could before he had to go.

"I was wondering if you'd like to come to church with me tomorrow." He hesitated. "I mean, if you don't have commitments where you attend."

Maya didn't answer right away, but then she said, "I don't actually have a church that I attend on a regular basis."

"Would you like to come to church with me then?" Gabe asked again.

"Yes, I would."

Gabe felt a wave of relief. He had thought maybe she'd say no. That she'd be uninterested in attending a church service. "I can pick you up, if you'd like."

"I'd prefer to drive myself." She smiled at him, lessening the sting of the rejection a little. "Just give me the address and the time. I will be there."

Gabe wondered why she kept refusing his attempts to give her a ride. Just one more curiosity about Maya that he hoped would be satisfied soon. "I'll hold you to that."

Once out of the car, Maya thanked him again then she headed for an SUV hybrid parked a couple rows over. As he watched her go, Gabe wondered when he'd be able to give her a hug when they parted from each other. It seemed like the right thing to do, but he knew it was too soon. Hopefully, it wouldn't be too soon…soon.

"WHERE HAVE YOU BEEN?"

Maya huffed out a sigh at her mother's words as the woman came from the direction of her dad's office. She was starting to absolutely hate those words. Maybe it was time to look into finding a place of her own. Despite the fact that Gabe was also living with his parents, she knew that it wasn't normal for someone her age who had the money for a place of their own to still be living with their parents.

"I met someone for lunch." Maya took off her jacket and put it over her arm.

Her mother's brows drew together. "Wearing that?"

"It was a casual thing." Disappointment seeped into her as she saw the disapproval on her mom's face. She wanted to share about her morning. She wanted to talk to her mom about her time with Gabe. About how he made her feel. But she knew she couldn't.

"Are you going out again? I would like to speak with you."

Maya stifled a sigh. "I'm not going anywhere. Did you want to talk now?"

"Yes. In the sunroom, please."

"Let me just put my stuff in my room, and I'll meet you there." She headed up to her room, taking her time as she hung up her jacket and put her shoes in her walk-in closet.

Though she didn't want to go back down, Maya knew delaying would just mean putting off the inevitable. She had wanted to get online and talk with Lainie about what had happened, but now that would have to wait.

Finally, she headed back down the stairs, popping her head into the kitchen to say hi to Elisse before continuing on to the sunroom that was at the back of the house. It looked out on a large expanse of lawn and the river beyond it that, at the moment, was covered in snow. Her room had a similar view, and one of her favorite things was to sit in her window seat and watch the sun set. That would definitely be something she'd miss if she moved out. She wasn't sure if she'd end up in a place with a similar view.

Her mom was seated at the glass bistro table with a couple of mugs in front of her as well as a plate of cookies. Maya frowned. She hoped it was tea and not hot chocolate in the mug. And the cookies were going to have to be a pass as well. Her mom didn't understand that she was trying to keep sugar out of her diet. It wasn't easy, but once she'd read a report about how sugar could feed cancer cells, she'd decided that it wasn't that important to eat sweets. Whether it was true or not, Maya had no way of knowing, but other things she'd read had said that removing sugar from her diet would also help with her immunity. Her mom might have been worried about protecting Maya, but she wasn't interested in something as simple as dietary changes to help her.

Maya settled into the chair across from her mom and looked at the mug. "Tea?"

"Yes. I had Elisse make you a cup of that herbal stuff that you like to drink."

"Thank you." No doubt her mom was hoping to get on her good side. Maya hoped she had the strength to stand firm in the face of what was likely to be her mom's determination to get her way.

"I want to discuss our trip to Paris," she began. "We leave next week."

Maya picked up her mug and took a sip, looking at her mom over the rim of the mug. "I'm not going."

Her mom waved her manicured hand dismissively in the air. "You have wanted to go for years. I have lined up an apartment in Paris. One that has beautiful views of the city."

Maya sighed. "Mama, I'm not going. You and Dad can go, but I won't be with you."

"I've gone to the trouble of setting this all up." Her mom's expression hardened. "You will be coming with us."

$\mathcal{M}$AYA WANTED TO JUST BURY her head in her hands and cry from the frustration of dealing with her mother's attempts to control and manipulate her. All she wanted was a chance to live her life and to share it with her parents. Her mom was making both as difficult as possible. Maya was starting to live parts of her life the way she wanted, but right then, she couldn't see how she'd ever be able to confide in her parents—especially her mom—about any of it.

"The last time I checked, Mama, I was of legal age. I'm an adult, and I can make my own decisions now. I have responsibilities here that I can't just abandon for a vacation to Paris." She took another sip of her tea, waiting for her mom's reply. When she didn't say anything, Maya continued. "I know the only reason you've set this trip up now is your hope that it will mean more to me than my job. Unfortunately, you've underestimated my desire to have a life of my own. A life that contributes something. Jetting off to Paris is no longer at the top of my wish list." She paused before adding, "But an apartment of my own is quickly moving up that list."

"You are not moving out," her mother said without hesitation, her expression a curious mix of fear and determination.

Sitting across from her mom, Maya remembered a different time, before hardness had overtaken every other expression. Even with the hardness, her mother was still a beautiful woman, but she was positively breathtaking when her expression softened, and happiness entered her eyes. However, seeing that was now a rarity, and Maya hated knowing that it was her mother's fear for her that had brought on the hardness that was so evident.

"Again, I'm old enough to decide for myself what I'm going to do, and I have the money to do it. I don't *want* to move out, but if you keep trying to thwart my attempts to live the life I want, I'll have no choice but to do that."

Her mother's brow furrowed. "You should never have been given access to that money. You were far too young."

"I wasn't. I'm not. I have tried to be responsible with what I have. I'm not frivolously spending my trust money. I've thought through the decisions I've made to spend money and I've worked hard to achieve the goals I've set for myself. I mean, it took me two years to get the diploma for my online course." Maya felt emotion clog her throat. "I just want you to see that I'm trying to embrace life."

"Hello, my girls." Her father's voice broke the thick silence that had grown between them. He bent and gave them each a kiss before sitting down on another of the chairs at the small table.

"She is refusing to go to Paris," her mother said, her voice tight.

"I know, my love." Her dad laid his hand over his wife's. "It's time to let it go. To let her go."

Her mom jerked her hand back and got to her feet. "I cannot accept that."

She turned sharply from the table and walked out of the sunroom. Maya's shoulders slumped as her dad sighed.

"She'll come around, sweetheart. You just need to give her time."

"I'm trying, but she needs to give in a little." Staring down, Maya ran her fingertips around the edge of her mug. "I can't keep arguing with her like this. I know her reactions are coming out of fear for my life as much as love for me, but I need a chance to live. To experience things other people my age experience."

Her dad nodded. "I know that. Don't believe for a minute that just because I'm agreeing to this doesn't mean I don't share your mother's concerns. If I had my way, you'd never go anywhere without a body-guard, and you'd be getting blood tests and scans every single month."

Maya's eyes widened at her dad's confession. Through all the cancer treatments, her mom had been the fearful and emotional one. Hearing her dad reveal his own fears for her made her feel like she was being selfish wanting to live her own life.

"But I realize that is unrealistic. Also, I have to believe that you didn't beat cancer twice just to sit in your room. I believe that you have a purpose beyond the walls of this mansion. So, I will support your decisions. I think we've raised you to think through things and weigh your options. I want to be a part of your life, and I don't think questioning all your decisions or trying to undermine your plans will facilitate that."

"You think Mama will come around?" Maya appreciated her dad's support, but she really wanted her mom's. Her mom had been by her side through every step of her cancer journey. They'd faced death together and won. Now she wanted her mom to appreciate her efforts to live the life they'd fought so hard together to save.

"I think she will. Just give her time. I will continue to do what I can to encourage her to give you a chance to live your life." He hesitated as if uncertain about continuing, which wasn't a common expression on his face. And Maya knew it wasn't one that anyone but those closest to him would see. "Please reconsider moving out though. I will do my best to get your mom to give you the privacy you want."

"Thank you. I would really appreciate that." She gave him a wry smile. "I'm getting a little tired of hearing *where have you been* every time I walk in the front door."

He let out a laugh. "Okay. Yeah. I can understand why that would be a bit annoying."

"Just a bit," Maya agreed.

Her dad took a cookie from the plate and bit into it. "How is your job going? Are you enjoying working there?"

"I am," Maya said as she cupped her mug in her hands. "It's a challenge at times, but I love the atmosphere there. Yeah, it's a business, but it has a very family feel to it. Of course, the employees I work with are all family, so I suppose that contributes to the unique atmosphere."

"It seems to be a business with a good reputation," her dad said.

"You checked them out?" Maya asked, not really surprised at the thought.

"Of course," he said with a smile. "I may be willing to let you get a job, but I do want you working for a reputable business. C&M Builders is very much that. Reports I received said only good things about their business practices, and people spoke highly of not just Steve Callaghan but also Bennett McFadden."

Maya felt a rush of warmth at the knowledge that her dad approved of the people she worked with and had come to respect so much. Maybe one day they'd meet. She kind of hoped that day would come sooner rather than later. Well, hopefully soon her mother would settle down a bit and accept her life choices.

"I need to go check on your mom," her dad said. He reached out and touched her hand. "You're okay now?"

"I am."

With a nod, her dad got to his feet. He pressed a kiss to the top of her head before leaving her alone in the sunroom. Maya remained at the table long enough to finish her tea, her gaze on the snowy expanse of lawn and the frozen river beyond. The river had frozen early as they'd had some cold spells already, and it hadn't been above freezing for the past three weeks. It was going to make the winter seem longer than usual unless they had an early spring.

Once her tea was gone, Maya gathered up the dishes and took them to the kitchen. She chatted with Elisse for a few minutes before heading up to her room. Once there, she took her laptop to her bed and opened it up to see if Lainie was online. When she didn't see her there, she spent the rest of the afternoon doing some reading and then trying to figure out what to wear to church the next day. Her parents headed out to another dinner party, leaving her alone in the house except for Elisse and Thomas. Gabe's text with information about the church came through around nine.

Gabe: *You still able to come tomorrow?*

Definitely. I shall be there with bells on.

Gabe: *Well, given the holiday season, you could probably get away with that.*

Maya laughed. *LOL Yes, I suppose that's true. I'll have to see if I have any bells stashed away in my closet.*

Gabe: *I'm glad you're going to be there. I look forward to seeing you again. Think you might be up for Sunday dinner out here at the house with the family?*

Maya bit her lip at the question. She wasn't sure she could spend that much time away from the house without bringing on another inquisition. And while she didn't want to let her mom dictate what she did, she wasn't interested in pushing more than necessary. Church would be one thing. Dinner afterward might be too much. Plus…she wasn't entirely sure she was ready to be included in a family dinner just yet. Didn't that mean something? Meeting the parents/family?

Thank you for the invite, but I'm not sure I'm ready for that just yet.

She went for refusal that would bring the least amount of questions. Surely he would understand that there would be some assumptions made if she went to dinner with him. They'd barely known each other a week. Family dinner needed to wait awhile longer. Plus, she was nowhere near ready to invite him to a family dinner of her own. The very thought made her shudder.

Gabe: *Yeah. I guess it might be a bit too soon…Although it's not like you don't know a good chunk of the family already.*

True, but…

Gabe: *Okay. I won't push…this time. ;) Text me when you get to the church tomorrow, and I'll come meet you at the doors.*

Okay. See you then. Have a good night.

Gabe: *You too.*

GABE CHECKED HIS PHONE to make sure that even though he'd turned off the ringer, it was still on vibrate. He didn't want to miss the text from Maya alerting him to her arrival.

"Waiting for someone?"

He turned to find Mitch standing next to him, his hands in the pockets of his pants. "Yeah, I invited Maya to church."

Mitch's face was expressionless as he looked at the large glass windows of the foyer. "She said she'd come?"

"Yep. I told her to text me when she got here." Gabe still wasn't convinced that Mitch didn't have a thing for her. Or that he wasn't bothered by the fact that Maya obviously was willing to spend time with Gabe when she hadn't been with Mitch. If Mitch had even asked her to. "Did you ever invite her?"

"No. I never did." Mitch looked back at him. "Not sure if Makayla did either."

His phoned buzzed in his hand, and Gabe looked at the screen to see a text from Maya.

Maya: *I'm here. Are you?*

Gabe smiled. *You said you were going to be here, so there's no place I'd rather be. Come on up to the door. I'll meet you there.*

Happy at the thought of seeing Maya again, Gabe strode toward the large doors at the entrance. He spotted her walking through the first set of doors and was there to open the door as she approached the inner set. The dual doors helped to keep the cold air from rushing straight into the building, but there was still a slight cold breeze that accompanied Maya into the building.

Wearing a black wool, double-breasted coat that fit her figure perfectly, Maya looked beautiful. The light purple scarf that was tucked neatly into the neck of the coat complemented her dark hair and eyes. She smiled as soon as she saw him.

"Glad to see you made it safe and sound," Gabe said as he came to her side.

"My GPS was a good help to get here." Maya tugged off her gloves then reached up and undid the button at the top of her coat. "So cold out there today."

"Yeah. Can't remember it being this cold so early in the season in recent history." Gabe rested a hand lightly on her back. "You can hang your coat up in there."

It didn't take long for Maya to remove her winter wear. Underneath it, she wore an outfit that matched the style of her coat. It was a forest green, long sleeve, double-breasted top that flared out over a fitted skirt ending just above her knee. The color was flattering to her and fit in perfectly with the season. She wore a simple gold chain with a teardrop diamond hanging down into the V of her neckline. Her earrings had matching teardrops.

She had such an elegant style, and Gabe was a little surprised how attractive he found it. Given that the lifestyle he led was anything but elegant, he'd always thought he'd be attracted to a woman who shared his passion for the outdoors and exciting adventures. Even though Maya had come to the gym to climb, Gabe couldn't picture her in the more extreme environments he was often in.

"Hello, Mitch," Maya said as Mitch joined them just outside the coatroom.

Mitch gave her a friendly smile. "Good morning. Nice to see you here."

"Hope you don't mind me crashing your church after seeing me all week at work."

"You never have to worry about that. You're more than welcome here."

"Should we head on in?" Gabe suggested when he noticed the foyer had begun to empty.

As they walked down the side aisle of the large sanctuary, Gabe noticed people turning their heads to watch them. He and Mitch often drew attention because of their matching looks and height, but adding Maya to the mix with her exotic appearance was attracting even more attention.

Mitch led them to a pew about halfway down. Makayla and Ethan were already seated there with Bennett, and they each showed varying degrees of surprise when they saw Maya. The surprise quickly changed to smiles as they settled into the pew. Mitch was seated on one side of Maya while Gabe took the other.

He hadn't told anyone he'd invited Maya, not completely convinced that she would show. If she wasn't a regular church attendee, it had been possible that she might not feel comfortable coming. Though she'd said she would be there the night before, Gabe had realized she might change her mind in the cold light of day. He was glad, of course, that she hadn't.

Though he tried to find churches to attend wherever he was in his travels, Gabe appreciated coming back to the church that had been his home for most of his growing up years. There had been changes over the years. A new senior pastor. A new worship leader. But it still felt at home to him. And he watched with pride as Dalton and Danica walked onto the stage with the worship team. They were the youngest members of the team, but Gabe knew that they were talented enough to be there.

He leaned over to Maya and pointed the two out to her, explaining who they were in a low voice. When she looked at him with a wide smile, he knew that his pride in his siblings had shown through. There wasn't time for any further conversation as the worship leader stepped behind the microphone and welcomed them to the service.

Gabe was thankful that given the time of year, Maya would likely know the majority of the songs they sang. He wanted this to be a positive experience for her. Any hope of having a relationship would be gone if Maya was opposed to what Gabe believed in. As it was, not knowing for certain where she stood spiritually came to mind fairly often. He knew his dad would be asking him about that for sure if things started to get more serious between them.

After the welcome and opening prayer, Dalton stepped to the microphone as a young teen made her way down the aisle with a candle. Without a single show of nerves, Dalton began the readings for the third Sunday of Advent. Gabe's sense of pride in his younger brother grew as he listened to him read the scripture for the Advent of Joy and then moved smoothly into the reading for the day. His tone had a melodious note to it, and Gabe was sure he wasn't the only one enjoying the reading—well, aside from family.

Gabe remembered when he'd stood at the podium to read one of the Advent readings as a teenager. To his chagrin, he recalled being more interested in the fact that the eyes of a lot of teenage girls would be on him. He'd made sure to look his best that Sunday, spending way more time on his appearance than on practicing the reading. From the look of things, Dalton had spent at least equal—if not more—time on practicing the reading as he had on picking out what he'd planned to wear.

As they stood singing *O Come, O Come Emmanuel* following the reading and candle-lighting, Gabe found he enjoyed the sound of Maya's voice as she sang along. He glanced down at her, his heart expanding in his chest at the joy he saw on her face. More than anything, it made him very much want to have a chance at something more serious with Maya. If he could just figure out how to balance his love for adventure with that desire.

MAYA WAS SURPRISED how much she enjoyed the service. Not that she had thought she might not, but it had been awhile since she'd last been in a church. If she recalled correctly, it had been for a wedding of someone who worked for her dad, which meant it had been a completely different experience from the service at Gabe's church.

She'd appreciated the Christmas music, happy that she could sing along with most of the songs. The décor of the church had been something she'd enjoyed as well. A large tree stood off to the side of the stage at the front. It was decorated with white twinkle lights and what looked like cream-colored ornaments. There were several Poinsettia plants on the outside of the stairs that ran the width of the stage.

As she listened to the minister's sermon on joy, her current struggle with her mom came to mind. Even when she'd been succeeding in keeping Maya sheltered, her mother had never seemed happy. The life they'd lived together hadn't brought her mother joy. In fact, the last time she remembered her mom having any sort of joy had been back before her very first cancer diagnosis. But even then, it had all been tempered with sadness that underlaid everything. Maya knew now it was because of the struggle her parents had faced to have more children. Each miscarriage her mom had experienced before and after her birth had seemed to take another piece of her soul. Was it possible for her to get joy back?

Maya really hoped so because both of her parents deserved to be happy with each other. To spend these later years of their life enjoying the time they had together. Right now, her mom's sadness was hindering that, and it was eating away at her dad too. It was only now as Maya was seeking things that brought her joy that she could see how things were for her parents.

As she listened to the minister, Maya began to frown but then quickly worked to smooth out her expression. His words suggested that no matter what she pursued in life—no matter how much she might enjoy what she was doing—she wouldn't know true joy without accepting God into her life.

Those words lingered with her as they stood to sing a hymn once the minister had finished with a prayer and stepped off the stage. The concept presented in the sermon wasn't something she'd heard before—or if she had, she'd heard it as a young teen and it hadn't sunk in—and Maya wasn't sure how she felt about it.

"Are you sure you can't join us for dinner out at my folks' place?" Gabe said when the service was over and they were making their way up the sloping aisle to the doors that led to the foyer. The others in their pew had exited the opposite end and had stopped to talk to people.

"I'm sure, but thank you for the invitation." Maya didn't feel that it was her place to join a family dinner since she still felt more like an employee than a family friend. Regardless of the time she was spending with Gabe.

Gabe nodded, as if he had already anticipated her response. "But we're still on for a movie this week?"

"Yep. I don't have any set plans for the week yet, so my calendar is wide open." Of course, her calendar was usually pretty wide open.

At one point in her life she'd spent a lot of time gaming, and in those situations, her guild had relied on her, so she'd had times she wasn't available for other activities. She'd been their best healer, and they didn't normally like to attack the dungeons without her as part of their party.

In the past six months, though, she'd been trying to move from a virtual life to a real one. That meant that while she did log in to help out at times, it wasn't as often as it had been at one time. Definitely not the daily occurrence it had been a year ago.

"Thank you for coming today," Gabe said as he held her coat for her.

Maya felt his hands linger on her shoulders after he'd lifted it into place, and she began to button it. Looping her scarf around her neck, she turned to face him with a smile. "I really enjoyed it. Thank you for inviting me."

With her scarf secure, she tugged on her wool-lined gloves, not all that eager to head out into the cold. She took her keys out and aimed the remote start fob toward the parking lot where her car would hopefully start. When she'd purchased it, she'd made sure it had a long-range remote start for situations just like this.

"I'll text you later about the movie," Gabe said as he walked by her side to the large doors. "But I might see you tomorrow."

Maya couldn't help but smile. "I'd like that."

When she walked into the mansion a short time later, Maya was already braced for a meeting with her mom. Because of the security cameras placed along the winding driveway, she could have spotted Maya's car as it approached the house if she'd been watching. Given how often her mom met her in the foyer, Maya no longer thought that she wasn't logging into the cameras to watch for her.

Even though she was standing in the foyer, her mom didn't say a word, but Maya knew it was probably taking every ounce of her control not to. It seemed her dad had had a conversation with her Mom as he'd promised.

"I was at church." Maya tugged off her gloves and unwound the scarf.

When her mom's finely plucked brows climbed nearly halfway up her forehead, Maya knew that of all her destinations lately, this one had surprised her mom the most.

"Church? Why would you go to church?"

Though she hadn't really been all that excited about it as a teen, they had attended church fairly regularly. But when they had stopped going, Maya hadn't really cared. Now she wondered if it had been more than just the struggle of attending church when she'd been undergoing treatment and trying to stay clear of germs and illness while doing so.

"I was invited by someone from work and thought I'd go. It's not like I had anything else going on this morning."

"Did you enjoy it?"

Her mom's question surprised Maya, but she went ahead and answered. "Yes, actually, I did. It was nice to sing the Christmas songs, and they had an Advent candle-lighting and reading. It was very lovely."

A smile briefly crossed her mother's face. "The Christmas music was always my favorite part of this season in church."

"I'm just going to go get changed then I'll be back down for dinner." Though they dressed for dinner when they had company, they were definitely more casual when it was just the three of them.

When she rejoined her mom and dad a few minutes later, Maya was happy to see that her mom seemed more relaxed. As they ate the meal Elisse had prepared for them, the discussion focused around their schedules for the upcoming week. Not surprisingly, her dad's was the most hectic with a quick trip to New York mid-week.

"Why don't you go with him, Mama? It's been awhile since you were last in New York." Maya told herself she was being altruistic, but she knew that wasn't necessarily the case. At least not completely. She did think the trip would be good for her mom, but there was no doubt that having her mom gone when she went on her movie date with Gabe would make her situation easier.

When her mom hesitated, her dad laid his hand on hers. "Come with me, love. I'll stay an extra day, and we can go shopping or to a show. Maybe I'll see if Ian and Margot are available to spend some time with us. Would you like that?"

Her mom's brow furrowed as she looked back and forth between them. "But what if Maya needs me?"

"I'll be fine, Mama. And if I need you, I'll call, and you can bring the jet back. You'd be home within hours."

"She's right," her dad said. "I'll make sure the jet is available if you need to come back in a hurry."

Maya knew her mom was tempted, she could see it on her face. New York at Christmas time was her mom's favorite, and it had been a few years since she'd last been there.

She turned her gaze to Maya. "You have to promise me you'll call if you need me. If you need me and you don't call, you'll never get rid of me again."

Maya didn't doubt those words at all. "I promise, Mama. If I need you for anything, I'll call."

And she would. She knew that in order for her mom to trust her judgment, Maya would have to call her if something happened. If she didn't, her mom would never trust her, and their relationship would continue to be strained.

"I have to be there for all of Wednesday, so we have to leave Tuesday, but we can stay until Friday. If you'd like."

Her mom seemed to consider it, and Maya held her breath, only letting it out when she nodded. Once that was settled, Maya happily participated in the conversation about what shows they might go see. There was a small part of her that wished she could go along. She loved Christmas in New York as well, but that really was just a small part of her. A much larger part wanted to have a week just on her own, going to work and out on a date with Gabe without her mother watching her every move.

Back up in her room after they'd finished dinner, Maya settled onto her window seat and pulled out her phone to send Gabe a message.

Had something come up. Best nights to go would be Tues, Wed or Thurs. Hope one of those works for you.

Gabe's reply didn't come right away, and Maya hoped she hadn't somehow upset him by narrowing down her available dates after telling him she was basically available all week. She didn't think she had, but really, they'd only known each other for such a short time that she couldn't claim to be an expert on all things Gabe Callaghan.

Chapter Eight

RATHER THAN DWELL ON IT or wait around like some lovesick girl, Maya got her laptop from the desk and checked to see if Lainie was around. When her reply came quickly, Maya settled back in the window seat and waited for their Skype video to connect.

They'd been talking for about thirty minutes when her phone chirped a text alert.

"Is that him?" Lainie asked, leaning closer to her camera as if she could see the phone screen from her vantage point.

Maya picked her phone up and stared at the screen. She glanced up at Lainie and smiled. "Yep. He *says any or all of those nights work for me*."

They laughed together then Lainie said, "Well, he's not making any secret of his interest, is he?"

"No, he's not, and I'm not sure what to make of it, honestly." Maya paused to type out a response. *Well, we can start with Tuesday and see how it goes. :-)*

"It is a little daunting to be going on first dates and having first crushes at an age when everyone else is more experienced," Lainie said. "And without going into a long explanation why, it's hard to deal with sometimes."

Maya set her phone down and turned her attention back to her laptop screen. "I know. I'm trying to appear like I know what I'm doing, but at times like this, I wonder if it's too much too soon. I mean, should I be playing a little more hard to get?"

"Sweetie, I think we both know that playing hard to get could be wasting time we might not have. Tomorrow isn't guaranteed to anyone. We know that more than most people."

"True. I just feel like I need to tell him about the cancer stuff, especially since I have another round of bloodwork and scans coming up."

"You're getting scans?" Lainie asked, a frown pulling down the corners of her mouth. "Has something come up?"

Maya sighed. "No, but it's been a year since my last scan so my parents are insisting on another one and are willing to pay for it at a private clinic in North Dakota."

"Do you think they'll ever accept that you're in remission or will they pay out for a scan each year?"

"I think it's a year by year thing," Maya said, though she had a feeling her dad would insist that she have a scan each year. "At some point, I suppose I could take control of my own medical care and just put my foot down. Unfortunately, I can't quite dismiss the small amount of fear I have myself. You know, the feeling that something could be growing inside of me, and I wouldn't know it until it's too late."

Lainie didn't have to say anything. By her expression, Maya knew that she understood.

Her phone chirped again, and Maya gave it a quick look.

Gabe: *That sounds like a plan. Still might see you tomorrow. ;-) Looking forward to it.*

As always, chatting with Lainie ran the gamut of emotions from laughter to more serious moments. She really was the one person that Maya felt understood what she was dealing with. Lainie had already experienced going on dates, but nothing had panned out for her. Both times, when she'd shared her history with cancer, the guys had ended up ghosting her. Lainie deserved so much better than that, and unfortunately, it had made her a bit gun-shy about going on dates for a third time.

Maya wasn't sure what she'd do if Gabe decided he didn't want to take on the chance of her cancer recurring. It wasn't like she could avoid him—or his family—unless she quit her job. Up until that point, she hadn't really been thinking about which she wanted more: a chance for something with Gabe or her job. Because if one went south, what would happen with the other?

"Only you can decide if the risk is worth taking, hun," Lainie said as she lifted one leg to rest her cheek against her knee. "I'm going to be avoiding men for the next little while. I don't need to have a crush right now. It clouds my judgment. I think I'd like to try being friends with a guy first. Maybe tell him about my history when we're still just friends, so he already knows should he decide to take the relationship beyond friendship."

This thing with Gabe was her first attempt at…something. She still wasn't sure if Gabe was interested in something more serious which made her reluctant to label it.

"So what's up with you and our receptionist?" Bennett asked as he sat down on the couch beside Gabe. "I'd really rather you didn't do anything that might make her want to quit. We need her."

Gabe frowned at him. "I'm not planning on that."

"Planning or not, it can happen, particularly since you don't have any intentions of putting down roots here." Bennett lifted a brow. "Unless things have changed?"

Gabe looked away. Things hadn't changed. He still had plans to leave Winnipeg after the holidays. Nothing could change since other people were relying on him for plans that had been made a long time ago.

"We're just getting to know each other. Enjoying doing some things together." Gabe hoped that Bennett didn't push because he really didn't know what he'd tell the guy. He figured he could play dirty and ask his older brother how things were going with Grace and the baby, but since he'd seen the heartache in the man's eyes, Gabe couldn't bring himself to do it.

Bennett sighed. "What are you doing, Gabriel?"

In the absence of Kenton, Bennett readily stepped into the role of sole big brother. Gabe had always respected the man. Probably more than he did Kenton, if he was honest. He respected Kenton for things like his drive to succeed as a hockey player and his willingness to take risks both on and off the ice. But when it came to personality and the ability to connect and care for those around him, it was Bennett that garnered Gabe's respect.

He wasn't sure how to reply to Bennett's question. What he wanted to say didn't make much sense given how he'd only known Maya for such a short time.

Bennett sat back into the corner of the couch, hitching an ankle on his knee. "Maya's a real sweet girl. I wasn't too sure about hiring her since she basically had no experience, but Makayla and...uh...Grace insisted on it. They'd met with her and thought that she'd be a good fit for the company. They were right. Even with Grace having to leave early, Maya has stepped up and done an admirable job." Bennett paused. "Because of that, I'd really rather you not lead her on or just play around."

"Are you planning to keep her on after Grace returns to work?"

Bennett nodded. "Yes. I think we'll have room for both of them. With the way the business is growing, we'll need strong admin support."

Gabe found that he liked the idea of Maya being part of the family business. Although that thought made it far too easy to imagine something more serious with her. But what would that mean for the life he currently led? He hadn't imagined that he'd be able to travel and experience risk-taking adventures for the rest of his life, but he had thought that he'd be able to do it well into his thirties. And then to a lesser degree, into his forties and fifties.

Love and marriage had been an abstract thing. Something he hadn't spent much time pondering. And when he *had* thought about it, he'd just assumed the person he ended up with would be part of the world he embraced. So instead of going on adventures alone, he'd have a partner. Someone to love and share the life he loved.

Unfortunately, he couldn't see Maya being that person. Which meant what, exactly, for their current situation? He didn't know.

"We're just getting to know each other. Doing some things together. She knows I'm only here for a few weeks."

Bennett didn't answer right away but then nodded. "Just think about what you're doing. For some reason, I get a real innocent vibe from Maya. Not just in the work place, but in life in general. Not sure how someone could be that way in this day and age, especially in their mid-twenties, but that's how she comes across. And in case she doesn't have an older brother looking out for her, I'm going to put myself in that role when it comes to this situation."

"She doesn't."

"Doesn't what?" Bennett asked.

"Have an older brother. She's an only child."

"Guess you discovered that as part of your getting to know each other?"

"Yeah. She mentioned that when I told her a bit about our family." Gabe turned to look at Bennett more fully. "I was surprised that she didn't know more about us all. I mean, she didn't even know that Mitch had a twin. Has she not been invited to family stuff?"

"She has," Bennett said with a tilt of his head. "But she's declined all invitations that fell outside work hours. She comes to our Friday staff lunches, but other than that, she's not come to anything else."

"She met me at the climbing gym on Saturday, and then we went for lunch. We're also going to a movie on Tuesday night."

Bennett sighed. "Just…be careful with her."

Before Gabe could say anything more, Mitch and Tristan joined them. Ethan settled into an armchair next to the couch, but he wasn't alone for long. Makayla came into the living room and sat down in his lap, leaning into his side. There was some discussion amongst his siblings about Kenton's latest game. He'd been injured at the beginning of the season and finally had his first game back after four weeks off.

Gabe hoped to catch a couple of Kenton's games during his travels. Being in different divisions meant that Kenton's team didn't play the Jets as frequently as other teams did. He had to wonder, after this latest injury, if Kenton was considering retirement, even though he was just thirty years old.

As the afternoon unwound, Gabe wondered what Maya was doing. How she filled her time when she wasn't at work. Did she have a lot of friends? Since he knew her family was small, maybe she filled the void of siblings with friendships. He found that he was curious about her friends and hoped that he'd have the chance to meet them.

Though he wanted to text or call her, Gabe decided that maybe that would be too much. Instead, he decided to see if she had a social media presence and would maybe connect with her that way.

AFTER WHAT HE'D SAID, Maya had anticipated that Gabe would show up at the office at some point on Monday, but around noon, her phone chirped with a text from him.

Gabe: *Not gonna make it to the office today. I'm in an all-day meeting with my business partners. Guess I'll see you tomorrow.*

Though she was disappointed, Maya knew that his presence would have been a distraction for her, so it was probably just as well. *Hope it goes well. Looking forward to the movie.*

Gabe: *Me too! Can we grab dinner before or after?*

Maya smiled at his suggestion. Since she'd be on her own at home, dinner out would be a welcome thing. Not that Elisse wouldn't cook for her, but it would give the older woman a break and would give Maya that much extra time to spend with Gabe.

Dinner sounds great. If we go to the late show, we can grab dinner first. Just tell me where to meet you. :)

Gabe: *Still not letting me pick you up?*

Maya bit her lip. She just wasn't ready to reveal that part of her life yet. It really had no bearing on their relationship or whatever it was they had. Given he was leaving in a few weeks—which would make anything between them temporary—she didn't think it was necessary to tell him everything about herself just yet.

Nothing personal. I just prefer to drive myself. Hope that's okay.

Gabe: *It's fine. All that matters is that you actually show up.*

No worries. I'll be there. Wouldn't miss it.

GABE WASN'T IN THE OFFICE the next day either, so as soon as her day was over, Maya headed for home. She wanted to change before heading to the Olive Garden where they'd agreed to meet before heading to the movie.

It had been snowing off and on throughout the day, so it took a little longer than usual to get home. Once there, she plugged in her flat iron and sat down at her makeup table to freshen up her makeup. After using the narrow flat iron to smooth the flyaways and curl the ends of her hair, Maya headed for her closet.

She really shouldn't have been worried about what she wore—about how she looked. But she just couldn't help it, so it took her longer than she'd planned to decide what to wear. In the end, she pulled on a pair of black skinny jeans and a soft rose colored sweater that hung low on her hips and had a cowl neck that draped over her shoulders. She tugged on a pair of boots that went to her knees and then took a minute to spritz some of her favorite cologne—Chanel N°5—before grabbing her purse and jacket.

"I'm off, Elisse," she called as she jogged past the kitchen. "Enjoy your evening with Thomas."

She heard the older woman's chuckle as she reached the door leading to the garage. She'd parked in the garage when she'd come home since it was snowing, and she didn't want to have to brush her car off again before leaving.

With the roads being more snow-covered than usual, Maya took her time on the long driveway and then the highway leading into the city. She was grateful for the all-wheel drive capabilities of her car. When she'd bought it, she'd made the decision herself after doing a lot of research, but she'd been happy when her dad had given his approval of the model she'd bought.

The restaurant parking lot was nearly full when she pulled in, forcing her to park a little ways away from the building. She tugged her hood up over her hair, then grabbed her purse and headed for the entrance. The hostess led her deeper into the restaurant when she gave her name. Apparently, Gabe was already there waiting for her.

As they approached the booth where he sat, Gabe got to his feet. He wore a pair of blue jeans and a long sleeved black T-shirt. He had a bit of scruff on his face, and Maya suddenly discovered that she had a real attraction to that look. She wondered what it would feel like if she reached out to touch his jawline.

"Hey!" Gabe said as she came to a stop next to him.

"Sorry I'm a bit late." Maya felt the urge to give him a hug but resisted it and slid into the booth opposite the side he'd been seated in. "That snow really slowed down the traffic."

"Yeah. It was a mess out there." Gabe smiled at her as he sat across from her, making butterflies came to life within Maya. "You look beautiful."

Heat rushed into her cheeks as the number of butterflies exploded. Maya couldn't help but return his smile. "Thank you."

"Thank *you* for coming out with me tonight. I'm really looking forward to it."

The waitress's arrival helped to keep things from getting awkward. Maya just wanted to get past the first part of the evening. The greeting where the hug seemed right but didn't happen, got them off to an awkward start. Hopefully, once they placed their orders, the conversation would flow more easily.

After the waitress left to get them their drinks, they discussed the meal specials and their experiences with different menu items. When the waitress brought them their drinks, they were both ready to order. Once that was done, and the menus were taken away, a few moments of silence settled between them.

"Did you have a good day at work?" Gabe asked.

Maya nodded, though for the life of her she couldn't remember exactly how the day had gone. She always enjoyed what she did for C&M Builders, but today, her thoughts throughout the day had been focused on the upcoming date.

Gabe got a mischievous glint in his eye. "So which of my siblings do you like working with the best?"

"You honestly expect me to answer that?" Maya asked with a grin. "I love working with all of them."

"Ah, c'mon." Gabe leaned forward. "I won't tell anyone. If you answer my question, I'll tell you who my favorite sibling is."

Maya laughed at that. "Pretty sure your favorite is Mitch."

"Okay, well, I suppose that was kind of obvious. Is he your favorite too?"

"I have favorites for different things," Maya said, trying to be diplomatic. "Bennett and Makayla were intimidating at first, but now they're not so bad."

"Yeah, they are the most intense of all of us. Tristan and Mitch are at the opposite end of the spectrum. They are probably the easiest going of us all. Well, Danica is pretty easy going too."

Maya took a breadstick from the basket the waitress had placed on the table. She hesitated to take a bite since she knew that Gabe had prayed before previous meals they'd shared.

He seemed to read her mind because he said, "Hold that thought. Mind if I pray for the food?"

Maya shook her head then closed her eyes as Gabe said a quick prayer of thanks for the meal. When he was done, she took a bite of the bread stick. Though she usually restricted her intake of stuff like bread and pasta, both were hard to avoid at a place like Olive Garden, and since she enjoyed both, she decided to just treat it as a cheat meal.

"I still can't believe that Bennett has feelings for Grace," Maya mused once the prayer was over, continuing the topic of Gabe's siblings. She thought of the sadness she'd seen in Bennett's eyes recently. "That must be so hard. To love someone and not have those feelings returned."

"You've never experienced that?" Gabe asked as he broke off a piece of a breadstick.

Reticent to give away how inexperienced she was in the world of love and dating, Maya said, "No. I mean, yeah, I've had crushes on people who didn't return the feelings, but never been in love like that."

Gabe's expression was thoughtful. "No, me either. And I wish Bennett didn't have to experience it. It's probably even more difficult because Grace is someone close to our family. She's Makayla's best friend, so it's not like she won't be a part of our lives. And, of course, they live in the same building."

The waitress appeared with their food, and once again the conversation shifted. Maya was glad that the topic moved on from love and relationships. For some reason, Gabe seemed happy to dominate the conversation with stories about his family. She appreciated the insight into the people she worked with. It made her feel even more like she was part of the C&M Builders family.

"Ready to go?" Gabe asked once they were done eating. "The movie starts in about twenty minutes."

Maya nodded then waited as Gabe took care of the bill. They walked out together, and Gabe, once again, offered to drive to the mall where the theater was and then bring her back. She agreed since it was just a short drive away. They were there in less than five minutes.

Her indulgence continued as Gabe bought them a large buttered popcorn to share and a drink for each of them. She was determined to enjoy the experience since she rarely went to movies. Not having friends to do things with, she usually waited for movies that interested her to come out on Blu-ray and then she'd watch it in the theater they had in the mansion. It was set up like a theater, so she kind of had a taste of going to the movies'.

But with Gabe there beside her, Maya realized just how lacking that experience had been. Sitting with her arm pressed against his, she wondered what he'd think about the theater in the basement of her home. It would definitely be a more intimate viewing experience. They could talk about the movie without having to worry about disrupting it for those around them.

She was glad that they'd chosen to watch an action-adventure movie instead of a romance. It would have been a bit uncomfortable for her if their first movie together had included a love story. Comedies were a hit and miss thing for her, and she hadn't wanted anything that might make her cry. Thankfully, they'd both agreed on the movie without much discussion.

By the time the movie ended, Maya wasn't sure that she'd remember much of the storyline, but the memory of being there with Gabe would linger forever. She'd remember the brush of their hands as they'd repeatedly reached for popcorn at the same time. The press of his arm to hers, its warmth a reassuring presence. And how, a few times, he'd turned to whisper a comment about the movie, the brush of air against her ear as he spoke giving her shivers. All of that and more would imprint this evening in her memory, even if whatever it was between them ended up being nothing more than a good friendship.

It was late when they walked out of the theater. The snow had continued to fall, so Gabe needed to brush off his vehicle before they could leave. He'd told her to get inside, and he'd started it, so warmth flowed out of the vents. Maya watched as Gabe used a long brush to scoop away the snow on the windows. After it was all clear, he climbed behind the wheel, flashing her a quick smile that disappeared from sight when he closed the door and the interior light went off.

He rubbed his hands together then held them out to the vents. "The temperature is dropping, I think."

"I'm not enjoying this winter too much," Maya said. "Usually it's not this cold until January."

Gabe pulled out of the parking spot. "Yeah. That's why I usually plan to be somewhere other than Winnipeg in January."

Maya didn't like the idea of Gabe leaving, but she didn't want to live in denial of what was to come. "So where are you headed in January?"

"Thailand, actually," Gabe said. "I'm traveling with a group other people to Thailand for a month."

"A month?"

"Yep. One of our group has managed to line up some very affordable housing for us, and we'll have three different home bases while we explore the country. It definitely won't be cold, that's for sure."

"Have you been there before?"

"Yeah, but it was only a quick trip with a specific goal."

Maya wanted to ask more, but Gabe was pulling into the spot next to her car in the nearly empty parking lot at Olive Garden. "Thanks for another fun time."

"You're welcome." Gabe turned the interior light on. "Why don't you start your car and wait here while I clean it off."

"You don't have to do that," Maya said, reaching for the door handle.

Gabe laid a gloved hand on her arm. "I know I don't have to, but I want to do this for you. It won't take too long."

Warmth that had nothing to do with the air from the vents flooded through Maya at his words. "Thank you."

Gabe made quick work of her car then leaned in to let her know it was good to go. She climbed out and circled around to where he stood. This time, Gabe reached out and pulled her into a hug. Maya's heart pounded as she wrapped her arms around his waist. Even though it was freezing, standing there with the snow falling all around them had suddenly become her absolute favorite moment. She didn't feel the cold as she stood there in Gabe's arms.

When he stepped back, his hands slid down to take hers for a moment. They were both wearing gloves so she couldn't feel his skin against hers, but still, she felt the strength in his grip on her fingers.

"Thank you again for tonight," Maya said. "I really, really enjoyed it."

Gabe smiled down at her, his expression soft in the light cast by the parking lot lampposts. "I did too. I hope we can do it again soon."

"Me too. Maybe we can talk tomorrow?"

"Definitely."

Though Maya didn't want the evening to end, the cold was starting to seep through her jacket. She turned and opened the door, glad that the car had warmed up a bit. Gabe held the upper edge of the door as she settled behind the wheel and did up her seat belt.

They said goodnight then Gabe shut the door for her and stepped back. With a final wave, Maya pulled out of her parking spot and away from Gabe. She glanced into her rear-view mirror and saw his truck follow her out of the lot onto the street and then the highway. She hated to see the end of such a perfect evening, but she had high hopes for the evenings together that she hoped were yet to come.

Chapter Nine

*T*HAT HUG BESIDE MAYA'S CAR set a precedence for their future meetings—except for the ones at the office—and Maya
found she had one more reason to look forward to seeing
Gabe. She'd taken advantage of her parents' absence and had done
something with Gabe Wednesday and Thursday nights as well.

On Wednesday, they'd met up at a Tim Hortons after dinner and
grabbed some donuts and hot drinks. Gabe had then driven them
through the Christmas light display that was set up west of the city.
Though she'd been through the display in previous years with her mom
and one of their drivers, going there now with Gabe had been far more
memorable than any of the other times had been.

Thursday night, they'd attended a Christmas dinner theatre that had
been put on by Gabe's church. His youngest brother and sister had been
part of the production that had started that night and would run through
Sunday night. She'd been so impressed by the performance and had
thoroughly enjoyed the evening even beyond just being with Gabe. His
parents had been at the table with them, as had Makayla and Ethan and
Sammi and her boyfriend. None of them had questioned her presence
there. They'd just welcomed her with friendly smiles as she sat down
on the chair Gabe had pulled out for her next to Makayla.

Though she'd been happy to see her parents when they returned on
Friday, she knew that having them home would change things up a bit
unless she was willing to tell them about Gabe. So she'd spent Friday
evening having dinner with them, hearing all about their trip to New
York. Saturday morning, she'd managed to sneak off to the gym to give
climbing another try. Nerves were non-existent this time around, but
the butterflies that seemed to always be present when she was going to
see Gabe had been out in full force.

She'd gone to church again on Sunday, and on the drive there, Maya
had realized she was thinking as much about the upcoming service as
she was about seeing Gabe again. Thoughts of the previous Sunday's
sermon had lingered throughout the week, coming to mind at the oddest
times. She'd been curious if the sermon for that Sunday would be as

impactful as the previous week, and it had been. Both Sunday services had carried a strong reminder of what Christmas really was about.

Unfortunately, in the remaining days leading up to Christmas, she hadn't managed to spend as much time with Gabe. Between family obligations on both sides, they'd had to rely on text messages and phone calls. If nothing else, the brief break from constant contact with Gabe had reinforced her growing feelings for the man.

Maya still had no idea when she should broach the subject of her health history. Though part of her had wondered if she had to at all, she had quickly acknowledged that all of that had played a role in who she was and how her life had unfolded from the moment she'd been given her cancer diagnosis. Her relationship with her parents had also been impacted as a result. So there really was no way to not have to share that history at some point if she really wanted something more serious with Gabe.

That was also assuming that a more serious relationship was what he wanted.

As Christmas Day drew to a close, quiet settled over the mansion. Not that it had been all that noisy since it was just the three of them, but her mom had set up a playlist of Christmas music that had drifted through every room all day. Presents were always a challenge for the three of them. What did you get the person who could afford to buy whatever they wanted? If her mom wanted a designer outfit or bag, she'd just buy it for herself. If her dad wanted a new car, he bought it. Two cars, if he wanted. So it had required her to think far in advance since whatever she got for them wouldn't be something she could just pick up off the shelf or order online.

In the end, she'd commissioned a painting from an artist who had taken a photo and transposed it onto a large canvas. The photo was of the three of them taken just weeks after Maya's birth and had always been her favorite. It was a professional photo of her mom holding her, and her dad with his arms wrapped around them both. Her parents had been gazing down at her, and it had perfectly captured the closeness of their family. And the artist had done a superb job of transferring their expressions from the photo to the canvas.

Maya knew that she'd done a good job in choosing that gift when both her parents had ended up with tears in their eyes upon unwrapping it. She'd gotten in touch with the artist early in the year, and the delivery had come the beginning of the month. It had been everything she'd hoped for and more.

Her parents had been discussing where they planned to hang it as they'd made their way up to their suite. Relieved that her parents had liked her gift, Maya was happy to retreat to her own rooms with her parents' gift to her.

Not too surprisingly, they'd given her more jewelry, but this time it was a piece that they had both had a hand in designing. The white gold necklace had a fine chain with a pendant that was the Japanese character for love set in the center of a circle of diamonds. Not all the strokes of the character touched, so slender fragments of the gold joined the broader strokes, giving the illusion that the small detached ones were floating. It was nestled right into the base of her neck, and Maya took a moment to admire it in the mirror, appreciating the nod to her mom's heritage.

She'd been uncertain about whether or not to buy a gift for Gabe, but when he'd brought up the idea of buying something for her, Maya had told him she didn't need anything, and that he hadn't needed to worry about it. He'd resisted the idea, finally accepting it when she agreed to let him bring her something back from Thailand. In the meantime, she was going to need to see if she could find a gift for him.

After a last touch to the pendant, Maya grabbed her laptop and settled on the window seat to see if Lainie was online. Her friend had been a great source of support and had been listening to her go back and forth on when she should tell Gabe about her health history.

Unfortunately, Lainie hadn't really been able to help except for being a sounding board. She'd shared her experiences with Maya, but all that had done had been to reinforce the feeling that she didn't want to have to tell him at all—which wasn't an option. Maybe if Maya had more experience with love and relationships, it wouldn't be so difficult. She was just scared of messing up her first—and if she had her way, last—shot at love. But what if Gabe didn't feel as strongly as she did? Maybe the time apart when he left in January would be a good thing. If he came back and seemed interested in continuing on, then maybe she'd tell him then. She needed to see where he thought things were going before she decided to reveal anything. He'd told her that he was leaving on January second, so they had just over a week left.

Not surprisingly, Lainie wasn't on, and there was no text or call from Gabe. Both of them had larger families they were hanging out with and would no doubt be tied up for the rest of the day. Having seen first hand how a larger family could be, Maya found herself really wishing that her parents had been able to have more children. But that was never going to happen, and she'd never voice her wish to her parents. Though they might not have had a huge family, she suspected that if they could have had more children, she'd have had at least two siblings.

Deciding that she would end the day doing something she enjoyed, Maya went into the spacious ensuite bathroom and began to run water into the large garden tub. She flicked on the switch to start the fireplace and then dimmed the lights. After adding a bath bomb and some oils to the water, she turned on the jets. There was a large window that ran the length of the tub that faced out into the forest, and the bathroom was high enough up that she wasn't worried about anyone seeing in. The window curved over the top of the tub so that she could see the stars in the dark night sky.

Even though there was a television at the foot of the tub above the fireplace, Maya opted to play some soft instrumental music. It was the second best way to close out a day that had ended up being pretty good. After she had sunk into the warmth of the water, she leaned her head back and closed her eyes, listening to the soothing sounds of the fireplace and the music.

Gabe had invited her to come out to their place for a Boxing Day gathering the next day. There was talk of ice skating and food, but Maya still wasn't sure if she was going to go. For one thing, she hadn't been on skates in more years than she could remember. Secondly, she wasn't sure how to get away from the mansion and her mom without having to fill out a questionnaire. She really wanted to see Gabe again, but she just wasn't sure she wanted to have to deal with her mom.

As if her thoughts brought it on, her phone chirped. She lifted it up from where it sat next to the tub.

Gabe: *So did you have a good day?*

Yes, we really enjoyed our day. How about you?

Gabe: *Hectic and out of control like most holidays. I can't even imagine what it's going to be like when the grandchildren start coming.*

That would probably be a lot of fun.

Gabe: *Fun, yeah, but still crazy!*

The more, the merrier, right?

Gabe: *You know it. That applies to tomorrow as well. Are you going to be part of the more? So it can be merrier?*

Maya stared at the screen. Trying to keep two parts of her life separate was starting to stress her out. But she just couldn't see the sense in telling her mom and dad about Gabe or Gabe about her family if their relationship wasn't going to turn into anything serious. Maybe knowing about her situation would make Gabe second guess a relationship with her. In that case, it would be better to know sooner rather than later.

Ugh…she just couldn't seem to stop her mind from going around in circles, and the reality was that she was most likely overthinking it all.

Yes, I think it will work for me to be there. Even though it's been ages since I've been on skates.

Gabe: *Well, that will just give me even more reason to stick close to you. *Wink* Wouldn't want you to injure yourself without proper supervision.*

LOL Yeah, wouldn't want that.

They texted for a few more minutes with Gabe promising to send her directions to the family home before they said goodnight. Now all she had to do was hope her mom didn't ask too many questions when she told her that she'd be going out for awhile.

GABE WANDERED INTO THE KITCHEN to see if his mom needed some help with the food for the group that would be gathering there later in the day. Most people would arrive in the early afternoon to do some skating before having a dinner together. There would be time for general skating, but Gabe was pretty sure that a hockey game would break out at some point.

His business partners, Tennyson and Forrest as well as Hunter and Brent would be coming. Some of them with significant others. Tennyson and Forrest's foster sisters, Noella and Erin would also be coming with their husbands. The group that gathered on Boxing Day was slowly growing as their friendship group expanded and relationships developed. Gabe was glad that this year, he was going to have someone special there with him for once.

Though Mitch had had a couple of girlfriends over the years, Gabe hadn't dated much at all since he'd thought he didn't have a lifestyle that worked well with relationships. So while his twin was open to love and marriage, Gabe hadn't been so sure it would work for him at that point in his life. Plus, he just hadn't met anyone he had been interested in devoting time to.

Until Maya.

"Can I get you to grate the cheese, sweetie?" his mom asked when she spotted him.

"Sure thing," Gabe said as he headed to the sink to wash his hands. When he'd finished, his mom gestured to where she'd set the grater and the cheese. In years past, they'd tried to convince her to just buy already shredded cheese, but she'd insisted that the stuff they grated themselves was better.

"We're having chili, right?" Gabe asked as he dried his hands.

"Yes. We've had it in the slow cookers for a few hours now. Your dad insisted we make a larger batch than we usually do."

"It smells wonderful," Gabe said as he began to move the block of cheese across the grater. "Dad's probably right that we need more. We had hardly any leftovers last year, if I recall correctly."

"You're right." She shrugged as she smiled. "But it's better to have too much than too little. If we do have leftovers, we'll be eating chili for awhile."

"Did you need me, Mama?" Dalton asked as he came into the kitchen.

"Yes. How about you mix up a couple batches of brownies?"

"Okay." Dalton turned to the cupboard and began to pull ingredients out.

"Do you make brownies a lot, Dal?"

His brother turned and scowled at him with a flick of his head to keep his hair off his face. "Don't call me that."

"What? Dal?"

"I'm not a doll." The young teen swung back to the cupboard to pull out a few more things. "And yes. Brownies are my specialty."

"Really?" Gabe watched as Dalton began to measure out ingredients into the bowl their mom had placed on the counter. "No recipe?"

"Nope. It's all up here." Dalton tapped his temple. "I've made it often enough that I don't need the recipe anymore."

Gabe felt a sense of regret that he was missing a lot of his younger siblings' growing up years. As much as he loved the adventures he went on, there was no question that it came with a few sacrifices. But he did try to make it home for the major holidays and any significant events. Which was more than he could say for Kenton. He rarely made it home once a year, if that.

By the time Gabe had finished his job with the cheese—which had been significant since they had a lot of people coming—Dalton was putting the first pan of brownies in the oven. Tristan—who still lived at home—came into the kitchen with Danica to offer a hand as well. Their dad had been out working on the ice rink he'd made as he did each year. Well, each year that it was cold enough before Christmas. There had been a couple years where it had been too warm in the run-up to Christmas to have a rink ready for Boxing Day.

The cold snap they'd had right before Christmas had broken, and the weather that day was promising to be a bit more mild. Not above freezing, but not in the deep freeze either. He had been afraid that if it was too cold, Maya would back out. When he'd texted her earlier, she'd still been planning to come, so he was happy about that.

"So you have someone coming out today, Gabe?" Sometimes it was uncanny how his mom seemed to be able to read his mind.

"Yes. Maya is coming." Gabe was sure she already knew exactly who he'd invited, but she seemed to delight in making them have to actually tell her if they hadn't already volunteered the information.

"She seems like a nice young woman. I know Bennett and Makayla speak highly of her and how she's stepped in for Grace."

Though Gabe was glad she was doing such a good job for the company, that was kind of the least of what he cared about when it came to Maya. "She is nice. A bit reserved though, so don't be surprised if she doesn't chat a lot."

"I'm sure you'll do your best to make her feel at home," his mom said with a wink at him. "And we'll try our best not to embarrass you too much."

"Well, see, if you drag out any embarrassing photos or such, I'll just claim it's Mitch. One of the benefits of having an identical twin."

"Maybe it's one of you together," Dalton offered. "Then what are you going to say?"

"That I'm whichever twin is being the least awkward or embarrassing in the picture."

His mom gave him a shake of her head as she took the bowl of cheese from him. "Well, since you've never brought a woman home before, I think we should probably do our best to *not* scare her off."

"I would appreciate that," Gabe said, and he really would. He got the feeling that while Maya was okay spending time with him alone or with the others at work, she was a little shy about spending it with his family in a social situation where there weren't a bunch of other people around. She hadn't hesitated to go to the Christmas party or the dinner theater with him, but invites to spend time with just his family had—up until Boxing Day—been refused.

He kept glancing at whatever clock was closest to see how much longer it would be until Maya arrived. When she'd asked what time she should be there, Gabe had been tempted to give her a time earlier than when everyone else would be arriving, but then he'd realized that it might make her feel uncomfortable, and that was the last thing he wanted. His goal was to get her comfortable with being around his family, and having her there ahead of time would most likely achieve the opposite.

Ethan and Makayla were the first to arrive, followed shortly after by Mitch and Bennett. In years past, Grace would also have been there, but this year, with her baby still in intensive care, she had decided to spend the day at the hospital instead. Gabe could hardly blame her for that, but seeing the sadness in Bennett's eyes was hard to take. Though Bennett was present at all the events he needed to be at, anyone with eyes could see that his heart wasn't in it. His heart—broken though it might have been—was with Grace and, from what he'd heard, her baby.

The first non-family members to arrive were Tennyson and Forrest though Erin and James weren't far behind. It was shortly after their arrival that Gabe caught sight of Maya's car pulling into the parking area that had been cleared of snow earlier that day. He abandoned his conversation with Tennyson and Forrest and headed for the front door, pulling it open just as Maya reached the top step of the wide porch that ran all around the house.

She wore a light pink beanie on her head that matched the scarf around her neck and the gloves on her hands. She had on a thick black jacket that would be perfect for when they were outside later on and fitted jeans that disappeared into knee-high boots. She carried a bag over one shoulder that looked like it was big enough to hold a pair of skates. But what she wore that drew him in more than ever was her smile.

Gabe stepped back to let her into the house. Before he could stop himself, he pulled her into a hug, relishing the feel of her in his arms, the scent of her shampoo a tantalizing bouquet.

"I'm so glad you made it," Gabe said as he stepped back from her.

Maya's smile grew as she took off her jacket. "Your parents have a nice place here."

"Yep. They had to build a place big enough for all us kids." Gabe took her jacket and hung it up in the closet while Maya slid her boots off. "Only four live here full-time now. I'm not sure what they'll do with all the space once the last of the kids leave home."

Maya looked around as they walked further into the house. "They could have a bed and breakfast."

"That's definitely a possibility." Gabe took her hand and led her into the living room where the others had gathered. "Come meet more of the gang."

As he was introducing her, Noella and Finn arrived, and conversation increased. Gabe settled Maya in a seat on the couch next to Erin.

"Did you bring dessert?" he asked Erin as he pulled an ottoman over to sit on in front of the two women. He turned to Maya and said, "Erin and Noella own a bakery in the city, and Erin is the head baker. She always brings the most amazing things to our gatherings."

"I did bring a few cupcakes. I tried out a couple new flavors over the Christmas season that were really well received, so I brought a few dozen out for you all to try."

"I should warn you that Dalton made some brownies, so you'll have to tell him how good they are when you try them." Gabe grinned. "He's apparently been making them a lot. He didn't even need a recipe."

Erin's blue eyes lit up as she smiled. "That's terrific. Is he interested in baking? If so, he could come by the bakery one day to do some work with me. I'm always happy to try and cultivate the interest of the next generation."

"Not sure if he has any interest beyond brownies, but you could always ask him. I know he already keeps busy with his music and videos."

"I'll talk to him and see." Erin turned her gaze to Maya. "So you're the one whose captured Gabe's attention."

Gabe grinned as Maya's cheeks flushed. "I guess you could say that. I didn't even know that Mitch had a twin brother, so the first day he came into the office, I was a bit surprised at the change in Mitch."

Erin laughed. "Yeah, Gabe is definitely more outgoing, but Mitch is a sweetheart in his own quiet way."

Maya nodded. "He always had time to answer any questions I had when I first started. He never made me feel like I was inconveniencing him or anything like that. Everyone has been great at the office, actually. I've been so fortunate."

"Well, from what I hear, the company is fortunate to have you," Gabe said, unable to keep from smiling. "Makayla sings your praises frequently."

"And that's incredible coming from Makayla," Erin said.

"Hey now," Makayla said as she dropped down on the couch next to Maya. "Are you saying I'm difficult to please?"

Erin and Gabe exchanged glances before they both nodded, and Gabe said, "I think that's what we're saying, yes."

Makayla frowned as she took in his response but then nodded and grinned. "Yeah, I can be difficult. It's a wonder Ethan puts up with me."

"Ethan definitely deserves a medal for that," Gabe said.

"I think the ice is ready, everyone." His dad's voice interrupted their conversation. "And we've got a fire going as well, so grab your gear and head out."

Conversation picked up as people got up and began to gather up jackets and bags. Gabe carried Maya's bag after helping her into her jacket. He'd grabbed his from the closet by the back door, and then they left the house. Bennett and Tristan were already on the ice with Dalton, music drifting from the speakers that were mounted at the back of the house.

"This is incredible," Maya said as Gabe led her to the fire beside the rink. There were log benches set up around the rink, and they sat down side by side.

"Do you want to skate?" Gabe asked, hoping that she would.

"Sure. I haven't skated since I was about thirteen, so hopefully, I don't end up falling more than skating."

Gabe tugged off his boots and pulled on his skates, making quick work of the laces. When he was done, he moved to kneel in front of Maya, not caring that the knees of his jeans were pressed into the snow. "Let me help you lace up."

"Uh…okay." It had taken Maya a little longer to get her boots off and her skates out of her bag, so she'd only just pulled one on.

Gabe worked the laces from the toes, tugging them firmly as he proceeded. "How does that feel? Too tight? Too loose?"

"Perfect."

At the tone of her voice, Gabe looked up to find her watching him, a small smile on her face. His chest got tight, and the air seemed to be squeezed from his lungs, leaving him breathless. He had to look away in order to catch his breath as he picked up her other skate and slid it onto her foot. Once again, he worked the laces quickly.

"How about that foot?"

"It's good," Maya said as she placed the blades with skate protectors on them flat on the ground and wiggled them side to side. "They both feel perfect. I don't think I ever laced skates quite that well."

"I've had lots of practice." Gabe got to his feet and held out his hand. "Let's go give them a try." He pulled Maya to her feet. "I probably should have asked before you put your skates on…but did you get them sharpened?"

Maya nodded. "When you first asked me last week, I bought myself a pair of skates and had them sharpened."

"Even though you didn't know for sure that you were going to come?" Gabe arched a brow at her. "Or did you know all along and just wanted to keep me guessing?"

Maya laughed. "Well, I think I knew I'd come. Just had to sort things out with my mom."

Most the others were on the ice when they got there, but there was plenty of room. The rink his dad made each year was a work of art. Though not arena size, it was close enough that they had gotten good practice on it over the years, and there was lots of room for people to skate without running into each other. Even though Kenton was the only one who had been good enough to play hockey professionally, all of them—including the girls—had learned how to play.

He spotted Sammi with her boyfriend Jayden as they skated by. He had his arm around her waist, and their strokes were synchronized. Sammi smiled up at Jayden, laughing at something he said. Gabe was glad to see her happy again. She'd had a long-term boyfriend in high school, but the guy had dumped her just before graduation. Since then, she'd focused on getting her nursing degree and finding work. Now it seemed she had the job she wanted and a man who made her happy. It was about time.

Maybe it was about time for him too.

Chapter Ten

AFTER REMOVING THEIR SKATE GUARDS, Gabe stepped onto the ice then reached back to take Maya's hand and help her. She seemed reticent to let go of the boards, but at his coaxing, she gripped his hand tightly and allowed him to guide her onto the ice. They stuck close to the outside of the rink so that others on the ice could easily pass them.

After a couple of laps around the rink, Maya had seemed to find her legs and was taking more confident strokes. Gabe still held her hand, enjoying how tightly she gripped his in return. Once it seemed she wasn't scared of falling, Gabe pivoted on his skates in front of her so that he could skate backward.

"Show off," Maya said with a grin as she reached to take his other hand.

Holding both her hands, Gabe began to stroke in time to the music. They were still playing Christmas music because…why not? As Michael Buble sang *Winter Wonderland,* they made their way around the ice. Maya smiled up at Gabe, her joy at being able to skate, and not just fall all over the place, clear on her face.

"Your brother is amazing," Maya said, her gaze following Dalton as he skated past.

"If he were any older, I might be jealous of him," Gabe said with a laugh.

Maya looked back at him and smiled. "Well, I think you're pretty amazing too."

Gabe felt something shift inside him as he gazed down at Maya. The joy and happiness on her face did so much for him. "I think you're amazingly amazing as well."

"But seriously. Is there anything your brother doesn't know how to do?"

"Well, he absolutely won't touch a hockey stick. Much to my dad's chagrin. When my dad told him he had to learn to skate, Dalton insisted on figure skating lessons instead of hockey. I think it's all tied to his artistic, musical nature. He has talent in spades with his music, and fig-ure skating allowed him to express himself artistically."

"Did he compete?"

"Nah. He didn't want to do it professionally. It was more like my dad wanted him to participate in a sport, and figure skating was the only one that worked for him. And now he can skate circles around the rest of us." Gabe laughed as Dalton approached them again and turned to skate backward beside Gabe for a few strokes. "Literally. Tristan also didn't want to play hockey, but he wasn't vocal enough with his objections, so he played…badly."

"I heard that," Tristan said as he skated by them.

"And yet you're not disputing it," Gabe called out.

"This is true!" Tristan spun to skate backward and gave them a grin, looking more relaxed than he usually did at the office.

They skated for awhile, enjoying the music and the good-natured jokes from the other skaters, before Mitch showed up on the ice with a hockey stick and a puck and began to skate with it, moving the puck back and forth in front of him as he glided over the ice.

"Is that a sign that it's time for a hockey game?" Maya asked. "Hopefully I can just be a spectator for that because I'm not sure I could skate that well without a hand to hold."

"Yeah, that doesn't work too well for hockey. And don't worry, the ladies usually just cheer us on. Sammi has played with us on occasion, but I have a feeling she'll be happy playing cheerleader today."

At the entrance to the rink, Gabe helped Maya put on her skate guards and then leave the ice. She joined the other ladies who were leaning against the boards that surrounded the rink as his dad handed out hockey sticks to the guys who remained on the ice.

"You gonna play today, Dalton?" Gabe asked as his little brother came to a stop in a spray of ice by the entrance.

Dalton gave him a look, eyebrows raised. "Nope. Maybe once I hit my growth spurt and can hold my own with you guys. I have no desire to get squished. I'm going to go help Mom with the food."

Gabe grabbed a stick and began to skate around the ice at a faster speed than when he'd been with Maya. He skated by Mitch and snagged the puck from him, talking a bit of smack as he stroked away. His dad called out the teams and tossed jerseys to each of them. Dark blue for one team and red for the other. The guys took off their jackets, leaving them along the boards before pulling on the heavy jerseys. Between the long sleeve jerseys and the exercise they'd be getting, there was no worry about getting cold.

His dad came onto the ice with a puck and a whistle and skated to the center of the rink. Each group got together to determine who their goalie would be and then those guys donned the goalie protective gear. Mitch was the goalie on Gabe's team while Forrest took the position for the other team. Once the goalies were in place, his dad dropped the puck at center ice, and the game began.

MAYA HAD NEVER WATCHED much hockey, and certainly never that close up. She found that she enjoyed cheering loudly for Gabe and his team. Gabe's youngest sister was manning a flip scoreboard on the opposite side of the rink which indicated that—for the moment—his team was winning.

She was surprised at how quickly skating had come back to her once she'd gotten on the ice. Not that she'd ever been all that great, but she'd at least been able to stay on her feet. With Gabe's help, she'd been able to gain confidence after not skating for over a decade.

And once again, Maya was feeling like this was the best day ever. Well, aside from the day when the doctors had told her that her cancer was in remission for the second time. She didn't know how to process all the new feelings and experiences she was having. At times like these, as she watched Gabe fly across the ice with his hair blowing in the wind and a broad grin on his face, she felt like she might explode from it all.

He was coming to mean so much to her. Too much? What if he wasn't feeling the same way. After all, these weren't new experiences for him. He was taking her out into the world in a way she'd never experienced before, and he didn't even know it. He didn't know the impact he was having on her life in so many ways. The thought of him leaving, even for just a month, made her heart ache if she allowed herself to dwell on the thought too much.

They still had a week together, and she planned to enjoy it as much as she could. And maybe, when he got back, they could have a conversation about their...relationship. Maya found that she didn't want to go on much longer without knowing how he felt about what was developing between them. If she was the only one feeling this depth of emotion, she needed to know sooner rather than later because her heart was already full of feelings for Gabe. She just needed to know that she wasn't alone.

As she watched them skate, her gaze was always drawn to Gabe. Something began to dawn on her as the game progressed. Gabe was by far the most aggressive of the skaters. He took risks, skating around the other players, ducking and spinning. But it wasn't just the risks Gabe took, but the expression on his face as he took them. Clearly, he thrived on it. His smile was huge as he slid between Bennett and the wall, snagging the puck from his older brother.

An uneasy feeling formed in the pit of Maya's stomach. She already knew from Gabe himself how much he liked adventure, but Maya was beginning to think that while she had thought it might be him liking to bungee jump, he might, in fact, prefer BASE jumping. That was more than just liking a little adventure, and that worried her.

If she'd been there with someone else, she might have just watched Gabe for a few minutes, noting the way he liked to play aggressively but then looked back to whoever she was there with. However, she was there with Gabe—couldn't take her gaze off him—so she saw what others might not have. He needed the thrill. She could see that now. While he'd been happy when he'd been skating with her, it was nothing compared to how he looked now as he played hockey with his friends and brothers.

Maybe this was the answer she'd been looking for. If Gabe thrived on the excitement of adventure, there was no way she could compete with that. With her lack of experience of life in general, Maya knew she was the exact opposite of exciting and adventurous.

"I'm always surprised that these games end without any broken bones," Makayla said as she came to stand next to Maya. "Especially Gabe. The only time it's worse than this is when Kenton is here. He and Gabe really go at it."

"Did Gabe ever want to play in the NHL like Kenton?" Maya asked.

"No. He wasn't interested in the practice schedule that he'd have had to keep in order to be good enough." Makayla backed up a bit as a couple of the guys crashed into the boards in front of them. "I think he probably had the talent—and he definitely had the nerve—but it wasn't something he was interested in. I think it was too restrictive. Set season. Set dates for games. Set places to be. That's just not Gabe."

Makayla's words just reinforced what Maya had been thinking. But now what did she do with the realization? Did she pull back? Or did she stick it out and hope that maybe Gabe would decide that being with her was more important than the adventures that pulled him away from his home and family in Winnipeg?

Not wanting to allow her thoughts to cast a shadow over the day, Maya pushed them aside. She wanted to recapture the feelings she'd had when Gabe had been holding her hands and guiding her around the ice. So she cheered with the other women who were standing along the side of the boards with her. Cheered and hoped that she was wrong in thinking Gabe wouldn't settle for a life that didn't include dangerous adventures.

It was no surprise when Gabe's team won. He'd scored three of the four goals his team had gotten during the game. Mitch had managed to stop all but two of the shots on goal. Maya couldn't deny that it had been an exciting game, and Gabe appeared super pumped that his team had won.

"Why don't we head into the house for some food?" Steve Callaghan suggested as the guys began to come off the ice. "We can come back out afterward. If you want."

The group returned to the log benches and began to remove skates and put boots back on. Gabe was there once again, helping Maya get her skates off, chatting about how the game had gone.

"That makes five years," Gabe said with a huge grin.

"Five years?" Maya reached for her boots and tugged them on.

"I've been on the winning team for five years now."

"Do you stick to the same teams?" Maya asked as Gabe pulled her to her feet.

"Nah. We never know who will be here, and my dad is usually the one who decides the teams." Gabe took her hand as they followed the others into the house.

A wall of warmth greeted Maya, the scent of rich spices heavy in the air. There was a huge table set up in the dining room, and people settled into seats around the table. Gabe led her to a seat and then disappeared into the kitchen along with Makayla and Ethan. Soon they reappeared carrying large bowls that they set on the table. Dalton and Danica appeared with smaller bowls.

Maya found it such a contrast. If this had been a meal at her parents' home, they would have been served by people they had hired. Her mother wouldn't have dared serve a meal herself. Elisse served them their meals when it was just the three of them, but as soon as they had more than two extra people, her mom hired extra help.

When the food was all on the table, the rest of the group found seats, Gabe dropping down onto the chair next to her. "Hope you like chili."

Maya smiled but didn't say anything since she had no idea if she liked chili or not. She couldn't remember the last time she'd actually had it. Her mom had something against ground beef and usually forbade Elisse from using it when she cooked for them. Even their sauce for pasta was made with ground turkey or chicken. And chili? Given her mom's heritage, they were more likely to have sushi than chili.

Once everyone was seated, Steve said a prayer of thanks for the meal, and then they all dug in. Maya found the chili to be very tasty and enjoyed the buns that Emily said she and Danica had made earlier. There were chili toppings of grated cheese and sour cream as well as crackers.

It was all new to her, but Maya wasn't about to confess that. She could only imagine how they'd look at her if she told them that she couldn't remember ever having eaten chili. That would lead to too many questions that she wasn't really ready to answer just yet. Those questions would have to be answered soon, though, if she continued to socialize with these people. Something was going to slip. Something was going to get awkward.

These people were so down to earth and easy going. She wondered what they would think if they knew the extent of her family's wealth. That jetting off to New York or Paris was something her family could do without much thought. And it wasn't just her dad. She was wealthy in her own right thanks to her trust fund. That was why she'd gone after a job, so that she could be part of a group of people who were contributing positively to the world.

She could have just chosen to donate money to organizations that helped people and then spent her time traveling and buying everything she wanted. Instead, while she did donate to shelters and other non-profit organizations and volunteered at a couple of them, Maya had decided she wanted to get a job. To be in a position where she was part of a group of people working toward a common goal.

After having worked at C&M Builders for five months, Maya knew that she would do what she could to keep her position there. She loved the work there and the people she worked with.

"Are you glad you came?" Gabe asked as he took a second helping of chili.

"Definitely." And she had enjoyed herself, aside from the moment of realization she'd had. "I'm just glad I didn't break a bone."

"You'd be in good company if you did. I think most of us have broken bones because of skating at one time or another over the years."

"Really?" Maya had spent a lot of time in the hospital but never for a broken bone.

"Yeah. I've had a few broken bones. Not all related to hockey." He lifted his arm. "I broke my arm in two places while skiing in Switzerland. That was not fun."

Maya didn't want to be reminded of the adventures he'd been on and was likely still going to go on.

"Gabe is definitely the one who has been injured the most," Mitch volunteered. "Even worse than Kenton."

Gabe shrugged. "I do my best to not get hurt, but stuff happens... It's the price I have to pay sometimes in order to have these experiences."

"You're still nuts," Mitch said. "That's the bottom line. You have to be more than a little crazy to do what you do sometimes."

"I think when our genes split, I got your dose of nerve."

Mitch just shrugged like Gabe had earlier, apparently not concerned about his brother's comment. "Well, if I don't have to deal with broken bones, I'd say that's no loss."

"One of these days I'm going to get you to go with me." Gabe pushed his empty bowl and plate away. "You really shouldn't knock it til you try it."

Maya looked back and forth between the brothers to see if there was really any animosity in their jabs at each other. She was not used to the type of banter among siblings like she was seeing with Mitch and Gabe. It didn't appear that they were truly upset with each other, so Maya figured this must be an old discussion between them.

Once the meal was over, they discovered that the sun had gone down, but it appeared that people were still planning to go skating again. Maya wasn't so sure she wanted to go back out there. If she was being honest with herself, she was feeling the need for a break. Given what she had learned about Gabe during the course of the day, she was beginning to think that spending a little less time with him might be a good thing. Her emotions were already so engaged in him that it was only going to get worse if she spent much more time with him.

Maybe it was a good thing that he was leaving for a little while. It would give her a chance to pull back from the intense emotions she was feeling.

"You want to go out and skate a bit more?" Gabe asked as he started to stack up the dishes that were around him at the table.

"I think I've skated enough for today." Maya handed him her plate and bowl. "Tomorrow I'm probably going to be feeling muscles I haven't felt in a very long time."

Gabe chuckled as he got to his feet. "Sadly, you are probably correct about that."

They carried stacks of dishes into the kitchen and set them on the counter.

"Can I help you clean up?" Maya asked Emily when the older woman turned toward them.

"Sure. Thank you for offering." Emily motioned to where Danica and Dalton were at the sink. "You can dry, if you'd like. Danica lost the toss so she has to wash and Dalton is rinsing."

Gabe went back into the dining room while Maya took the dish towel Emily held out to her and lifted a plate from the dish drainer and began to dry it.

"Did Mom say you could go to the party?" Dalton asked as he put another dish in the drainer.

"No," Danica said with a frown. "At least Sierra's not going either. Ethan and Makayla said no."

"Are you really surprised?" Dalton asked.

"I suppose not, but Devon is going."

"Jealous?"

Danica let out a sigh. "No. Well, I don't know who else is going to be there."

"Devon is my friend, but seriously, you know he's a little too impressed with himself sometimes."

"Hah. Like you aren't?" Danica said with a snort.

"I'm not too impressed with myself. I don't expect girls to throw themselves at me because I can sing or play an instrument."

Maya smiled as she listened to two more siblings in the Callaghan and McFadden family go back and forth. As she looked at them, she realized that Dalton was close to the age she'd been when she'd gotten her first cancer diagnosis. The things they were talking about were things she had ended up missing out on. Not that she would have gone to many parties. She'd been attending an all-girls school to start with, so there weren't many opportunities to meet boys. Then as she'd gone through treatment, she'd been tutored to minimize her exposure to germs while her immune system was compromised, so her contact with teenagers had been narrowed even more.

"Was your mom strict?"

It took a second to realize that Danica had been asking her the question. "Oh, yeah, she was probably more strict than your mom."

Danica turned to look at her, her hands still in the soapy water. "More strict? I didn't realize that was possible."

"Oh, it's possible. I'm pretty sure that my mom would win the title if there were a strict mom pageant."

"Can you imagine? Like seriously." Danica laughed. "So you didn't go to a lot of parties as a teen?"

"I went to no parties." Maya hoped her admission didn't lead to more questions, but she was so enjoying the conversation with the teens.

"Okay. Yeah. You win," Dalton said with a smirk. "Danica is usually allowed to go to parties if they're kids from the church, and Mom and Dad know their parents."

"Do you go to parties?" Maya asked Dalton.

"Nah. I'm not interested in parties, to be honest. There are a million other things I'd rather be doing than hanging out with people whose only goal in life is to try and out-cool each other."

"Give it a rest, Dalton." Danica rolled her eyes. "You just know that no one would want to talk to you."

While Maya had thought the teen boy would get defensive at his sister's jab, he just said, "You're not wrong about that, but then I don't really want to talk to them either. Or excuse me…they would actually want to talk to me but only because they'd want to be in my videos. Devon has already tried to get me to let some of his friends into the videos, but that's not gonna happen. If they want to impress the ladies, they're going to need to go to a different channel for that. Ours is about music and sharing our songs with the world."

"So does it bother *you* that Devon is going to the party instead of hanging out with us here?"

The pause before Dalton answered his sister's question spoke louder than the words he eventually said. "I'm not in charge of his social calendar. He can hang with whoever he wants."

Maya wondered who exactly Devon was and how he fit into their lives. She knew that if she'd had the opportunity as a teen to hang with kids like Dalton and Danica, she would have skipped the party for sure.

Gabe set the dishes he'd carried in from the dining room next to Danica then looped an arm around each of their shoulders. "Well, Devon has pudding for brains if he'd rather hang out with anyone but you two."

Maya smiled at his words and the sincerity behind them. It was so interesting to her how they could take digs at each other, but when push came to shove, they were there for one another. For some reason, she'd thought that exchanging those types of words with someone meant that they didn't like each other. Given that she'd never had a sibling to joke around with, she'd been unaware of how the dynamics could play out.

"You have to say that," Dalton grumbled as he lifted a couple more plates from the rinse water. "You're our brother."

Gabe straightened. "I am your brother, true, but I don't have to say that. I do happen to like hanging with you all. Why else do you think I stay here instead of with Mitch?"

"Because you don't like sharing a bed with him?" Danica asked and then jostled Dalton's arm with a laugh.

Maya enjoyed watching Gabe interact with his younger siblings as she dried the dishes Dalton was putting into the rack. What would her life have been like if she'd been part of a family like this one? On the one hand, she was glad that she hadn't had siblings while going through treatments. Her mother had been absolutely devoted to her, rarely leaving her side when she'd been in the hospital. If there had been other children, her mom might have been torn about where to focus her attention. Or she'd have focused on Maya, and the other children would have suffered. So maybe it was best that she'd been an only child, but at moments like these, she sure wished she'd had a brother or sister.

There was a steady flow of people through the kitchen, most making their way out the back door once again. Maya momentarily wondered if she should stay to skate again, but then remembered why she had decided to leave. The teasing between siblings continued, some of it in passing as they walked past the ones doing the dishes on their way out the back door. Emily chided a few when it got a little too pointed, but for the most part, the older woman was silent as she handed off stacks of dishes to Gabe and Tristan who had come into the kitchen to help.

"I think I'm going to head out," Maya said once the kitchen had been cleared up.

Gabe frowned. "Already? You don't want to stay for dessert? I know you don't want to skate anymore, but we can just sit down and talk."

Maya was tempted, but she knew it was best for her to head for home. She had work the next day anyway. Gabe's brow furrowed when she shook her head. "It's been a great day, but I really need to get home."

"Okay. If you're sure." Maya nodded again. "Well, I'll be working in the office again this week, so I'll see you there. Let me walk you out."

Gabe got her jacket from the back mudroom and held it out for her to slide her arms into. It didn't take long for her to get her things together and then at the front door, she pulled on her boots. Gabe had also grabbed his jacket and boots and followed her out into the cold night air.

There was a tall light pole that illuminated the parking area, so they had no trouble getting to her car. Once there, Gabe opened the door for her, but then held out his arms for a hug. Maya stepped into his embrace, relishing the feel of his arms around her. This was the only good part of saying good bye.

"Thanks for coming out," he murmured against her ear. "It was a lot of fun."

It had been…until she'd seen that he'd had even more fun when the hockey game had started. How he'd really come to life when he'd had the chance to skate with speed, taking risks, and crashing into the boards. And from the conversation she'd heard that day, that had been mellow for him.

Though her heart wanted to love Gabe, Maya just couldn't allow herself to love a man who so thoughtlessly put his life at risk when she'd fought so hard to save hers.

Chapter Eleven

G ABE WATCHED AS THE TAILLIGHTS of Maya's car disappeared as she turned onto the highway. He couldn't shake the feeling that something was off. He'd noticed that she'd spent lots of time observing the stuff going on around her. Whether it was how the other couples interacted or the conversations between him and his siblings, she had watched them all. It made him wonder about her social life in light of her lack of siblings. Maybe he should have asked her to bring a few friends of her own. She might have been more comfortable if she'd had some people she knew well there too. It was her first time to be submerged into his family so much, and maybe it had just been too much for her.

Turning, he headed back into the house, the snow crunching beneath his boots. Though he would have preferred to spend the remainder of the evening with Maya, Gabe was still going to enjoy himself. He grabbed his skates from the mud room and went to the log benches to put them on once again. He grabbed a stick and a puck and stepped back out on the ice. While most the others were moving slowly around the ice to the music that was playing again, he and Mitch skated around them more quickly and passed the puck back and forth.

By ten o'clock, most everyone had left, and the house was quiet. Mitch was still there, making himself a cup of coffee. Gabe sat across the island from him, just the two of them in the kitchen.

"Want one?" Mitch asked as he pulled his cup from the Keurig machine.

"Sure. Why not?" Gabe watched as Mitch got another mug from where it hung on the spinning cup holder next to the Keurig. Once it was done, Mitch slid the mug across to him, knowing he took it black. "Thanks."

"Is everything okay with Maya?" Mitch asked as he leaned a hip against the island counter. "I noticed she didn't stay to skate again after supper."

"Yeah. She hasn't skated in awhile and figured she'd be sore enough as it was." Gabe wasn't sure that was the real reason, but it was the one she'd given him, so it was the one he gave Mitch. "And she's an only child. I can only imagine how overwhelming our family must be for her."

"So it's been a couple of weeks now, have you told her yet that you spend less than two months out of the year here?" Mitch lifted his mug and took a sip.

Gabe scowled at his twin. "She knows I'm leaving."

"Yeah, but does she know that you're not coming back for awhile?"

"What is your problem, bro?" Gabe asked, not appreciating the way Mitch was pressing.

"My problem is that Maya deserves to not be led on," Mitch said.

"She's a grown-up. She's not your responsibility."

"No, but she *is* my friend." Mitch met his gaze without flinching. "And for some reason, I feel like I need to protect her from you."

Gabe and Mitch hadn't physically fought since they were youngsters, but right then Gabe felt like throwing a punch. "I'm not planning to hurt her."

"Best laid plans…" Mitch let him finish the thought.

Gabe sighed. "What am I supposed to do? I mean, I feel things for Maya that I've never felt for anyone else."

"What are you supposed to *do*?" Mitch scoffed. "Change your lifestyle. Like seriously. How is that not even crossing your mind?"

It *had* crossed Gabe's mind, more than it ever had in the past. He just didn't know if he could sustain that change. He thrived on the lifestyle he'd chosen. The heart racing, blood pumping, adrenalin high was what he lived for. Was it even possible for him to switch to a less exciting lifestyle without feeling a constant restlessness?

THE NEXT MORNING, Gabe headed into the office to meet with another of his teams. This group worked with him conducting social media revamping for companies and also working on the app company he'd taken over. His business interests were as varied as his entertainments. Between the gym, his work with Tennyson and Forrest and the social media/app company, Gabe never found himself getting bored with his work.

Maya wasn't at her desk when he came in, but it looked like she was somewhere in the building. Makayla's door was closed, so he assumed she was in with her. Gabe pushed aside his disappointment and headed for the boardroom where Bennett had agreed to let him work with his employees.

He'd told his team to text him when they arrived, so when his phone chirped with a text from one of them, Gabe made his way to the front door to meet them. The other two showed as they stood talking in the area in front of Maya's desk.

"C'mon back, guys." Gabe motioned for them to follow him.

His social media team was made up of three people. Sophia was the senior member of his team. She was a whiz with web page and app design. Jonathon also worked on the web and app design. Amberly took care of the social media side of things, helping companies build up a positive presence online. Thankfully, they all worked well together and required minimal supervision from him which was a bonus since he was usually somewhere other than Winnipeg for the majority of the year.

Just like Mitch had pointed out the night before.

Prior to the meeting, the trio had sent him a list of the things they wanted to discuss, and Gabe had added his own topics. Thankfully, none of them were into a lot of chatter, so they moved through the agenda quickly. As they worked together, Gabe wondered if he could do this full-time. Bring his focus in business and life in general back to one solitary place. He'd chosen the businesses he had because of his interest in them and because he'd had partners willing to work with him. He'd been able to deal with them from afar with his partners' help. Being in Winnipeg would mean doing more hands-on work with the businesses which wouldn't necessarily be a bad thing.

But on a personal level, was there enough in Winnipeg to keep him entertained? For the first time, he was thinking that maybe there was. But beyond the entertainment factor, for the first time, there was some-*one* that might be enough to keep him there.

When lunchtime rolled around, Gabe went out to see if Maya was available to join them for lunch. He thought it would be nice for her to meet his team. Unfortunately, the front desk was still empty, and now he wondered if Maya was really there in the office at all. Makayla's door was open, so he headed over there.

"Hey, sis," Gabe said as he walked through her door.

Makayla glanced over at him as he sat down in the seat across from her. "Hey. What's up?"

"Do I need a reason to stop by?" Gabe leaned back, stretching his legs out under her desk.

She laughed as she punched a couple of keys on her keyboard then turned to face him fully. "No, probably not, except in this case, I'm thinking you do."

Gabe shrugged. "Okay. Sure. I was wondering if you knew where Maya is."

Makayla frowned at his question. "Did you text her and ask?"

"No. I just saw she wasn't at her desk and thought you might know where she is."

"As it happens, I do know. She's out with Mitch visiting a couple of the job sites. She's been doing it on occasion to get to know that side of the business and what it is that C&M Builders does. Being in the field also gives her the opportunity to meet some of the people she's been doing things for with regards to some of the HR projects we've been handling."

She was out with Mitch? Neither of them had mentioned that the previous day. Gabe wasn't sure what to do with the information. It meant he likely wouldn't get to see Maya as he was heading out to meet with Hunter after lunch. He'd hoped to have lunch with Maya and then go to his meeting, but now he wasn't sure what to do. Well, he did know what to do. He'd go to lunch with his team, and then he'd go meet Hunter.

And hopefully, he'd at least talk to Maya later in the day.

"I have to meet my team for lunch," Gabe said. "And then I'm meeting Hunter, so I'll just text Maya to let her know I was sorry to not see her."

Makayla gave a nod. "Sounds like a plan." She hesitated. "Am I correct in assuming a few people have asked you recently what exactly you're doing with Maya?"

Gabe huffed out a breath as he got to his feet. "Yeah. No worries there."

He could tell Makayla wanted to say something more, but he wasn't in the mood to deal with her input on the subject of Maya. Makayla could be like a dog with a bone if she got it in her mind that something deserved her attention, and he didn't need that at the moment.

After saying goodbye, Gabe left her office and went back to the boardroom to gather up his things. He'd made arrangements to meet the other team members at a nearby restaurant, so he left right away since he didn't want to keep them waiting.

"WANT TO GRAB A BITE to eat before we head back to the office?" Mitch asked as they left the last job site. "It's a little bit late, but I'm hungry."

"Sure we can stop somewhere. Makayla told me she'd cover for me until mid-afternoon."

Maya had thought they might be back to the office in time for her to see Gabe, but she suspected that she'd missed him. She didn't mind going to lunch with Mitch since she'd always thought he was a nice guy, friendly and respectful.

"So, I know it's probably not my business," Mitch began once the waitress had taken their orders. "But are you hoping for something serious with Gabe?"

Maya felt apprehension rise within her. She looked at Mitch, seeing the sincerity in his gaze as he watched her. "I think it would be foolish of me to have that hope."

Mitch's brows rose slightly. "I'll admit I'm surprised to hear you say that, but it is a relief. I mean, I love my brother with all my heart, but he's a bit of a rolling stone. Never staying in one place for very long." Mitch paused. "I do think meeting you has given him pause. For the first time, it seems that he's found someone he enjoys spending time with."

"Do you think he would ever settle down?" Maya regretted the question as soon as she asked it. She didn't want to let herself hope for something that *might* happen in the future. There was no way she should allow herself to be tied up in something that was strictly a distant possibility.

"Maybe." Mitch's shoulders slumped a bit. "I know we're identical twins, but in this aspect, I just don't understand his need to constantly be off on one adventure after another. And not just regular adventures either, he goes for the extreme ones. The more dangerous, the better, apparently."

It was the confirmation that Maya needed for what she'd thought the previous night. She really hadn't needed to hear Mitch say the words, but maybe it was a good thing that she had. It wasn't that she would no longer spend any time with Gabe, but she would just keep in mind what she'd discovered and use it to build a wall around her heart. She couldn't afford to let her emotions get involved with someone who had no intention of settling down. Even with her.

The thought hurt, but it also helped her to answer the question of whether she should tell him about her family and her medical history. This relationship was going to be a lighthearted, casual thing. Too bad this was her first experience with relationships and love. She really had no idea how to keep things lighthearted and casual, but she was going to have to figure that out if she was going to survive this.

It probably was a good thing that he was leaving in less than a week. Hopefully, that meant she would be able to find a way to accept that the man her heart felt so strongly attracted to was more interested in his next adventure than he was in staying with her.

Her phone buzzed as the waitress brought their food, and Maya pulled out her phone to check it.

Gabe: *Sorry I missed you at the office today. I'm off for a meeting with Hunter so will try and call you later. :)*

Sounds good. Sorry I wasn't there when your meeting finished. I was out to a few job sites with Mitch. Hope your meeting goes well.

Gabe: *Don't believe anything Mitch tells you. ;) He likes to think he's the better twin, but really, I am.*

Haha Well, I have to say you both have many redeeming qualities.

Gabe: *As long as you like my redeeming qualities better, it's all good.*

LOL. No worries there.

Maya let out a sigh as she typed her reply. She kinda wished that she felt about Mitch the way she did about Gabe. It would have made everything so much easier, but that wasn't how it had worked out. The unfortunate thing was that Gabe's over-the-top zest for life was a big part of what had attracted her to him. The very thing that would take him away from her was the thing she lo—uh…—liked the best about him.

Gabe: *Heading into the meeting with Hunter. Will chat with you later.*

They spent the rest of the meal just chatting about the previous afternoon and evening. Mitch filled her in a bit on the friends that had been there that Maya hadn't known. It was a nice way to spend a meal once they had finished talking about her relationship—or whatever it was—with Gabe.

She really did want to forge friendships with the people she worked with. It might not have been something she'd have done in a different sort of workplace atmosphere, but at C&M, with so many of them related, friendships didn't seem to be a thing to avoid. She just hoped that whatever she'd had during the holidays with Gabe would just sort of fade away in the minds of the people who had witnessed them together. That wasn't how it was going to work for her, but hopefully, that's how his family—and Gabe—would view it.

It wasn't until much later that night—after she'd finished her work day, after she'd eaten dinner with her mom, after she'd had a brief text conversation with Gabe—that Maya finally allowed the feelings that had been building up slowly over the course of the day to break free. She'd run herself a bath and as she sat in its warmth, the tears she'd held back since the previous night began to slip down her cheeks.

Maya hadn't known that heartache was real. She hadn't realized that it could spread to every part of her body. That it was a real overwhelming pain that couldn't be ignored. Bits of pain had caught her off-guard throughout the day, but it was nothing like what she felt then. Her chest tightened, squeezing the breath from her lungs and not allowing her to draw air back in.

Though Maya hadn't known for sure if she was in love with Gabe, the heartache she was experiencing made her think she was. But if this wasn't love, she never wanted to experience the heartache of things not working out with someone she *did* love.

In the seclusion of her bathroom, Maya let her pain out in sobs, knowing that she'd have to be strong in the days until Gabe left, and she didn't have to face the prospect of seeing him on a daily basis.

"DON'T YOU HAVE A FACEBOOK or Instagram account?" Gabe asked as they sat side by side at the weekly Friday staff lunch. "I did a search for your name but came up empty."

Maya fought the urge to laugh. Facebook? Who on earth would be her friend beside Lainie and now maybe the Callaghans and McFaddens? She had never felt the need or desire to have any sort of social media presence. "No. I don't have any social media accounts."

Gabe gave her a perplexed look. "Why not?"

She shrugged. "I don't have that many people I want to be aware of the goings-on in my life."

"Well, I, for one, would totally like to be aware of the goings-on in your life."

It was a painful reminder that he was going to be watching her life from afar. "Or maybe I should have said that I don't have much goings-on worth putting on social media for the world to see."

"You should at least follow my social media accounts then," Gabe said. "My accounts are open, so you don't even need to get an account of your own to see my stuff."

"Okay. Send me the addresses, and I'll check them out." And she would…for this trip anyway. She had no desire in the future to see him posting pictures of himself with the woman who either was brave enough to join him on his adventures or who captured his heart so completely that he was finally willing to make one place his home.

"But if you want to comment or like photos and videos, you'll have to create an account." Gabe smiled, causing the heartache to bleed through the walls she was struggling to keep in place. "And you'll really like my videos. Dalton edits them for me, and he does a great job."

"Edits them? You mean like for YouTube?"

"Exactly!" Gabe said with a nod. "I have a YouTube channel where Dalton uploads them then he links each video on my social media so you can find it from there."

The conversation around them turned to plans for New Year's Eve, and Maya was very relieved to have a solid reason to turn down the invitation that was issued to her for the party at the Callaghan and McFadden home.

"I'm sorry I can't make it, but I'm going to be spending the evening with my parents."

Maya didn't miss the disappointment on Gabe's face, but she just couldn't allow herself to be drawn in even further when he had given no indication that anything was going to change in his lifestyle. Ringing in the New Year with the man her heart yearned for when they had no future just seemed like she was setting herself up for even more heartache.

"Well, you're missing the party to end all parties," Mitch said with a laugh.

As the others around the table recounted events from years past, Maya had to admit it sounded like a lot more fun than where she was headed. She'd asked if she could leave at noon on New Year's Eve, and Makayla had agreed without hesitation. Maya had needed the time because she and her mom were headed to New York City to spend New Year's Eve with her dad.

They had a large party to attend which wasn't Maya's first choice, but after she'd bailed on the Paris trip with her mom, she didn't feel it was right to refuse to attend the New Year's Eve party. Especially since they would be taking the jet and her mom had promised that she would be back on New Year's Day so she could be at work on January second.

"Can we go out for dinner tomorrow night?" Gabe asked as they left the restaurant a short time later. "Since I won't see you on New Year's Eve."

Maya knew she should say no—she knew it—but instead, she found herself agreeing. The relief on Gabe's face left her confused though. Was he that upset at the thought that they couldn't spend time together before he left? Did that mean…?

No.

She wasn't going to try to read anything into his obvious relief. This would just be a fun evening before he headed off for his next adventure.

"Is there anywhere special you'd like to go?" Gabe asked.

Maya rubbed her gloved hands together before shoving them into her pockets. "I'm going to say the only thing I want for sure is some place warm."

Gabe chuckled. "Okay. No winter picnics then."

"As interesting as that might be, I would say, no. No winter picnics."

"I'll surprise you then," Gabe said. As they reached her car, Gabe opened the door for her. "Any chance you'd like to come to the gym tomorrow to climb?"

It hadn't even crossed her mind to go, but she had really enjoyed it, and she wanted to maintain contact with the people there because she hoped to continue to go even after Gabe left.

"Sure. Maybe if you don't pick a fancy restaurant, we could meet up at the gym first and then head out for dinner afterward."

"Sounds good. I'm not really about fancy restaurants anyway, to be honest."

Maya smiled as she slid behind the wheel of her car. "I would never have guessed."

"I know. My penchant for wearing expensive suits would definitely seem to say otherwise." His words made her smile even more, but it was his grin that warmed her heart. "How about we meet at three at the gym?"

"I'll be there," Maya said then waited as Gabe stepped back and closed her door before she backed out of the parking spot and headed back to the office.

GABE WAS NO MORE SETTLED watching Maya drive away this time than he had been on Boxing Day. Something had happened that day, and he still didn't know what it was. Since then, he'd tried to get together with her, but it just hadn't worked out until she'd agreed to go to the gym and out to dinner the following day.

He knew that Mitch had spent some time with her, but when he'd tried to pump his twin for information, he'd been suspiciously tight-lipped. There was a part of him that wondered if Mitch had somehow managed to undermine him with Maya. Mitch had said that he didn't have feelings for her, but he also had seemed very defensive of her. Like he had to protect her from Gabe—just as he'd said the other night. That didn't sit well with him.

But he had a promise of some time with her the next day, and Gabe was going to grab hold of that. And hope she didn't cancel.

Gabe went to the gym around two the next day, partly to have some time to climb himself, but also to just touch base with Hunter one more time before he left in a few days. He had complete confidence in his partners at the gym, but he always liked to make sure there was nothing that might need his attention while he was gone. Especially on a month-long trip where the internet might be sketchy at times.

Once he was done meeting with Hunter and Brent, he headed out for the wall he preferred to climb on. Brent worked with him, as he started up the wall. Usually, he found himself zoning out, focusing on nothing more than what handhold to reach for next and where to put his foot. It was just him and the wall for the time it took him to make his way up it and then out under the overhang.

But for once, he found thoughts of other things intruding on his zone-out. Well, other things meaning Maya. Though he still managed to reach the top, he didn't feel as relaxed as he usually did when he climbed. And he had to focus twice as hard to keep his attention where it needed to be in order to complete the climb.

It wasn't until his feet were back on the ground after reaching the top that Gabe realized that Maya was there, watching him.

"Still can't believe how you guys can do that. You make it look so easy," Maya said as he walked to her side. "I think a straight up and down wall is about the extent of my climbing experience."

"Well, let's get you ready to climb," Gabe said and led her back to the office. It was amazing to Gabe how settled he felt just seeing her again.

This time around, he had no problem keeping his attention on the wall, making sure that Maya was safe as she made her climb. She was a lot more confident this time around than she had been the first time she'd come to the gym. Though she still wasn't fast—and at this stage in the learning process, that wasn't the goal—she definitely took less time between moves than the first time she'd climbed.

He wondered if she'd continue to come to the gym while he was gone. Hopefully, she would. Climbing had been something they'd done together in the short time they'd known each other, and he thought that they had connected even more because of it. He didn't want to lose that connection while he was gone.

Chapter Twelve

HEN MAYA REACHED THE POINT where she'd stopped previously, she didn't even seem to consider stopping there this time. Gabe grinned as he watched her move a couple more times, her feet now at her previous high point for her hands. Seeing the way her legs were trembling, he knew that she was going to be stopping soon. There was no need to push it when she was just starting out. He would push himself past the point of exhaustion because that's what he did with his life: pushed himself. But he didn't think that was the case with Maya.

When Gabe finally lowered Maya back to the ground, her legs gave out almost immediately. He went to kneel beside her, glad to see a smile on her face.

"You did even better this time around," he told her, not sure that she was aware of that.

"Really?" Maya tilted her head back, her silky dark hair sliding over her shoulders. "How far did I make it?"

Gabe told her the color of the handhold she'd last gripped before letting go, pointing to it on the wall. "Your foot was level with where your hand was last time."

"Wow!" She looked over at him, her eyes wide and sparkling. "I never would have imagined. I mean, I have been trying to increase my strength."

"You have?" Gabe sank cross-legged onto the mat beside her. "What have you been doing?"

She looked away from him, tipping her head back again to watch someone else head up a nearby wall. "Just some more walking and a little lifting, and exercises that might strengthen my core. From what I've read, a strong core is important for climbing."

"Yes. It definitely is." Gabe found that he was strangely thrilled at the thought that Maya had taken it upon herself to try to make her body stronger and better able to do wall climbing. "Clearly what you're doing is working."

"It could also be that I'm not as scared this time around." She gave him a small smile. "I was pretty nervous that first time."

"Most people are," Gabe reassured her.

"Were you?"

"Uh. Well, let's just say that I'm not most people in this regard."

"Something tells me you say that about a lot of things."

"How long have we known each other?" Gabe asked with a laugh.

"Long enough for me to have picked up on that."

Gabe flopped onto his back, spreading out his arms to the side. "Well, the mystery is gone."

"On your end maybe," Maya said, humor lacing her voice.

He sat back up, wrapping his arms around his knees. "Do tell."

She laughed at that. "Doesn't that kind of defeat the purpose of retaining some sense of mystery?"

"In every other situation, sure, but in ours, I think it's important that you reveal everything."

"Oh, not gonna happen."

Gabe sighed. "You're gonna make me work for it, eh?"

An unrecognizable emotion passed over Maya's face before she smiled. "You bet."

"Okay. On that note, let's go spend some more time together." Gabe jumped to his feet and held out his hand for Maya.

After she grasped it, Gabe pulled her up. She walked to a nearby bench and picked up the duffle bag that was sitting there. "Is there some place I can freshen up before we head out?"

"Sure." Taking hold of her hand, Gabe walked with her to the office. "We have a private set of change rooms in the back. You can use the one Cathy usually does, but you'll have to ask her for the key." Gabe grinned. "She absolutely will not let any of the male gender set foot in *her* change room."

"Smart woman," Maya said as they approached the front desk.

"Hey, Cath," Gabe said to the woman behind the desk. "Can Maya borrow the key to your inner sanctuary?"

Cathy's gaze went back and forth between the two of them before settling on Maya. "You know that no one with an XY chromosome is allowed inside it, right?"

Maya nodded. "Gabe told me you don't allow guys into the changing room you use."

"He is quite correct. So I will give this key to you only, and you must return it directly to me." She held the key ring up and shook it. "No male hands must touch this. Those guys leave a mess behind. Old gym socks. Sweaty shorts and T-shirts. It's nasty. I don't want any of that where I'm changing."

"I absolutely promise that I will be the only one who touches the key to your room."

"Then you may use it." Cathy held the ring out.

Gabe made a grab for it, but her reflexes were quick, and she jerked it back with a frown in his direction. He sighed and crossed his arms. "Fine."

This time when she held the ring out to Maya, he allowed her to take them without any interference. "How about I show you the room as well?"

"I'm going to talk to Hunter in the office," Gabe said with a smile. "Come find me when you're ready to go."

Gabe watched the two women head for the door down a little further from the front desk. Once they'd disappeared inside, he walked to the office and dropped down into the chair across the desk from Hunter.

"You ready to head out in a couple of days?" Hunter asked him.

"Yep. We've been planning this trip for ages, so it will be good to finally get it underway."

"Are you connecting with the group somewhere this side of the ocean or just meeting up in Thailand?"

"We're all flying into Chicago and then will make the rest of the trip together."

Hunter gave his head a shake. "I just can't imagine flying around the world the way you do, never mind doing the things you do. I'm so thankful to just go about my boring life here in Winnipeg."

"And I'm thankful for that," Gabe said with all sincerity. "It gives me peace of mind to know that you and Brent are here keeping things running smoothly while I'm off gallivanting around the world."

Hunter gave him a quick smile. "Just stay safe. Well, as safe as you can be, and yes, I know…"

"Safe isn't fun," they both said together then laughed.

That had been his motto for as long as he could remember. It had all started when his mom —and then later his stepmom, Emily—would tell him to stop doing something because it wasn't safe.

Don't climb so high in the tree, it isn't safe.

Don't go so fast on your skateboard, it isn't safe.

Don't put the bike ramp so high, it isn't safe.

Don't skate so fast or *don't play with the bigger players, it isn't safe.*

But seriously, skating with other six-year-olds had been beyond boring for him. He'd much preferred skating with Kenton and his team who were in the ten to the twelve-year-old range. It seemed that every-thing fun that he wanted to do had been squashed because it wasn't safe.

Eventually, he'd started telling his parents that safe wasn't fun. They hadn't agreed and had continued to prevent him from doing anything they viewed as unsafe. But the moment he'd turned eighteen, every penny he'd saved from working with his dad at C&M Builders had gone to pay for his first skydiving jump.

His parents had continued to object, but since he was of legal age, they couldn't threaten to ground him, take away his electronics or confiscate his bike or skateboard. All through his university years, he'd continued to work hard to save money for his adventures. His parents and grandparents had set aside some money for each child to go to university but had expected them to save half of all the money they earned working for the company business to put towards the remainder of the cost of their education. While Mitch had spent his half of the money he'd earned on a car and all the associated costs, Gabe had saved every dime he could for his adventures.

He knew his parents had hoped his desire to travel the world in search of adventure would change once he graduated. But as luck would have it, he had been able to land jobs he could handle remotely, and then he'd started posting his videos on YouTube and had built up quite a following. The videos had brought in some money for him, and before he knew it, he was also fielding offers from companies wanting him to try their products—such as rock climbing gear and workout equipment—or their resort or destination.

This trip to Thailand was, for the most part, something he had planned with his friends and had paid for himself. There was one activity that they'd be doing that had been sponsored by a company, but the rest of the itinerary was full of things that they'd chosen and planned together. And then he and another guy he often did stuff with had a sponsored trip planned in February, just a few days after they got back from Thailand.

"You just need to come with me on one of my trips," Gabe said. "Then you, too, would learn what real fun is."

"No, thank you," Hunter said, shaking his head firmly. "Not gonna happen. Climbing a wall here is about the extent of risky behavior for me. I'll just watch your videos on YouTube. I'll even sit through the commercials, so you get the ad revenue."

Gabe chuckled. "You are a true friend, Hunter. A true friend."

Hunter leaned back in his chair with a grin. "And don't you forget it."

Voices drifted in through the open doorway, quickly getting close enough that Gabe could recognize them as Cathy and Maya's. He pushed to his feet and then rapped on the desk. "You going to be out at Mom and Dad's for New Year's Eve?"

"Yep. I have a new recipe that I want to prepare and get your mom's opinion on."

"Just don't poison us, and we're all good." He turned to the open doorway and smiled as Maya appeared. "Ready to go?"

"Yes, I am." She smiled at Hunter and said hi to him.

"Are we going to keep seeing you while Gabe's gone?" Hunter asked as he got to his feet.

"I hope to be in a few times. Surprisingly enough, I'm coming to really enjoy the climbing."

"You aren't the first person to make that discovery," Cathy said. "We'll be happy to step in for Gabe in his absence."

After they said goodbye, Gabe led her from the gym. "Still okay to take one car? I can bring you back here afterward."

"Sure, that's fine. Just let me put my bag in my car."

Gabe walked with her through the cold afternoon air and waited as she popped the trunk and dropped her bag inside. "Nothing in there that will freeze? We could leave it in the gym if you want."

"No, there are no liquids in there. I kept them in my purse." She turned slightly so he could see the slouched bag that bumped against her hip. "This thing has room for a lot of stuff."

Gabe reached for her hand as they walked across the parking lot to where he'd parked earlier. He felt her fingers flex against his, and for a moment he wondered if she was going to pull away, but in the end, she didn't. It just made him wonder once again what was going through her head. His experience with Makayla and Sammi had made him well aware that a lot of women didn't tend to just spill whatever they were thinking. Even though a lot of the women he met through adventuring tended to just say whatever came into their head, he knew better than to assume all women would be that way.

He'd debated where to take her, wanting it to be casual but not fast food casual. So he ended up pulling into the parking lot of Mongos. "Is this okay?"

"I've never been here before," she said. "But I'm up for trying anything."

"I can't believe you haven't been here. It's a more interactive form of eating. You choose what you want from their buffet, and then they cook it for you."

"Sounds fun. As long as they cook it for me. I'm not much of a cook."

He hopped out of the truck and rounded it to open the door for Maya. "Hopefully they're not too busy. We're here early enough that it should be okay."

As they stepped into the restaurant, they were immediately met with a low hum of conversation and the aroma of spices. The hostess wasn't at the entrance but appeared a couple of minutes after they arrived. She showed them to a table that was bistro height with one side being a booth and the other side having chairs. Maya slid into the booth side leaving Gabe to settle into the chair across from her.

The waitress came, and even though Gabe had been there before, he let her give her spiel since it was Maya's first time, then they were up and on their way to the buffet area. They took their time with Gabe telling her what he usually chose, but he noticed that she tended to avoid the seafood, while loading up on vegetables, chicken, and beef. She did put some noodles in her bowl, her eyes going wide at how high the pile of food was.

"You need to add some sauces to all of that, or they'll add them for you," Gabe said as they approached the last section before the huge round area where staff waited to cook the food. "If your food doesn't include a lot of sauce or oil, it will burn."

"Teriyaki. Soy sauce. Garlic oil." Maya's brows drew together as she read the labels. "What do you usually add?"

"Well, I like my stir-fry a little on the spicy side, but for your first time, if you're not sure, the less spicy sauces and oils might be a good idea." Gabe pointed out the ones he thought might work, and she chose mostly the less spicy ones with the exception of one. He hoped that she liked the flavors she'd picked. It had taken a few visits for him to find the combination he really liked. Unfortunately, he didn't get to come to Mongos too frequently.

They stood together at the cooking area, watching as four guys moved around the large round flat grill, working the food back and forth with large cooking utensils. He glanced over when he heard Maya laugh after a couple of the guys tossed bowls to each other. Her smile lit up her face and made her eyes sparkle. He loved seeing her excitement and once again was struck by her innocent, wide-eyed fascination with the world. It was a rare—but welcome—find in someone her age.

When their turn came, they handed over their bowls and watched as the contents were dumped on the large grill. It didn't take too long before the cooks were handing back the cooked stir-fry on a plate with a bowl of rice on the side. They returned to their table where the waitress had brought their drinks while they were getting their food.

Maya paused, her hands folded, looking at him expectantly, so Gabe bowed his head and said thanks for their meal.

"That was so cool," Maya said as she poked at the pile of food on her plate.

"It is very entertaining," Gabe agreed. "I really enjoy coming here."

"I've never been to a place like this before." She took a bite and hummed in apparent appreciation, if the smile curving her lips was any indication.

"So did the oils and sauces you chose work?" Gabe asked.

Maya nodded with a smile. "This is amazing. Seeing them cook the food I chose was really fun. And yes, the sauces you recommended are perfect. Thank you."

Though he didn't understand why she seemed so inexperienced with the world, he liked introducing her to things that she came to enjoy. The things they were doing weren't at the level of adventure that he was going to set out on in a couple of days, but they still filled him with a deep sense of satisfaction.

"I've had to do some experimenting during my visits, but I've finally found my favorite combination of oils and sauces." He took a bite of his stir-fry and once again appreciated the flavors that he'd chosen for his own food.

"This might just be my new favorite restaurant," Maya said.

Gabe smiled. "What was your previous favorite?"

"Um…" Maya tilted her head and frowned. "I guess it was probably Montanas or Olive Garden. I don't eat out a lot actually, but in the past, when I have, I've chosen one of those two. Now I'll have three places to choose from."

"So you don't do much cooking?" Gabe asked, wanting to delve into her life a little bit more.

"No. Since I live with my parents, I don't really have to cook for myself." She paused, her gaze on the plate in front of her. "I probably should learn since I won't live with them forever."

"Are you planning to move out?"

Maya shrugged, her dark eyes serious. "I'm not sure. Some days I want to get away. My mom can be a little overprotective since I'm her only child."

"My mom can be overprotective too, and she has ten kids. Somehow, I think that something like that is possibly just engrained in certain people, regardless of the number of children they have." They ate in silence for a couple of minutes before Gabe asked, "So what are you and your folks doing for New Year's Eve?"

Maya's gaze met his for a moment before focusing on her food again. She jabbed her fork into the stir-fry and lifted a forkful up but didn't put it in her mouth. "We're going out of town to meet with some of my dad's business acquaintances. We'll be back on New Year's Day. What does your family usually do?"

"We don't do anything too formal. There's lots of food, and the evening is open to whoever doesn't have any other place to be. At some point, we usually gather and share thoughts on the past year and hopes for the new year, and then spend some time in prayer. And then if it's not too cold, we sometimes shoot off some fireworks to ring in the new year."

"It sounds fun. If I wasn't already committed to going with my parents, I would have come."

The disappointment Gabe had experienced when he'd first heard she couldn't join them resurfaced. For some reason, he'd just assumed she'd be there. He'd been counting on starting off the new year with Maya, so to hear that that wasn't going to happen was disappointing. Maybe next year.

"You think you're up for another bowl?" Gabe asked as he pushed his empty plate to the other side of the table.

Maya leaned back in her seat. Her dark eyes were shining as she smiled at him. "I'm not even sure I can finish this one, but don't let that stop you from going back for more."

Though Gabe would have liked to have her with him, he left the table alone and moved quickly through the buffet. Thankfully, there wasn't much of a lineup, so it didn't take too long to get back to the table and Maya.

The waitress came and refilled their drinks and took away his empty bowl, then left them to continue to talk. Gabe didn't want the evening to end, knowing that this was their last time together before he left for a month. Though he still sensed that she had some reservations, she seemed to be relaxed during their time together.

They continued to talk as they ate, but Gabe found he still wasn't finding out that much more about Maya. For every question he posed to her, she gave a brief answer and turned the conversation back on him. It was equal parts frustrating and intriguing. It felt like she was hiding something, but at the same time, she seemed so innocent that he didn't think she'd be lying to him about anything.

As the evening had progressed, more people had streamed in the front door and the tables around them had filled, so they didn't linger too long once the meal was over. They headed out into the cold to Gabe's truck. He'd started it from inside the restaurant, so it wasn't freezing cold when they climbed inside. Back at the gym parking lot, he had Maya start her car while they sat together in his vehicle.

"I guess I won't see you again before I leave," Gabe said, gazing out the front windshield.

"I might be at church tomorrow," Maya said. "So I'll see you if you're there."

Gabe smiled, relieved to know he didn't have to say goodbye to her yet. "Yeah. I'll be there."

They walked to her car, and when Gabe gave her a hug, Maya held tightly to him. Gabe had planned to make it quick, but he wasn't going to complain if she wanted to hug him longer. She felt good in his arms, the silkiness of her hair pressed beneath his cheek.

She pulled back a bit but didn't let him go. In the light from the tall lamppost in the parking lot, Gabe could see the seriousness of her expression.

"Please don't go," she said softly, the words barely audible.

Her request caught Gabe off-guard. For some reason, he hadn't thought that she would try to keep him from going. They'd only known each other for less than four weeks, and yet it felt so much longer. The truth was, he wasn't sure that he wanted to go either, but he had no choice.

Gabe moved his arms and cupped her face in his hands. As he looked down into her face, he felt his heart skip a beat. "I wish I could stay, but I have obligations."

Her lips tightened briefly, and he felt her swallow hard. "I know. I just wish…"

He wasn't sure which one of them moved—maybe it was both of them—but as Gabe's lips touched Maya's, a sense of rightness swept through him. He placed soft kisses on her lips, relishing the moment as they shared their first kiss. Maya had dropped into his life at a time when he hadn't been expecting it, but she'd become important to him in a way that no one else ever had. If there was a person who could get him to abandon his adventures, it was Maya.

She was asking him to do just that, but he couldn't do it yet. And he was scared that, even without obligations, it might not be something he could give up forever. He didn't want to become bored and resentful of Maya if he gave it up now and then realized later that he just couldn't live a life without some kind of excitement. Could they somehow compromise? Maybe that was something they'd have to discuss when he got back. The reality was that he had commitments that he just couldn't abandon right then. People and companies were counting on him. He had contracts that he couldn't breach by backing out of what had been set up for him to do.

But he was so tempted.

Maya's hands tightened on his back as Gabe continued to share soft kisses with her. He couldn't remember the last time he'd felt the warmth…the affection…the desire the way he did as he kissed Maya. The longer he held her in his arms, the longer his lips lingered on hers, the more convinced he became that he had never experienced anything like them before.

As the realization sank in that he was beginning to chase the physical connection more than the emotional one, Gabe lifted his head and stared down at Maya. The vulnerability and emotion on Maya's face tugged at his heart. This month away was going to be a challenge. Sure, he missed his family whenever he left, but in the short time they'd known each other, Maya had carved out her own place in his heart and being away from her would definitely leave a void inside of him.

"I'm going to miss you." He rested his forehead against hers, swallowing hard against the tide of emotion rising within him. "We'll talk when I get back."

"Okay. I'm going to miss you too," Maya whispered. "Stay safe."

Gabe wished he could promise her that nothing would happen. It was just like with his mom when she said the same thing when he was leaving, but it wasn't a promise he could make. "I'll do my best."

With a final kiss, Gabe released her. "I'll see you tomorrow."

Her arms slid from his waist as she stepped back. "Yes. I'll be there."

Gabe opened the door for Maya and waited for her to slip in and put on her seatbelt before saying goodbye and closing the door. Since the air was cold, Gabe didn't linger, watching Maya's car drive away this time. As he headed home, Gabe had to acknowledge that for the first time in his life, he was torn between staying and going.

Chapter Thirteen

AYA HEADED TO CHURCH the next morning even though it was freezing cold and staying home where it was nice and warm would have been preferable. She found Gabe waiting for her just inside the doors to the foyer. Memories of the kisses they'd shared the night before came flooding back, causing her cheeks to flush. As she'd curled up in her bed after leaving Gabe, she had replayed it all over and over again in her head.

Her first kiss.

While she was still confused about where things were going for the two of them, she was glad that she'd shared that with Gabe. What she felt for him was so strong, stronger than she'd ever imagined feeling for a man.

"Good morning," Gabe said as he approached her with a smile.

Maya returned his smile and relished the feel of his embrace as he drew her in for a hug. Leaving one arm around her back, he walked with her to the cloakroom where he helped her take off her coat and hung it up for her. When his gaze swept over her, his eyes lighting with appreciation, Maya was glad she'd taken extra time with her hair and makeup. She'd also tossed aside several outfits options before choosing the long-sleeve peplum top in deep rose that she wore with a pair of tailored black pants.

"You look beautiful," Gabe said, his hand moving to rest on her back as they left the cloakroom. He also wore a pair of black slacks, but his were paired with a long-sleeve, royal blue, button-down shirt that brought out the color of his eyes, and a paisley tie that happened to have a small swirl of a color that matched her top. It was almost as if they had coordinated their outfits.

"Thank you." Maya looked up at him as he guided her through the foyer. "And you look handsome yourself. I love your tie."

He ran a hand down its length as he smiled down at her. "I'm glad you like it. I hoped you would."

Gabe's words took Maya off-guard for a moment. He cared about what *she* thought? "Well, I do. Very much."

When he grinned, it was one of satisfaction, as if he derived fulfillment from her appreciation the way she had from his. It hadn't even crossed her mind that he would feel that way too. She found she liked the idea…

"Ready to go in?"

Maya nodded, and together they walked into the sanctuary and down to a pew near where they'd sat before. She enjoyed the services she'd been at so far, and Maya hoped to continue to attend the church, even after Gabe was gone.

The pastor that day was talking about glancing back over the old year and looking forward to the new. That was something she hadn't really dwelt on much in previous years. There were times when she'd been only too happy to see the end of a year while hoping that the one ahead would be better. That it would be free of cancer. Of pain. Of isolation and loneliness.

"Don't let the mistakes of this past year, the hurts you may have faced, weigh you down as you look forward to what God has in store for you in the new year. In Lamentations, we are reminded that *through the Lord's mercies we are not consumed because His compassions fail not. They are new every morning: Great is Your faithfulness.*"

The verse popped up on the screens on either side of the stage. Maya quickly jotted down the reference because the words really spoke to her, and she wanted to be able to look at them again in the future. There had been a time when all she'd wanted was to just live to see another day. Then another week. Another month. And now she was looking forward to the next year without the cloud of cancer hanging over her.

Though she did have a scan and bloodwork coming up the end of January, Maya was trying not to dwell on the possibility of what might be to come. She couldn't live in the shadow of death any longer. It was time to accept that her life might not be cancer-free forever, but it was right then, and she was going to just live her life day by day. And as the pastor spoke, Maya realized that there was a part of her life that had been shoved aside because of the cancer and her mom's reluctance to return to church after her first diagnosis. Though her mom had never said the words, it was as if she was angry at God for allowing her only child—the one she'd waited so long for—to get sick.

"I'd like to call Dalton Callaghan up here to read a poem that I want us to take to heart as we look forward to the new year and the plans we're making. It was written by C.T. Studd who passed away in 1931, but the poem is still so applicable for us today."

Dalton stood from his seat in the front row and walked up to join the pastor behind the pulpit. After resting a hand on Dalton's shoulder and giving him a nod, the pastor went to a seat off to the side of the stage.

Dalton didn't seem nervous at all as he set the paper he held down on the pulpit. He looked out over the congregation before he lowered his gaze to the paper and began to read.

Two little lines I heard one day,
Traveling along life's busy way;
Bringing conviction to my heart,
And from my mind would not depart;
Only one life, twill soon be past,
Only what's done for Christ will last.

Only one life, yes only one,
Soon will its fleeting hours be done;
Then, in 'that day' my Lord to meet,
And stand before His Judgement seat;
Only one life, 'twill soon be past,
Only what's done for Christ will last.

Only one life, the still small voice,
Gently pleads for a better choice
Bidding me selfish aims to leave,
And to God's holy will to cleave;
Only one life, 'twill soon be past,
Only what's done for Christ will last.

Only one life, a few brief years,
Each with its burdens, hopes, and fears;
Each with its clays I must fulfill,
living for self or in His will;
Only one life, 'twill soon be past,
Only what's done for Christ will last.

When this bright world would tempt me sore,
When Satan would a victory score;
When self would seek to have its way,
Then help me Lord with joy to say;
Only one life, 'twill soon be past,
Only what's done for Christ will last.

Give me Father, a purpose deep,
In joy or sorrow Thy word to keep;
Faithful and true what e'er the strife,
Pleasing Thee in my daily life;
Only one life, 'twill soon be past,
Only what's done for Christ will last.

Oh let my love with fervor burn,
And from the world now let me turn;
Living for Thee, and Thee alone,
Bringing Thee pleasure on Thy throne;
Only one life, "twill soon be past,
Only what's done for Christ will last.

Only one life, yes only one,
Now let me say, "Thy will be done";
And when at last I'll hear the call,
I know I'll say "twas worth it all";
Only one life, 'twill soon be past,
Only what's done for Christ will last."

Maya was mesmerized by the sound of Dalton's voice as he recited the poem in a way that brought the words to life. They flowed effortlessly from him with a cadence that drew her in and—by the looks of the people around her—she wasn't the only one so affected.

As Dalton returned to his seat and the pastor came back to stand behind the podium, Maya found the words echoing in her mind, and she planned to google the poem for herself when she got home later.

Only one life, 'twill soon be past,
Only what's done for Christ will last.

The service ended with a prayer and a song, and then they were filing out of the sanctuary. Maya knew that Gabe was most likely going to ask her if she wanted to join them for dinner following the service, but she was going to decline. After what had happened between them the night before and then listening to the pastor's words, Maya felt like she needed a little space.

The poem Dalton had read had been a strong reminder that she really did only have one life. And it was a life that she had fought hard for. When the pain—the endless pain—had worn her down so low that she hadn't known if she could find the strength to go on. When it had felt easier to just stop fighting. To stop the treatments. To let the cancer win. She'd somehow found the resolve to go on. To fight just one more day. And then another. Her life was precious to her. She loved her life and wanted to do something meaningful with it. What that was, she wasn't sure yet, but more and more, she was coming to realise that it *wasn't* being with a man who courted death with the same passion she'd fought to live.

Being close to Gabe weakened her resolve to not get in even deeper with him. The kiss—her first—the night before had already made her want to just chuck her resolution to take things slow, right out the window. So she wouldn't go to dinner, and she would say goodbye to Gabe without the little bit of a meltdown like she'd had the previous night. He wasn't going to stay, that much was clear, and there was no way she would beg him again.

When they reached the foyer, Gabe rested his hand on Maya's back and guided her off to the side. He looked down at her with a smile that went right to his eyes, crinkling the skin at the corner of them. "Can you come for dinner at Mom and Dad's?"

Maya shook her head. "I'm sorry. Not today."

Disappointment dimmed the smile on Gabe's face. "Are you sure?"

The pull was there to cave in, but she couldn't. "No. I'm sorry."

"Okay, guess this will be goodbye then?"

The knot tightened in Maya's stomach. She didn't want it to be goodbye. She didn't want to think about what he was leaving to do. She didn't want to think about what could possibly happen to him.

"I'm sure you'll have a good time." Maya hoped her smile looked steadier than it felt. "At least you'll be warm!"

Gabe looked at her closely, his blue eyes serious, then nodded. "More like hot, and the humidity is usually really high."

"Do you have trouble adjusting when you go from one extreme to the other?" Maya asked, finding it a bit ironic that they were discussing the weather.

"It can take a couple of days, but it usually isn't a big factor." Gabe paused then said, "I'm going to text you my social media information. Even if you don't have social media yourself, you can still see the pictures and videos from the trip. But if you do set up an account on anything, be sure to follow or friend me."

"Okay. I'll do that. I might set up accounts even though I don't really have a lot of people I want following my life." Maya laughed. "I'm truly not that exciting."

"Well, to some people you are. Post pictures of you on the climbing wall at the gym. That's definitely exciting."

"True," Maya said then shrugged. "I'll see."

Gabe grinned at her. "You could post pictures of what you're eating for breakfast, and I'd find it interesting."

"I've managed to go this long without taking pictures of the food I eat, I think I'll probably go a little while longer. But who knows, I might post one for you."

"Well, that makes me feel special," Gabe said, his eyes sparkling with laughter once again. "I'll probably post some food pictures from Thailand since they have some great food over there."

"Hey, Maya."

Mitch's greeting interrupted their conversation, and Maya saw a flash of irritation on Gabe's face. "Hey, Mitch. How's it going?"

"Going good." When he smiled at her, Maya noticed how different Mitch's smile looked from Gabe's, and it certainly didn't fill her with warmth the way his brother's did. "Are you coming to dinner?"

"No, not today. Though I do appreciate the invitation."

Gabe and Mitch exchanged a look that apparently contained enough conversation that Mitch turned back to her with a smile. "Well, I hope you have a good New Years. I'll see you at work again later this week."

"Happy New Year to you too," Maya said with a smile. "I hope that you have a good holiday."

Gabe watched his brother walk away then looked back at Maya. "I guess I should probably go home so I'm not late for dinner." He paused and tilted his head with a small smile. "Are you sure you can't come?"

"I'm sure," Maya told him. "I need to get going too."

"Then let's get our coats, and I'll walk you to your car."

Gabe again placed his hand on her back, and Maya savored the feel of it—the connection between them seemed so strong even though they hadn't known each other that long. It scared and intrigued her in equal measures. Which was why she needed to say goodbye and go home.

When Gabe held her coat, the thought that her mother would love that he had good manners crossed her mind and made her smile. As she buttoned up her coat, Gabe grabbed his own and pulled it on. The crowd in the foyer had thinned out, and the cars were lined up to exit the parking lot.

The wind blowing across the parking lot was frigid, so when Gabe offered her his elbow, she slid her gloved hand into the curve of his arm and buried her other hand in her pocket as they walked. Walking close to Gabe seemed to offer a little warmth, and Maya savored it, knowing it was going to be the last time with him for a little while…maybe forever if it seemed that his adventures were more important than she was.

When they reached her car, Gabe took her hands in his and squeezed them. "Take care of yourself."

Maya smiled though she felt her lips quivering. "I think that's my line for you."

"I know," Gabe said with a slight nod. "But I want you to take care of yourself too."

He pulled her in for a hug, and Maya wrapped her arms around him, her hands grasping handfuls of his coat. She blinked rapidly, trying to keep the tears at bay. Why was she crying over this man she'd barely known for a month? It didn't seem possible for her heart to ache the way it did at the thought of him leaving.

"I'll see you again in a few weeks," Gabe said as he stepped back. "So, we're not saying goodbye, just…see you later."

Maya nodded. "See you later."

Gabe reached past her to open her door. "You need to get in out of the cold."

Feeling sad at the thought of driving away from Gabe, Maya hesitated then slid behind the wheel. After she was seated, Gabe bent down and used his fingertips to turn her face toward him. He stared at her for a moment, then pressed a quick kiss to her lips. "See you later, beautiful."

He straightened and closed the door, ending their moment of saying goodbye. Maya sat with her hands clenching the steering wheel and stared in her rear-view mirror, watching as Gabe walked to where his truck was parked. She closed her eyes, let out a long breath and then opened them up, blinking to clear the moisture that had gathered there.

She made the drive home in silence, not even turning on the radio. The tumult of emotion within her was nearly overwhelming her. She desperately needed someone to talk to, so as soon as she got home, she checked to see if Lainie was online. When she wasn't, Maya changed out of her church clothes and pulled on a pair of leggings and a baggy sweatshirt. She went downstairs to see what she could find to eat for lunch.

There was no sign of her parents, but that didn't mean they weren't home. Her dad's favorite spot in the house was his office, and her mom's was the sunroom with her plants. Maya was just as happy to not have to see either of them so she didn't have to explain why she wasn't in a great mood.

After making a sandwich using the multigrain bread that Elisse had baked and some slices of chicken, tomatoes, and cheese, Maya headed back to her room. She ate her sandwich while sitting on her window seat, looking out over the snowy forest behind the house. When she was done, she leaned her head back against the window and closed her eyes.

What was she going to do about Gabe? Was there a way to get used to saying goodbye all the time while he went off on his adventures? The more her emotions became engaged with him, the more difficult it would be to say goodbye while he traveled the world. And while she did want to go on some adventures herself, she wasn't sure that they were the same types of adventures he would choose.

Her phone chirped a short time later, and Maya picked it up to see a message from Gabe giving her a bunch of links to his social media pages.

Gabe: *Be sure to follow/friend me if you set up any accounts for yourself. ;-)*

A sudden rush of tears caught Maya off-guard, and she had to blink away the moisture in order to tap out a reply to Gabe. *I will. Thanks for the links.*

She set her phone back down on the seat beside her, uncertain that she wanted to see anything about the adventures that were taking him away from Winnipeg. Maybe when her mindset was in a better place, she'd have a look.

GABE LOOKED AROUND at the people gathered with his family to ring in the New Year. He really wished that Maya had been able to make it, but he knew that he had no right to request that she prioritize him over her family. They hadn't even defined their relationship. All Gabe knew was that her not being there had created a feeling of missing part of himself.

"Everything okay?"

Gabe looked to his side and saw that his mom had come to stand beside him. She looked up at him, concern on her face. He gave her what he hoped was a reassuring smile. "It's all good."

The way she quirked an eyebrow at him told him that she wasn't buying it. "Are you having second thoughts about leaving?"

Was he? He didn't think so. There was still excitement about the trip, it was just that he didn't like the idea of leaving Maya behind. However, while he did get the feeling that she had some interest in adventures, he didn't think her interest would be on the same level as his.

"I'm looking forward to it. It's been awhile since I've wandered around Asia. I think it will be fun."

"And dangerous," his mom added with a frown.

"Not all of it," Gabe tried to reassure her. "It's not really dangerous to ride on an elephant. I mean, they had elephant rides at the zoo when I was younger."

"Oh, I remember that, and I wasn't too thrilled about you riding on one even then. Although that didn't stop you."

Gabe grinned. "Of course it didn't."

She gripped his upper arm and rested her head against his shoulder, staring out at their family and friends. "Nothing ever really has stopped you. I thought maybe a certain someone might have been enough."

"We've not even known each other a month, Mom," Gabe said, though the words felt wrong even as he said them. It was like he was dismissing the connection they shared as something so much less than it was.

"Time doesn't necessarily define the depths of what two people can feel for each other. For some people, time will never deepen what they feel for one another. For others, that deep connection comes on much more quickly." His mom hesitated, her grip tightening briefly on his arm. "I've never seen you like that with any other woman."

"That's probably true, but I have dated—just not here. You haven't seen me with those women."

When she didn't reply right away, he glanced down to see her looking at him. "I don't think I need to."

Gabe let out a quick sigh. "I don't have any choice but to leave, Mom. You and Dad have always impressed on us the importance of following through on commitments we make. I have signed contracts with companies for this trip and a few more after it. There's no way I can just drop everything."

"Will you consider *not* signing any more contracts after that? Maybe it's time you think about settling down."

Was it time to settle down? For the first time in his life, Gabe didn't immediately dismiss his mom's suggestion. That, more than anything, showed just how much he felt for Maya.

"I might consider it. I'll see how things go with the next few trips." He was already in discussions with a couple of other companies for future adventures, but nothing had been signed yet, so those could possibly be passed over. But did he really want to do that?

Maybe it was time to start looking at how he could balance his love for adventure with his desire to be with Maya. He knew that a relationship would never work if he wasn't present for ten months out of the year. It was unrealistic to expect Maya to put her life on hold for him, but the thought of letting her go and maybe her finding a guy who was willing to give her priority ate at his gut. He couldn't just let her go without at least trying to see if a relationship would work.

"This may be the year for change," Gabe murmured to his mom. "We'll see."

"I think it might be a year of change for a lot of people, not just you."

Gabe turned slightly so he could look her squarely in the face. "Is there something going on?"

His mom smiled then shook her head. "Nothing but a whole lot of prayer."

Her answer was no surprise to him. Gabe knew that his parents prayed daily for all of them. His parents' prayers weren't something he took for granted. In the course of his life of adventure, he'd come across plenty of people who were estranged from their families. Some had left their family of their own accord. Others had been kicked out of their family's homes for a variety of reasons.

After having met those people and gone on to call some of them friends, Gabe knew he was beyond blessed with the life he led and the family he had to support him. Yeah, his mom wanted him to stop his adventures, but when push came to shove, she'd see him off the next day with a hug and a smile and a promise to pray for him. There wasn't much more he could ask for when it came to supportive parents.

"I'm sorry Maya couldn't make it tonight," she said, once more turning her attention to the room.

"Yeah, me too, but she had plans with her parents. They're out of town right now."

"Maybe next New Year's Eve," his mom said, squeezing his arm.

Gabe laughed. "Yeah, maybe."

Strangely enough, he could actually picture being in that same place a year from then, getting ready to ring in the New Year with a kiss from Maya. The mental picture settled deep into his heart, and he knew that it would keep coming to mind until things were official between him and Maya. As the clock edged closer to midnight, Gabe resolved it would be something he'd talk to her about when he came back in four weeks.

Chapter Fourteen

ITH THE KNOWLEDGE THAT GABE was no longer on the same continent as she was, Maya took her time driving to the office on the day after she'd gotten back from New York. It was a sad thought for her, and she was full of regret that she hadn't just ditched the trip to New York so that she could have spent New Year's Eve with him. But it was too late now. And her resolve to keep her distance from him no longer mattered because he was gone.

Pulling her collar up around her ears, Maya sighed, envying the fact that Gabe was someplace warm, and pushed open her car door. She grabbed her purse and got out, slamming the door behind her. Thankfully, it was a quick walk to the front door of the building, and soon she was within its warm interior. The Christmas decorations were still up, and the lights on the tree glowed warmly in contrast to the cold, gray day outside.

As Maya walked toward her desk, her footsteps faltered then came to a stop at the sight that greeted her. On her desk sat a beautiful floral arrangement. It was an explosion of colors with flowers of blue, pink, yellow, red and white all arranged together. Maya smiled as she continued to her desk, rounding the corner of it to reach her chair.

Keeping her gaze on the bouquet, Maya unbuttoned her coat and hung it up on the rack behind her desk. Setting her purse on the desk, she sank down onto her chair. She reached out and touched the petals of a daisy before letting herself pick up the large envelope that was propped up against the bouquet. Her name was scrawled across the front of it, and she traced the letters, realizing this was the first time she'd seen Gabe's handwriting. It was nothing like Mitch's, which was much more compact and neat.

Smiling, she slid a finger under the flap of the envelope and gently pulled out the card that was inside. The front of the card was yet another beautiful floral explosion of color. When she opened it, Gabe's scrawl filled the page.

Dear Maya,
Happy New Year!

I hope you had a good start to the year. My year is off to a great start because you are now a part of it. These flowers are my way of showing you how my life looks with you in it. Bright. Cheerful. Beautiful. I hope they made you smile because the world needs you to smile more. Seeing your smile has certainly brought me much joy.

I haven't even left yet, and I already want to be back. I can't wait to see you again.

Take care of yourself.

Gabe xoxo

Maya lowered the card and stared at the flowers again. Her first flowers from a man. Her first card from a man. Well, her dad had given her flowers on a few occasions and a card to go with them, but that was totally different from something like this. These were given without any reason other than the fact that Gabe liked her and wanted to give her something to show that. She had all the money she'd ever need and the ability to buy herself anything she wanted, but at that moment, none of that compared to how she felt about a simple card and a bouquet of flowers. Definitely priceless.

"I see you found Gabe's gift."

Maya turned to see Makayla standing just outside her office, her arms crossed and a smile on her face. "Yes, I did. How on earth did he arrange this with the holiday and everything?"

Makayla moved to the front of the desk and looked down at the flowers. "He picked up the bouquet on New Year's Eve since the stores were still open and then my mom made sure to keep it cool until this morning when I brought it in with me. Now when he bought the card, I have no idea."

Maya grinned. "This is such a beautiful surprise. A shock really. Thank you for your part in getting them here."

"Well, now that I've got a man of my own, I'm all about helping out romance where I can." Her smile faded into a frown as her gaze went to the hallway leading back to the offices. "Wish there was something I could do for Bennett and Grace. I love them both so much, but it is hard to see Bennett hurting because Grace won't acknowledge the feelings between them."

"Do you think Grace really does love Bennett?" Maya had heard bits and pieces of their story over the time since she'd started working at C&M, but she had no idea if it was really a case of unrequited love on Bennett's part or if Grace did love him in return but chose not to be with him for some reason.

"Has she ever said the words? No," Makayla said. "I think her crazy belief that everyone she loves and lets into her life will die on her is what's keeping her from letting herself get close to Bennett. In the past few months, she's been relying on him a lot, and they've grown close. I don't think she even realized how often she talked about him, or how her eyes lit up when she did. He was also the one she called when her labor started. They need each other. Bennett has realized it, but Grace is living in fear and denial. Never a good way to live life."

Maya thought about her mom and the way she had been so over-protective of Maya for so long. She knew fear was her mom's motivation as well, and Maya had lived that way too, but she was trying her best to move past that. So far, she felt like she was successful in her efforts.

"Anyway," Makayla said, her smile coming back, "I was happy to give Gabe a hand."

"Thank you again. This is amazing."

The office phone rang, and when Maya answered it, Makayla gave her a quick wave and headed back to her office. Mitch and Tristan walked in a short time later, and the business day was underway. It was surprisingly busy considering a lot of businesses were still in holiday mode, but each time she glanced at the bouquet, she couldn't help but smile.

Maya wasn't sure if Gabe had access to text messaging while he was in Thailand, but she went ahead and sent a message to thank him for the flowers. Nothing came back from him right away, so Maya set aside her phone and focused instead on work. It wasn't until around seven that night that she received a message from him.

Gabe: *I'm so glad you liked them!*

Maya smiled and quickly tapped out a response. *They are beautiful. Definitely brightens up my room!*

Gabe: *Just the way you do!*

She shook her head at his comment. Never had Maya felt like she was the "light up the room" type of girl. In fact, her parents had worked hard to make sure that she wasn't the center of attention. It wasn't until later in her teens that she'd understood why she and her parents had different last names. Her dad had done that to create some distance between them as a precaution against kidnapping attempts. She hadn't realized how much her dad had hidden her connection to him until she'd googled herself and found nothing. And when she'd googled her dad, there was mention of her mom but nothing about Maya.

So to be told that she brightened up a room was something new and a bit unbelievable.

How is Thailand?

Gabe: *Hot! And wet! But we're heading out to the Mahawangchang Elephant Camp to go on an elephant trek.*

That didn't sound too dangerous. In fact, Maya thought that perhaps she might like to try that herself some day. Maybe people were exaggerating his need for dangerous adventure.

Hope you have fun! Say hi to Dumbo for me.

Gabe: *LOL I will! Check out my FB page for pics and vids. : D*

I will.

Gabe: *Guess I better run. The day starts early here, and I want some breakfast before we start out. Take care of yourself. <3*

Maya stared at the heart at the end of the text before tapping out her reply. *You take care of yourself too. Stay safe.*

Gabe: *Will do!*

Maya let out a long breath, sort of relieved that Gabe's leaving didn't mean losing all contact with him. She was still incredibly confused by how she felt about Gabe. The differences in how they lived their lives seemed almost insurmountable. She didn't expect him to change his life for her, but Maya wasn't sure that she could be in a relationship with someone who traveled as much as Gabe did. Her dad traveled a lot less than Gabe did, and still, she and her mom missed him tons. She couldn't imagine being with someone who was gone even more. And then there was the matter of what he did while he was away. The danger he placed his life in on a regular basis.

Then she'd shown up at work and seen that bouquet, and she'd been ready to chuck all her reservations out the window. Maya turned her head and looked at the floral arrangement that sat on her desk. She'd managed to sneak it into the house when she'd arrived home from work earlier. Makayla had helped her cover it all up so that the frigid temperatures couldn't nip at the delicate blooms. Now it was safe in the warmth of her room where she could enjoy it for as long as it would last.

The sound of an incoming Skype call had Maya rolling off her bed and heading for her desk. Since there was only one person who ever contacted her that way, she leaned over and accepted the call even before sitting down in her chair.

"Hey, Lainie!" Maya said with a big smile. "Happy New Year!"

"Happy New Year, sugar," Lainie said as she appeared on the screen. Her blonde hair was piled in a messy knot on the top of her head, and she looked happy and relaxed as she stared into the camera.

"How was your New Year's Eve?" Maya asked. They hadn't connected much over the holiday, partly because Maya hadn't wanted to explain why she was on a private jet or, later, in an opulent hotel in New York City. "How was your party?"

"Oh, girl, it was incredible," Lainie said. "As it turned out, my cousins brought some of their friends who didn't have anywhere else to go. I met someone!"

"You did?" Maya leaned forward, staring at the excitement on her friend's face. "Tell me all about him."

"His name is Stewart, and he's a resident at the hospital with my cousin, Darcy. We spent the whole time just talking about life, and even when I would leave to get something to eat or drink, he'd search me out again."

"Oh, hun, I'm so glad you found someone you connected with," Maya said, meaning every word since she had a new understanding of what that could really mean for someone.

"And that's not the best part," Lainie said. Her friend seemed to be practically bouncing in her seat. "The best part of it is that he already knows all about my history with cancer. Darcy has known him for a couple of years and talked to him about me early on in their friendship. She told me after the party that he knew exactly who I was. He knew who I was and *still* wanted to spend time with me. It was amazing!"

"I'm so happy for you, sweetie. I know that was something that you were worried about."

Lainie let out an audible breath. "I honestly didn't think I'd find someone who would be willing to take a chance on me given my past and the risk in my future. And even though I never thought I'd be interested in someone in the medical community, I can see a benefit since he would understand things more than the average person. You know how people can be when they hear the word *cancer*."

"Yeah, a doctor would understand what remission is and what it means." Maya wondered once again how Gabe might react to the word. Would she ever find out? "Are you going to be seeing him again?"

"Yes! I thought maybe I'd imagined things, but he texted me just a few minutes ago to ask if we could meet up for coffee on the weekend." Lainie squealed and clapped her hands. "I told him yes, so we're going to be going out on Saturday afternoon."

"That's so great!" Maya was genuinely happy for Lainie given the heartache she'd experienced in her past attempts at a relationship. She really hoped that she wasn't going to have to endure similar heartaches before finding someone she could spend her life with. If that was even part of what was in her future.

After they had talked about Lainie's new guy a bit more, she asked about Gabe and how Maya's New Year's had been. Maya took advantage of the opportunity to spill her most recent feelings about him, and then she showed Lainie the bouquet.

"That is seriously beautiful! And the card too," Lainie said with a grin. "Gotta love a guy who gives a girl flowers."

"Yeah," Maya agreed with a sigh. "But I'm not sure that's a good thing for me. I have no idea how our lives would mesh. He's been after me to get on social media."

"Do it! I've told you for awhile now you should get a Facebook account at the very least." Lainie paused then leaned forward a bit. "Can you send me his social media information? I won't try and friend him or anything, but I'd like to see what's public anyway."

"Sure, I'll do that." Maya picked up her phone and found the message that Gabe had sent her with the links. She took a minute to copy and paste it into a message for Lainie and then sent it off. "I haven't had much chance to look at it. Truthfully, I'm a little scared to."

Lainie scrunched up her nose as the alert on her phone went. "Scared? Why?"

"There have just been some comments made, and after watching him on the climbing wall, I realized that he's much more into dangerous adventures than I'd realized. I guess I don't really want to watch his stuff and see my fears confirmed, especially while he's on this trip to Thailand."

"Do you want me to check it out for you and let you know," Lainie offered.

Maya considered her offer then said, "No. I think I'll have to watch it for myself and make a decision."

"If you change your mind, you know I'll do that for you."

Maya did know that. She and Lainie had been there for each other for so many things—well, as much as they could be when they lived so far apart. Maybe one of these days she'd fly to meet her. It felt like the strings her mother had held around her life were finally loosening. Or maybe the knife she'd been using to try to cut through them was finally fraying the ropes. Either way, she was just glad that things were changing for the positive in her life.

They talked for a bit longer before Lainie had to go. Maya went down to the kitchen and got herself a cup of tea then went back upstairs to take a bath before bed. While in the tub, she used her phone to make a Facebook account and then found Gabe's. She went ahead and sent him a friend request even though she wasn't one hundred percent sure whether she wanted to follow his trip through his pictures and videos just yet.

THROUGHOUT THE NEXT WEEK, Maya received a few texts from Gabe, but there was no regular schedule for when they would come through. She was still on the fence about her future with Gabe. She'd look at the card or the bouquet that was still looking beautiful on her desk at home and would feel like she could happily spend the rest of her life with the man. But then she'd remember that his texts were coming from Thailand, where riding an elephant was probably the mildest adventure he was going to experience, and she'd feel as if there was no way they could make their lives mesh.

Saturday was the first day that she hadn't received any sort of text from Gabe. When, by Sunday night, she still hadn't gotten anything from him, worry began to flourish within her. Horrible scenarios began to filter into her mind. Though she knew she shouldn't do it, Maya sat down at her laptop and pulled up the message Gabe had sent her with links in it and clicked on the one to his YouTube channel.

Maya had spent a lot of time on the website over the years, since, for a long time, it was her way of connecting with people's lives virtually when she couldn't do it in real life. Watching people's vlogs of their everyday lives had always been a huge fascination for her. She had never watched anything like Gabe's though.

The first one she watched was of him in a shark cage from a few years earlier. It was among the first he'd done. He was holding up what she assumed was a waterproof camera, showing the shark that was headed straight for the cage. Maya stared in shock as the cage shook with the impact of the shark hitting it. As the shark moved away, Gabe swung the camera toward his face, and through the mask he wore, she could see the familiar crinkling of his eyes as he reacted to the attack. Even without being able to see his mouth, Maya could tell that he was beyond excited about what was happening.

And the footage that followed the cage dive, when he was back on the boat, confirmed it. His hair dripped water down his tanned skin as his smile reached from ear to ear, his blue eyes sparkling with excitement. It was a look she became acutely familiar with as she continued to work her way forward through his videos. Some of the adventures were fairly mild—at least by Gabe's standards—but most were things a normal person wouldn't even consider trying. He seemed to intersperse his more dramatic adventures with milder ones, but still, there was a disturbing pattern that Maya couldn't ignore.

It wasn't until she reached a video labeled VOLCANO BOARD-ING-FAIL that she finally paused. For some reason, she wasn't sure she wanted to see it. The unease that was already present in the pit of her stomach grew as she considered what the video might show. Obviously not his death since Gabe was walking around alive and well—at least as of the last time she'd heard from him.

She glanced at the clock on her desktop monitor. 12:15 AM. She'd spent the last four hours watching the videos on Gabe's channel. She had to be up for work in less than seven hours, and she still had one more to watch. Or did she?

Maya read the title once more, wishing it was clickbait, but given that Gabe hadn't seemed to be in the habit of doing that for other videos, she doubted he'd done it for this one. She reached out and clicked the mouse to start the video.

It started out like most his videos did, with an explanation of where he was and what he was doing. There were others with him, just like in his previous videos, some of them even looked familiar to her now. She was beginning to see that he traveled with a lot of the same people. These were the people who—like Gabe—lived for the adrenalin rush only the most dangerous activities could bring.

"I'm here in Leon, Nicaragua with Matt, Eric, Alex, Jill, Nathan, and Sue. If you've been following my vlogs, you've been able to see a bit of this beautiful country as we've traveled around. I figured that what we're going to do today deserves a vlog all of its own. We've done a few crazy things in our time, but this is a new one for us." Gabe paused to turn the camera away from him to face the view. Out in the distance, a mountain rose high and dark. "This is Cerro Negro which means Black Hill. It's an active volcano—the youngest in Central America at the age of one hundred sixty-seven years old—but its last eruption was in 1999. We are going to be climbing to the peak, and then we'll be heading back down on what is basically a short wooden board."

The group joked around for a bit, each talking about what they were looking forward to in the day's adventure.

"Well, I can tell you what I'm not necessarily looking forward to," Jill said. "The walk up to the top and then trying to not get blown away."

"Just remember how they said to hold your board, and you should be good," Gabe said. "But if you start to feel like the wind is going to carry you away, just grab onto Eric. You know he's the one with the lead foot."

"Hardy. Har. Har." A tall, dark-haired man scowled as he crossed his arms. "A couple of speeding tickets and suddenly I'm the butt of all the jokes."

"Well, you can enjoy your need for speed today," Gabe said as he focused his camera on the volcano once again. "It's going to take about forty-five minutes or so for us to walk up it. And once we get to the top…" He turned the camera back on himself and grinned. "The adventure begins."

Up a live volcano? Just so they could slide down the side of it? That wasn't Maya's idea of adventure. That was plain foolishness.

As she watched, the video went into about a five-minute sped-up time lapse as they made their way up the volcano. Every once in awhile, it would return to regular speed, and Gabe would ask someone a question about their hike before going back to the time-lapse speed. As the climb progressed, Maya could see the wind picking up, and the two girls were struggling against it.

When they got to the top, the time lapse slowed to normal speed, and Gabe panned around where he stood. He showed Eric down on one knee feeling the ground around the edge of the volcano, expressing how it was hot to the touch.

Again, Maya just shook her head at why someone would want to be that close to an active volcano. Gabe turned around and then slung his arm around the shoulders of one of the girls—Jill—and held his camera out, so they were both in the frame.

"Still got both feet on the ground, I see, Jilly." Gabe grinned down at her. "Hanging in there?"

Jill looked up at him and returned his smile, and Maya saw something there that made her frown. The woman was looking at Gabe with clear adoration on her face. Had the two of them dated? Her name sounded familiar. Maya paused the video and went to Gabe's Facebook page and the post he'd made before leaving for Thailand. That had been the only post she'd read so far.

Met up with the gang in Chicago! Next stop….Bangkok, Thailand! Looking forward to this next adventure with Eric, Sue, Alex, Damon, Matt, Jill and Annie! Stay tuned for pics and vids!

There she was. *Jill.* Almost two years later and the majority of the group traveling together was still the same. Did the woman still have feelings for Gabe?

Maya sat forward in her seat, staring at the picture that Gabe had included in the post. She immediately spotted Jill—standing right next to Gabe, her arm around him while he had his around her and one of the guys she recognized from the earlier video.

This was definitely not something she'd thought much about, which, when she considered it, was pretty ridiculous. Gabe was handsome, energetic and outgoing. No doubt he drew people to him. So why had he zeroed in on her? Or was she just reading more into it?

Maya sighed and slumped back in her chair. This was when she really, really hated how inexperienced she was when it came to relationships. She had no clue what was going on, and she *still* didn't know what to do from her own perspective of what she wanted in a relationship. Watching the videos gave her a glimpse into his life, but she still wasn't sure it was a glimpse she wanted. However, if she was going to make a decision on whether to continue on with him or not, she needed all the information she could gather.

She stared at the social media page, still not familiar with its setup. Just one more thing that she knew nothing about. Maya knew this was largely her own fault. Her mom might have let her on social media—at least in a limited, supervised capacity—but Maya had been reluctant to let anyone get too close. Being in and out of the hospital had made it difficult to want to open her life to anyone.

In the online role-playing games she'd played, Maya could become someone she wasn't in real life. A healthy someone. Then, once she'd gotten older but her friend-circle hadn't expanded, she hadn't felt that there was a need to join social media.

She reached out to tap the touchpad of her laptop to shut down the Facebook browser window, but then paused when she noticed a red circle with a 2 in the middle of it. She clicked on it and saw that one was a notification that said that Gabe had accepted her friend request. The second said *Jill Danes wants to connect with you.*

Maya hesitated only a moment before clicking on it. If this was the Jill from Gabe's photo, she wondered why the woman would be contacting her. How she'd even know to contact her.

I'm sure you have no idea of who I am, and until a week or so ago, I had no idea who you were either. It has come as quite a surprise to those of us who consider Gabe a close friend that he is interested in someone who—from what he's said—has no interest in something he spends the majority of his life doing. I'm not sure if Gabe is just experiencing a passing infatuation or what, but unless you're prepared to join him on his adventures, I think you're doing both of you a disservice. He may decide to stop traveling for your sake, but honestly, that will kill his soul. We have all been traveling together for a long time, and there's no way that Gabe could just leave this life behind without it costing him a part of what makes Gabe who he is. I would challenge you to consider this before asking Gabe to make such a huge change in his life. It would truly be a selfish thing to do.

Maya stared in shock at the note then let out a huff of laughter. Like Jill's note hadn't been selfish at all. Maya had a hard time buying the idea that the woman was being strictly altruistic with her note. However, that didn't mean that the points she made were invalid. It had been something Maya had been considering as well.

Would Gabe be happy without his adventures?

According to someone who claimed to be his friend—and really, how could Maya argue that particular point because Jill had been in his life a lot longer than she had been—Gabe wouldn't be Gabe without his adventures. She had to admit that it was Gabe's zest for life that had attracted her to him, and it was possible he'd lose that if he couldn't do something he clearly enjoyed.

And worse than that, Gabe might end up resenting her for influencing him to make the decision to leave that life behind to be with her. But there was no way she could be with someone who viewed life so flippantly. She had fought for her life so hard, but now what she saw of Gabe's life seemed to say that he wasn't living his life to the fullest...he was chasing death. How could she be with someone like that?

The simple answer was...She couldn't.

Chapter Fifteen

ABE LISTENED AS THE WORLD came to life outside his room at the Airbnb where they were staying in Phuket City. Nancy, the person who had helped arrange their whole trip, had booked them an Airbnb in the city located in southern Thailand. It was a large space with beds for all of them. The women in the group had their own room with a double and single bed and bathroom while he and the other guys had beds that some of them had to double up in, but they were used to that. The cost of the place had worked out to about ten dollars a night per person. So they'd booked it for eight days as their base camp while they explored the area.

They were halfway through their time in Asia and had just returned the previous day from a three-day kayaking trip. It hadn't been a dangerous adventure, but he'd still enjoyed the beauty of kayaking in Phang Nga Bay and then exploring some caves as well as snorkeling and swimming in lagoons. They'd camped on beaches and eaten sunset dinners on the escort boat.

It had been a beautiful trip, but all Gabe had been able to think about was how much he wished that Maya was there with him. He knew she would have appreciated the beauty of nature that he and the others had seen. There was a keen desire within him to experience these things with Maya.

Once everyone was up, they were planning to do some sightseeing in the area before taking a trip on a liveaboard for two nights to do some diving. Then it would be up to Chiang Mai in the northern part of Thailand for another week. That was where they'd be doing some of their more dangerous adventures. Though he wasn't scared of what was to come, Gabe found he wasn't anticipating those adventures the way he usually did.

He was more distracted than usual too. He knew that had to do with Maya, and he'd had plenty of time to think—and talk—about her over the past week. In fact, he was almost certain that his group was pretty tired of hearing about her. But that was too bad. So much of what he felt for Maya, he'd never felt for anyone before, which both scared and excited him. He had no idea if she was interested in something long term, but he couldn't commit to anything until he finished his contracts.

And he still had to decide if he was ready to make a major change in his life. Though he'd known that he'd have to make that change at some point, Gabe hadn't anticipated it happening before he had even hit thirty.

With a sigh, Gabe shifted onto his side and grabbed his phone from the window sill next to his bed. He'd been out of touch for the past three days as they hadn't had an internet connection while on the kayaking trip. Eric had purchased a SIM card for local use, but the rest of them had decided to just focus on the trip unless they actually had access to the internet through wi-fi at the place where they were staying.

He looked at the display, seeing several notifications that had come in while he'd slept. When they'd arrived back the previous night, he'd been able to upload all the video footage he'd shot on the three-day trip. Dalton would work his magic and then send the video back to Gabe.

When Dalton had first offered to help Gabe do videos for his channel, Gabe had taken him up on it because honestly, video editing was not something he enjoyed. But it hadn't taken long for him to realize that Dalton was actually a whiz at it. As the quality of the videos on Gabe's channel improved, so did the number of people who subscribed. All people who wanted to live vicariously through him. People who would probably start to complain if his videos lost their edgy content.

Gabe scrolled through his notifications from social media, keeping a look out for a message from Maya. He felt disappointment thread through him when he found nothing from her. After a quick calculation of the time difference, Gabe knew it was nine o'clock on Sunday night in Winnipeg.

He pushed into a sitting position and stared at the message screen on his phone, trying to formulate a message to Maya. But before he could start, Matt poked his head in the door.

"Well, it looks like Sleeping Beauty is up," the man said with a grin.

Gabe had groups of friends spread all throughout the various areas of his life, but generally speaking, there was one person in each group that he was naturally closest to. In the family, that was Mitch. At the gym, it was Hunter. In his work, it was Tennyson. And on the adventure team, it was Matt.

"Even sleep couldn't improve on what nature bestowed on me." Gabe pushed back the sheet and swung his feet over the edge of the bed. He rubbed a hand over the beard that had grown thicker while they'd been out on the kayaking expedition. Shaving wasn't high on his priority list while on trips like this, but nor did he want to look like a caveman by the end of the trip. He would have to shave before they headed out on the liveaboard.

"So did your princess have a message waiting for you?" Matt asked as he dropped down on the single bed across from Gabe's, the one he'd slept in the night before.

"No," Gabe hated to admit. "Part of that could be my fault. I kind of forgot to let her know that I wouldn't have cell or internet access while away."

"Not used to having to be accountable to someone, eh?" Matt said as he scooted back across the mattress to press his back against the wall, bending his knees to rest his arms on them. "You gonna be leaving us?"

Gabe took up a position mirroring his friend's, his cell phone on the bed beside him. He let his gaze drift to the window looking out over the city. "I don't know. How do you do it with Em?"

Matt shrugged, his gaze dropping at the mention of his girlfriend's name. "I'm not sure I *am* doing it with her."

That wasn't what Gabe had wanted to hear. "Not going well between the two of you?"

With a long sigh, Matt dropped his head back against the wall. "She doesn't like me heading off on these trips. In fact, she's kind of issued an ultimatum. Her or the trips."

"I thought she was okay with them." Gabe frowned. "Isn't that what she told you?"

"Yeah. When we first started to date, she said that she was fine with the travel. She said she'd just look at it like I was going on business trips."

"Well, that is kind of what it is," Gabe pointed out. "I mean, you have even more sponsors than I do for your travel blog."

"True, but Em isn't interested in me traveling so much anymore, especially doing what I do."

"What do you think changed her mind?"

Matt grimaced as he lowered his head to look at Gabe. "Her best friends. One got married and the other—who was already married— just had her first baby. I think Em is now wanting that for herself, and she doesn't see my lifestyle as being a good fit for either of those things." He sighed. "Honestly though, tension in our relationship was already cropping up before the wedding and the baby. She was getting tired of attending events by herself, said she felt like a fifth wheel without a date of her own."

"What are you going to do?"

"Apparently we're taking a *break* while I'm on this trip."

Gabe's shoulders slumped. "Why didn't you say something?"

"I don't know. Maybe saying it makes it real." Matt cleared his throat. "I kind of get the feeling that she might have someone ready to take my place. That this break is just a stepping stone to ending things."

Gabe had a sick feeling in his stomach. He'd wondered if his life-style could continue even after getting into a relationship, and this seemed to be his answer. If he'd thought he could continue on with things the way they were while trying to build a relationship with Maya, he was quickly realizing that was not going to happen.

Matt suddenly pushed himself to the edge of the bed and got to his feet. "Let's go get something to eat. The woman Nancy arranged to cook for us has been working magic in the kitchen for the past hour."

Gabe got off his bed, tugging up the shorts he'd worn to sleep in before pulling on a T-shirt. He followed Matt out of the room and immediately inhaled the rich aromas of their breakfast. They found most of the rest of their team in the kitchen when they got there. After saying a prayer for the food—not all the group were Christian, but they didn't object when he, Matt or Sue said grace before eating—they began to fill their plates from the large platters of food on the counter.

Once seated at the table, Gabe found himself distracted by the conversation he'd had with Matt. When Jill sat down beside him, he gave her a quick smile before focusing on the food on his plate. He wasn't really in the mood for conversation with her. She'd seemed to be next to him every time he turned around this trip which wasn't working for him because he'd had a lot on his mind and didn't want to have to make conversation with her.

Though Jill kept trying to start a conversation, Gabe gave short replies and eventually, she turned her attention to Sue. He finished his breakfast—which had been as tasty as Matt had promised—and headed back to his room to get ready for the day. It had felt good to sleep in, but now it was time to get the day underway.

Though the kayak trip, which had included sleeping on the beach, had been fun, he hadn't gotten great amounts of sleep. That wasn't unusual on trips like these which was why they always made sure to build some rest and recoup days into their schedule. If the trip had been short, they would have been on the go every day, but since they had a whole month, they'd added down days between the more active stretches.

After a shower, Gabe got dressed in a pair of knee length shorts and a tank top since it was going to be hot when they left the house. He knew that there was a plan to hit up some of the markets, and he hoped to find some stuff for his family—and Maya. The more he thought about Matt's story, the less weight he gave it in relation to his own situation with Maya.

Until he had a chance to talk to her, trying to analyze what the future might hold for them was a bit ridiculous. It was entirely possible that she just wanted to be friends. Sure, he hoped that she wanted to be more, but he also hoped that she might be more accepting of his lifestyle than Em was of Matt's. Maybe she'd agree to him taking just one or two shorter trips a year, returning to Winnipeg in between instead of the constant travel he was currently doing, spending his sparse down time in Colorado or Whistler.

In the meantime, he'd continue to pray for her and for wisdom, all while texting her when he could, hoping that when he got back to Winnipeg, they could have a good conversation before his next trip.

MAYA LOOKED UP from her phone as her mom sat down across from her. She lifted her eyebrows, unused to seeing her mom in the kitchen. "What's up?"

"I was wondering if you wanted to go to New York City for Valentine's Day."

"Valentine's Day? That's not a real holiday, Mama. I think it even falls in the middle of the week, and I don't get the day off from work."

"Okay. I just thought you might like a trip somewhere." Her mom frowned. "You seem a little…down."

"I'm okay," Maya said, a bit surprised her mom dropped the idea of a trip so quickly. "You know how it is when I have a check-up looming."

This time her mom's shoulders slumped. "This Tuesday."

It wasn't a question. They both had had the date marked on their calendars since the appointment had been made. It was hard not to allow it to loom over them like a huge cloud because there was no guarantee that the tests and the scan would be normal.

"I took the day off for the trip to Pembina for the MRI." Maya set her phone down on the counter and picked up her cup of tea. "And also Friday afternoon for my doctor appointment."

She'd gone in for the bloodwork already so the doctor would just give her the results of both the bloodwork and the MRI on Friday. Though she would have been able to get an MRI in Manitoba since she was booked for one far in advance, she usually went across the border simply because her dad could afford to pay for it and doing so would free up the spot for someone who couldn't afford to pay for an out-of-province MRI.

"Everything will be fine." Her mom said it as if her word was law. If only.

"Mama? Why did you stop going to church?" Maya knew the question probably came out of left field for her mom, but she'd been thinking about it a lot over the past month and even more since the pastor's sermon that morning. She'd continued to go to church each Sunday since Gabe had left, and the sermons had resonated with her. They had focused a lot on the fact that it was the beginning of the year, and he'd spoken on resolutions, making plans and how God should factor into all of it.

"It was hard to believe in a God who seemed to delight in keeping from me the thing I wanted the most. Or, He'd answer my prayer to get pregnant only to allow the pregnancy to end in miscarriage. And then when He *did* grant me a child, He allowed you to get so very sick. Not just once, but twice. I just…couldn't."

Maya understood where her mom was coming from. It was hard to understand why God would allow bad things to happen like what had happened to her. And yet...He had also allowed the treatments to be successful, and she reminded her mom of that. "So many people weren't as fortunate. Their children weren't helped by the treatments."

"Yes, that's true, but it just seems so unfair that you had to go through that." Her mom frowned as she lifted her mug that no doubt held coffee heavily laced with cream and sugar. "It hurt me so much to not be able to take all that pain and suffering from you."

"I'm okay, Mama." She reached across and rested her hand on her mom's arm. "And you were the best mom ever through all of that."

The corner of her mom's mouth lifted. "But not now?"

"Well, now you're a little overprotective," Maya said it with a smile, hopefully taking the sting out of the words. "But you're getting better."

And she had been. Her mom had stopped trying to track her every move and had even begun to ask her a bit more about the work she did at C&M. It was a good feeling, and Maya didn't feel the need to keep her distance from her mom like she had at the end of the year. Of course, not having Gabe around to spend time with had helped, but he was due home the same day as her scan, so that might change.

That was another thing that was kind of weighing her down. Watching the videos and coming to understand what Gabe did and how dangerous it could be—such as the accident he'd had on the volcano slope when he'd broken his arm and collarbone—had made it pretty clear to her that their lives would never mesh. Like with the revelation she'd had during the hockey game, while viewing the videos, Maya had seen the joy that overtook Gabe when he was engaged in the risky adventures he went on.

She would never ask him to give that all up—and even if he offered to, she could never accept that. When she saw how much joy those things gave him, why would she want him to give that up? The flip side to that was that she couldn't be with—love—someone like Gabe. She had fallen hard for him even in such a short period of time, and now she was getting ready to have her heart broken.

"Are you sure you don't want me to come for your scan?"

"Yep. You know it's a boring drive, plus we won't be getting the results then." Maya paused. "But if you want, you can come with me to the doctor's on Friday."

Her mom smiled, but it wasn't a happy smile, more like a resigned one. "I'll be there." She slid off the stool and came around to press a kiss to Maya's forehead. "Love you, sweetheart."

Maya slid an arm around her waist and gave her a squeeze. "Love you too, Mama."

She picked up her mug and glided out of the kitchen with silent steps. Maya took a sip of her tea as she stared out the large bay window next to the breakfast nook. It had been a long time since she'd last dreaded something like she was dreading the week that lay ahead.

On the one hand, Maya wanted Gabe to come home so that she knew he was safe, but on the other hand, she didn't want him to because they were going to have to talk. And it wasn't just her thinking that. Gabe had sent a text stating the same thing. So now, in addition to her appointments, she had to prepare herself mentally for the conversation with Gabe.

She finished the last of her tea then put her mug in the dishwasher. After picking up her phone, she left the kitchen and retreated to her room. She hadn't been sleeping well, so after spending some time trying to relax in a hot shower, Maya crawled into bed, determined to get some sleep, so she wouldn't drag into work the next morning.

Just one more day to get through before the scan and Gabe arrived home.

GABE LOOKED AT MAKAYLA in surprise. "Maya's not in today?"

"No. She's taking a couple of days off this week. Said she had some appointments that she needed to go to." Makayla leaned back in her chair, swinging it from side to side. "She actually booked the time off not long after she started working here."

It wasn't any of his business, but Gabe couldn't help but wonder what the appointments were for. She hadn't mentioned anything about them during their texting sessions. Mind you, their text messages recently hadn't been very in depth...particularly after he'd told her that he wanted to talk with her when he got back. His biggest regret about the trip was not having taken the time to share with her about what was in his heart *before* he left.

"Did you come straight here?" Makayla asked, her gaze traveling up and down his body, no doubt taking in his wrinkled clothes and the scruff that was thicker than normal on his face.

"Yeah. I thought I'd stop by and see if Maya wanted to grab some lunch."

Makayla frowned. "Are you still trying to get something going with her?"

"I had hoped to talk to her about things." Gabe sighed, letting his breath puff out his cheeks. "I've missed her." He paused, his brows drawing together. "Do you think she missed me?"

Makayla caught her lower lip between her teeth for a moment then said, "To be honest, I'm not sure. She hasn't talked much about you."

Well, that wasn't exactly what he wanted to hear. He'd hoped that she'd take advantage of his siblings to learn more about him. That she hadn't done that, made him rethink how he should approach her.

"To be fair though," Makayla began, "she really doesn't talk about personal stuff at work. Not about herself. Not about you. She's very focused on her job, and rarely mentions anything that's not work related."

Gabe tried to take some comfort in Makayla's words, but he just couldn't. "You haven't seen her outside of work?"

"Yes. I've seen her at church a few times, but whenever I've invited her to dinner at the house, she's declined." Makayla gave a small smile. "She's a private one, that girl. I've wondered if she's hiding something, but it can't be anything too serious."

At Makayla's words, Gabe recalled how he'd gotten the same sense from her, reinforced by how she seemed to always change the subject without giving much information about herself. Perhaps he needed to ask more direct questions. Although he wasn't sure that he had that right.

He pulled his phone out and brought up his text messages.

Dropped by the office after the plane touched down. Missed seeing you!

Though he hoped for a quick response, Gabe didn't think he would get one since she had taken the day off for appointments. He slid his phone back into his pocket and got to his feet. "Guess I'll head to Mom and Dad's. Might try for a bit of a nap too. Jet lag is going to be a killer."

"Better you than me," Makayla said without an ounce of sympathy.

"Love you too," Gabe said over his shoulder as he left her office.

He wandered down the hallway to where Bennett's office was. His brother was focused on his monitor as he typed rapidly. Without announcing himself, Gabe wandered in and dropped down into the chair next to Bennett's desk.

Bennett glanced over, his gaze widening. Abandoning whatever he'd been working on, Bennett swung his chair around to face Gabe. "Hey! I didn't know you were back already."

Gabe looked his brother over, noticing that the strain on his face from the last time he'd seen him was gone. His smile, which hadn't reached his eyes before, was now filled with joy. "Yep, I'm back. For a few days, anyway."

Bennett's brow furrowed at that. "Just a few days?"

"Yeah. I'm heading to Colorado, and then I'm off with Matt and Damon to do some snowboarding for a sponsored video."

Bennett leaned back in his chair. "Something tells me it's not just regular snowboarding."

Gabe hesitated before nodding. "Yeah. We're being taken somewhere in a helicopter and dropped off on a mountain top."

"Really, Gabe?" Bennett said with a shake of his head. "Why?"

"I have a contract with a company for this."

"When are you going to stop with the adventure stuff? It's not like you need the money."

"I'm thinking of scaling back." For the first time, Gabe voiced the words that had been rolling around in his head for the past month.

Bennett nodded. "I think that's a good idea."

Of course, he did. Bennett—and the rest of his siblings—had never really understood Gabe's need for the adrenalin rush. So while he was willing to consider cutting back, he didn't think he could go forever without that rush. Which was something he really hoped that Maya would be okay with.

"I hear things have turned around for you," Gabe said, trying to move the focus of their conversation off him.

Bennett's face brightened. "So much! I couldn't believe it when Grace showed up with Olivia Joy and let me know that she wanted me to be a part of their lives."

"That is so cool. I'm happy that you guys were able to work things out." And he hoped that he, too, would have a similar result with Maya. "I can't wait to see Grace and the baby. The pictures on Facebook are great, but seeing them in person would be much better."

"I'm sure we're going to be out at Mom's at some point while you're here." Bennett paused. "How are things going between you and Maya?"

And wasn't that just the million-dollar question. "Well, we've been texting a bit while I was in Thailand, but we didn't really have any good conversations. I'm hoping we can talk while I'm here." Gabe paused. "I have been praying about everything with her."

Bennett had a serious expression on his face as he looked at him. "That's good. I hope you're able to work things out."

"Me, too. I feel things for Maya that I've never felt for anyone before." Gabe huffed out a breath. "I just want to see where the relationship might go."

"Just remember that sometimes love requires sacrifice. If you're not willing to do that, you need to step back from her now."

"I know. I just want to make sure that she knows how I feel and see if she feels the same way."

Bennett's cell rang, and he hesitated a moment, his gaze going from Gabe to the phone.

"Go ahead and get it," Gabe said as he got to his feet. "We'll chat later."

Bennett nodded as he picked up his phone.

Deciding he didn't really want another round of questioning by a sibling, Gabe headed out to his truck. Mitch had agreed to pick him up from the airport with his truck, so he was able to go home without having to arrange a ride. Thankfully, when he'd arrived at the airport, Mitch had known better than to pursue too much conversation since Gabe had just spent the past thirty-three plus hours en route from Bangkok through Taipei and Toronto where he'd had a ten-hour layover before flying into Winnipeg just before ten in the morning.

Though he'd gotten a few hours rest here and there, Gabe really was exhausted, and if he wasn't going to be able to see Maya, he was going to get some sleep. Hopefully, they'd make contact later in the day. It was that thought that got him through the drive home, a quick chat with his mom and a shower before crawling between crisp, clean, wonderfully scented sheets to fall asleep.

Chapter Sixteen

*W*HEN GABE WOKE, he lay there for a moment, trying to figure out where he was. The room was dark and cool, and
the bed was familiarly comfortable. *Home*. He turned onto
his stomach and reached out for where he hoped his phone would be.
Thankfully, his hand landed on it, and he wrapped his fingers around it.

With a groan, as his stiff muscles protested the movement, Gabe
rolled onto his back and lifted the phone to look at the screen. He
blinked a couple of times to bring the screen into focus then smiled
when he saw that he had received several text messages. He also saw
the time and realized he'd been asleep for a solid twelve hours, which
meant it was almost midnight. A bit late to call Maya, particularly since
her text had a time stamp from around ten o'clock.

Gabe slid out of bed, went to the bathroom then headed downstairs
to the kitchen, hoping his mom had put aside some food for him. The
house was quiet and dark, the only light coming from the bulb above
the stove.

With an easy familiarity, Gabe flicked on the overhead light and
went to the fridge. He smiled when he spotted the large plate covered
with plastic wrap sitting on one of the shelves. After removing the garlic
bread and the small bowl of salad, Gabe stuck the plate with the lasagna
on it into the microwave. Once it was heated, he settled down in the
breakfast nook and after a quick prayer of thanks, took a bite of his
mom's delicious food. While he'd loved the food in Thailand, his taste
buds were thrilled at that first bite of one of his favorite dishes.

As he ate, Gabe began to read through his messages.

Jill: *Hope you made it home safe and sound. Guess I'll see you in
Colorado in a couple of weeks. Can't wait!*

Matt: *Guess the break was a permanent thing in Em's eyes. She's
moved on already. No need for me to turn down any more contracts.
Gotta look on the bright side.*

Damon: *Give me a call when you get this. Or maybe text me first
to see if I'm awake. Jet lag is killing me this time.*

Maya: *Welcome home! Glad you're home safe and sound. Hope to
see you soon.*

Gabe stared at the message. It gave him some hope that she wanted to see him soon. He was disappointed, though, that he couldn't call her right away given the late hour. So he settled for texting Damon to see if he was awake, and when his phone rang right away, he contented himself with chatting with his friend instead of with Maya.

Once that call was over, Gabe put his dishes in the dishwasher then stood for a moment trying to decide what to do. He was wide awake, but everyone else was sound asleep. It was possible that Matt and Jill were awake as well, but he really had no interest in talking with either of them.

He wasn't sure he wanted to talk to Matt because he didn't want to think about the difficulty of having a relationship while balancing the lifestyle he wanted to lead. And Jill... He wasn't sure how to deal with her. The Thailand trip had been different with Jill than previous trips. She'd seemed to be around him all the time. And she'd started hinting that she wanted something more with him, which was especially annoying because he'd talked about Maya and how he felt about her. Had she really thought he was just joking around about Maya?

The awkwardness had lingered throughout the trip, and even some of the others had noticed it, which had added to the awkwardness, so he'd definitely not be calling Jill. And if she didn't let this go, he'd have to talk to her directly about it, which wouldn't be comfortable for either of them.

Gabe shut off the kitchen lights and went back to his room. With nothing else to do, he pulled up the page for his YouTube channel and began to read comments on the videos Dalton had edited and uploaded for him. There were the usual negative, trolling comments, but most were positive. Some asked questions about different aspects of the trip, wanting more information on places they'd visited. A few asked if he and some of the others in the videos had significant others. Gabe always laughed at those comments but never responded to them.

After checking the video comments, he moved on to taking care of some of the financial stuff needing his attention. Sent some emails to Tennyson and Hunter. Checked his online accounting program to see how the businesses were doing. His accountant took care of the financial side of his businesses, once again freeing him up to travel and be away from work, but he always liked to check through things after an extended period of time away.

Finally, he settled back down in the bed, thinking if he could sleep a couple of hours, he could then make it through until the next night. He needed to get his days and nights straightened out as quickly as possible.

Before he shut off the lamp beside the bed, he looked at his phone for a bit then tapped out a message to Maya.

Can't wait to see you. Can we go out to dinner tonight?

He didn't expect an immediate response, so he put the phone back on the nightstand and then stretched out beneath the blanket to try to get a bit more sleep.

MAYA WISHED SHE COULD have taken the whole week off work. The days between having blood work done, the scan completed and the doctor's appointment to hear the results stretched on interminably. Before—when she hadn't had a job—she'd spent those 'waiting' days playing online games, pretending to be someone else. Someone who wasn't waiting to see if their bloodwork was clear. Someone whose scan hadn't picked up something that shouldn't be there.

But she had to be Maya and go to work and pretend that nothing was wrong. The *what-ifs* were on an endless loop in her head. *What if this is the appointment when the doctor tells me the cancer is back? What if the battle I thought I'd won isn't over? What if I have to fight this battle all over again? What if I can't do it?*

The door leading into the building opened, and Maya looked up to see Gabe walk through the door. There was no mistaking him for Mitch this time around. Her heart leaped at the sight of him. His tan had deepened even further, and his face bore a bit more scruff than when he'd left. But his smile was the same. Bright and engaging as he quickly came around the desk to where she sat.

She got to her feet and found herself engulfed in a chilly but welcome embrace. Gabe's jacket bore the crispness of a cold February day, but along with that was the scent that she recognized as his. Maya sighed, letting herself sag against him in relief that he was really okay and home once more.

"It's so good to see you again," Gabe said, his voice close to her ear, his arms tight around her.

Tears pricked at the back of her eyes, as she held him close, knowing that she wouldn't have the right to be that close to him much longer. Her heart hurt at that realization, and made her hold him even more tightly. "It's good to see you again too."

When he moved back a bit to look down at her, Maya was finally forced to loosen her embrace. He cupped her face in his hand. "I've missed you."

"I've missed you too," Maya said, feeling a bit like a parrot as she kept repeating what he was saying to her.

His blue eyes were intent on her, filled with emotion she'd longed to see, but at the same time, feeling the hurt at finally witnessing it, knowing where things were going to end up. It would make what she had to do that much harder.

"You still on for dinner tonight?" he asked, his hands sliding down to take hers.

Maya really didn't want to be in a restaurant while having the conversation she knew they needed to have, but she wasn't sure where else they could talk. They certainly couldn't meet at either of their homes.

"Uh, sure," she said, still wishing they had another option. "Where are we going?"

"I'm still trying to decide." He grinned at her. "Can I pick you up here?"

Maya nodded. "As long as you bring me back to get my car afterward."

"Of course. Though one of these days, I hope you'll let me pick you up at your home."

Maya hoped that whatever was on her face looked like a smile to Gabe because it sure didn't feel like one to her. "Maybe one day."

When the phone rang, Maya turned to answer it, telling the person on the phone that Makayla was out of the office for the day.

When she hung up, Gabe said, "Makayla's off today?"

"She sent me an email saying she wasn't feeling well and wouldn't be in. Weird though because Ethan is out today too."

"Both of them?" Gabe frowned. "Hope they weren't felled by the flu or something."

"Bennett might have more information," Maya said, also concerned about the two people who had become important to her.

"I'm going to go talk to him and see if he knows what's up. I'll talk to you again in a bit."

Maya watched him go then sank back down into her chair. She swung around to face her monitor, but she didn't see what was on the screen. Instead, all her focus was on the way her heart ached. It was an ache like she'd never felt before. Deep, intense, and reaching into every area of her heart. She pressed a hand against her chest and tried to take a deep breath, fighting against the constraints her emotions had wrapped around her.

The pain was all encompassing, but she knew it was necessary. She could accept this pain if it meant that Gabe could continue to do what he loved. She wouldn't hold him back from that.

When Gabe returned from Bennett's office, he looked a lot more serious. "I'm going to head over to Makayla's. I'll be back to pick you up for dinner, okay?"

Maya nodded. "Tell them I'm praying for them."

From the look of Gabe's expression, Maya was beginning to think it wasn't the flu that had kept Makayla and Ethan from coming in. That added another layer to the emotion she was already feeling. And it scared her. The inability to control things—especially for the people she cared about. She didn't want them to hurt. She didn't want them to be facing difficult things. But there was nothing she could do. Nothing but pray that God would give them what they needed to face their situation.

GABE GRIPPED THE WHEEL of his truck tightly as he drove to the apartment building that his dad owned. He thought of Bennett's words, of his suppositions on why both Ethan and Makayla were out for the day. Though he supposed that Makayla might not necessarily want to see him, Gabe felt the need to offer his support. Too often he'd been far away when things had happened with his family. If he had the opportunity to help this time around, he was going to take it.

During the drive there, he prayed that Bennett was wrong in his assumptions. He parked in Mitch's spot and used his code to get through the security door. Taking the steps two at a time, he moved past the second floor that held the two apartments where Bennett and Grace each lived to the third floor where Makayla and Ethan lived with Ethan's teen sister, Sierra.

He knocked on the door then stepped back and waited to see if they'd answer. Quicker than he'd imagined, the door opened to reveal Ethan. He wore a sweatshirt and faded jeans, and his usually friendly expression showed signs of strain.

"Hey, Gabe." Ethan rested a hand high on the door frame. "Welcome home."

"Thanks. I'm glad to be back."

There was a beat of silence before Ethan said, "What can I do for you?"

"I was just worried when they said both of you were away from work because you weren't feeling well." Gabe paused. "Is everything okay?"

Ethan glanced over his shoulder then back at Gabe as if contemplating his response, then he stepped back and waved for him to enter. Once

Gabe was inside, Ethan closed the door and walked to the kitchen. "Can I get you a cup of coffee?"

"If you're having one, sure, but if not, I'm good."

Ethan began to go through the motions of making coffee in the pot that sat on their counter. "Did you enjoy your trip to Thailand?"

"I did. It was nice to have it all come together after we'd been planning it for what felt like forever."

"I watched a few of your videos." Ethan went to the fridge and pulled out a container of half & half then set it on the counter. "What was your favorite part of the trip?"

Gabe knew he'd get the question a lot, so he was prepared. "I loved the kayaking trip we went on, but the diving we did was even more incredible."

"I can't even imagine going on trips like that." Ethan poured coffee into two mugs and slid one across the counter to Gabe. "Does the prospect of danger not cross your mind?"

Gabe shrugged. "Safe isn't fun."

"Seriously?" Ethan arched a brow at him. "What does that even mean?"

Between sips of coffee, Gabe told him how he'd come up with his life motto. "The adrenalin rush has always been what drives me to do things."

"What are you doing here, Gabe?" Makayla's question caused them both to turn to where she stood. Her hair was pulled back from her pale face, but there were wisps of it all around her head in uncharacteristic messiness. She wore a baggy sweatshirt that looked like it might be Ethan's and a pair of leggings.

When she shuffled closer to Ethan, he set his mug down and reached out to take her into his arms. Makayla leaned against him, and Ethan stood firm as he supported her weight. She regarded Gabe with weary eyes that had dark circles beneath them.

"I was worried about you when you both called in sick today." Gabe paused, cupping his mug in both hands. "Everything okay?"

Makayla tilted her head back as Ethan looked down, then she let out a sigh. "The whole purpose in not telling people right away was so that if the worst happened, we wouldn't have to tell everyone."

Ethan pressed a kiss to her forehead. "They're family, babe. You know they want to support you through the good and the bad."

"What happened?" Gabe asked.

The two exchanged another look then Makayla shrugged before resting her head on Ethan's chest. The man looked up and met Gabe's gaze.

"Makayla was pregnant, but she started bleeding last night, and after a trip to the hospital, they told us that she was miscarrying." Ethan swallowed hard and leaned his head down against the top of Makayla's. "We just got home a couple of hours ago."

Gabe's heart clenched at the thought of a little life lost. His niece or nephew never even had a chance at life. Abandoning his mug, Gabe circled the island counter and wrapped his arms around them both as best he could. He felt Makayla take a shuddering breath as Ethan wrapped an arm around Gabe's shoulders, holding the three of them together.

When Makayla's soft sobs reached Gabe's ears, he didn't even bother to hold back the tears that slid from his own eyes. He and Ethan both murmured words of comfort. Not *Everything will be okay.* Or *You'll be able to have another baby.* Or even *This was God's will.*

No, the words of comfort they offered were just to reassure her of their love and their support because that's all they could do for her. They couldn't take away her pain—physical or emotional. They couldn't change how things were unfolding. They couldn't give her back the baby that was being taken from her prematurely.

Gabe could see the grief on Ethan's face too, reminding him that the loss was there for his brother-in-law as well. Though it was Makayla going through the physical loss, Ethan was also losing the child he would no doubt have loved as deeply as Makayla.

"I'm so very sorry this happened to you," Gabe said when Makayla finally looked up at him, her eyes ringed with redness.

Makayla gave him a sad smile. "Thank you."

"Is there anything I can do for you guys?" Gabe asked as he lowered his arms and stepped back a bit. "Do you need anything?"

"We've got everything we need." Makayla remained in Ethan's embrace as she shook her head. "We just needed a day off."

Gabe's respect of Ethan grew even larger as he watched the man care for Makayla. And it spoke volumes about how much Makayla trusted Ethan by being so vulnerable with her emotions. It wasn't something Makayla did easily.

"I won't be sharing this information," Gabe assured them. "It's for you to share as you want."

"Thank you," Ethan said.

"You can tell Maya if you're talking with her."

Gabe nodded, acknowledging to himself how much he did want to share this with her. His own feelings of loss, even though on a much lesser scale than Ethan and Makayla's, were real and painful. He hoped that even if they didn't tell everyone in the family, that they at least would tell their mom and dad.

After a final hug for them both, he made his way down to Mitch's apartment where he decided to take a quick nap before heading back to the office to pick up Maya. Unfortunately, he had a difficult time falling asleep as his mind spun with so many thoughts. Usually, the most stressful thing after a trip was recovering from jet lag. This time around, however, so many other things were demanding his attention.

Finally, Gabe gave up any attempt to sleep and got up and left Mitch's apartment. Though it was just after five, the office parking lot was empty of all but Maya's car.

With his thoughts having been preoccupied with Makayla and Ethan's situation, Gabe hadn't given a lot of thought about where to go to eat. He kind of wished that he had a place of his own where they could go, but he knew that his dad would caution against doing something like that. It was just that he didn't feel like sitting in a restaurant to discuss things like the miscarriage and where their relationship might be going.

The snow crunched beneath his boots as he walked toward the front door of the building. It was hard to think that just three days ago, he'd been walking around in a tank top, shorts and flip flops. Though he didn't usually hate winter, right then, the cold seemed to have seeped right into his bones.

As soon as he stepped into the office, he spotted Maya sitting at the desk, her head bent over her phone. She looked up as he approached, and right away he noticed a wariness in her gaze that hadn't been there earlier. That coldness he'd felt as he walked from the truck suddenly had tendrils wrapping around his heart.

"Do you think we could just talk here?" Maya asked as she got to her feet, her phone gripped in her hand. "In the lunchroom?"

"You don't want to go out for dinner?" Gabe asked, the sick feeling that had lingered from his time with Makayla and Ethan intensifying.

She hesitated before shaking her head. "I'd rather be able to talk to you here, where it's quiet."

Since he had been thinking the same thing, Gabe could only nod and then follow her as she led the way to the small lunchroom. Once there, she turned to face him, her arms crossed tightly across her body. What had happened in the few hours he'd been away?

"What's wrong?" Gabe asked, torn between needing to know what was going on and fearing what was causing Maya to act the way she was.

Maya sank down on one of the chairs and waited until Gabe did the same before meeting his gaze. "I want you to know that I…care more about you than I have for anyone outside of my family."

"But?" Gabe prompted. He saw tears well up in her beautiful brown eyes before she looked away, blinking rapidly.

"I just don't think this can work out between us." The words were laden with a sorrow that echoed deeply within Gabe.

Chapter Seventeen

"W HY?" GABE ASKED, unable to get more than that word out beyond the tightness of his throat.

"There's something you don't know about me," Maya said as she turned her gaze back to his. "I'm a cancer survivor. Twice."

Air rushed out of Gabe's lungs at the thought of what she must have gone through, and he couldn't find the words to respond.

"My parents have been very protective of me, so it's only recently that I've been able to spread my wings. With the job here." She waved her hand to indicate the room. "With church. With things like the rock climbing. With you."

"And you don't want a relationship?" Gabe asked, struggling to understand what she was telling him. "You don't want to tie yourself to someone so soon?"

"No, it's not that at all." She sat for a moment in silence as if trying to formulate her next words. "Last year, I decided that I wanted to have new experiences. Things I'd missed out on for so long." The corners of her mouth quirked up briefly. "You gave me the opportunity to do that with things like going to your gym and spending time with your family at Christmastime."

"I don't understand." Gabe frowned. "Then what's the problem?"

Maya's mouth tightened as her brow furrowed. "In that time, I saw what it was that truly brought you joy and happiness. You enjoyed skating around that rink with me on Boxing Day, but you absolutely lit up when it came time to play the hockey game, and it seemed that you got a rush from the danger that came with skating fast, fighting for the puck and the slams into the board."

Gabe couldn't argue with her. Playing hockey like that always lit a spark in him, but skating with her had lit him up in a different—but no less enjoyable—way. When he opened his mouth to tell her that, she held up her hand to silence him.

"I realized something more as I watched your videos on YouTube— and I've watched every single one—and that is that while I spent months…years…fighting to live, what brings you the greatest joy is flirting with death. I just…" She paused and looked away from him, lifting a hand to brush away a tear that had spilled over onto her cheek. "I just can't be with someone like that. Life is something precious to me, and I can't even contemplate any type of relationship with someone who gambles with theirs on a regular basis. I just can't. No matter how much I might…care for them.

"The day I just took off? I did it to have a scan to see if there were signs of cancer growing within my body again. I also had bloodwork taken a couple weeks ago, and on Friday, I'll be going to my doctor to see if I am going to be faced with another battle or if I'm in the clear for now. I have no guarantee that I will live to a ripe old age, but I do know that my death will not come by my own hand or a desire for adventure."

Gabe stared at Maya, shaken to his very core. Looking at things from her point of view, he could see why she felt the way she did. He'd never considered things from that perspective. Chasing death? No, that wasn't what he did. On each of his adventures, he'd stared death in the face and won. He wasn't chasing death. He was challenging it.

But still, if that was what stood between them, he suddenly found himself ready to give it all up. "I won't go on any more of the dangerous adventures. Just give us a chance. Please."

More tears spilled from Maya's eyes as she shook her head. "I won't ask you to do that. I've seen with my own eyes how much you love those adventures. I won't be responsible for taking away something that clearly brings you so much joy."

Gabe felt desperation fill him. He didn't want to lose her, but how could he convince her that she would be enough for him? They hadn't known each other long, but already she meant more to him that he'd thought possible. The thought of losing her was tearing his heart apart.

"Please, Maya," Gabe said, unable to believe he was prepared to beg. He'd never thought he'd beg a woman to be in a relationship with him, but suddenly, the thought of losing Maya overrode any thought that begging was beneath him. "Give me a chance to prove that you mean more to me than any adventure possibly could."

She shook her head again. "I can't do it. I know you're an honorable man and would stand by your word. If you said you wouldn't go on any more adventures, you wouldn't, even if the longing for that excitement ate away at what you might feel for me." She looked away from him as her shoulders hunched forward and her breath caught on a sob. "I've seen how I've already robbed my mom of the joy she might have had in a child because of my health problems. I'm not going to do that to another person."

"But the cancer wasn't your fault," Gabe said, the anguish he saw on Maya's face piercing his heart. "Surely she never said that to you."

When Maya lifted her head, the shattered look on her face took Gabe's breath away. "She didn't have to. The woman she was before my first diagnosis was completely different from who she is now. She'd tried so hard to have me, and those first thirteen years after I was born, she was happy. We had a lot of fun together, doing things as mother and daughter, but after I was diagnosed with cancer the first time, everything changed. Even to this day, five years since I was declared in remission, she hasn't shown that joy she had before cancer entered our lives. It's like she's just been waiting…" She swallowed, pulling her shoulders back as she lifted her chin. "I can't watch the same thing happen to you. Please don't ask that of me."

Without waiting for him to respond, Maya pushed to her feet, and after one last look at him, she left the room. Gabe sat at the table, feeling as if he'd just been beaten up. He'd always been the easy-going one. The one who drifted through life without experiencing much emotional upheaval in his life. He had his family. He had his friendships. The previous times he'd dated, he never felt anything like what he felt for Maya, and now she was walking out of his life.

Except that she wasn't. Any time he visited his family, he would be faced with her presence in the company. Constantly reminded of what he'd lost because she had seen something that he hadn't even realized he put out there through the lifestyle he had chosen.

He wanted to prove to her that she was wrong, but how could he do that when he still had commitments to carry out? As he sat there alone in the silence of the office, the thought of those commitments didn't bring forth any of the excitement he'd felt when he'd signed the contracts for them. Back then, he'd been thrilled at the prospect of working with the various companies, doing what he loved. Now, the thought of it left him feeling hollow inside.

Getting to his feet, Gabe made his way to the front of the office then paused when he realized he needed to lock up but had no idea how to do that. He called Bennett to ask him what to do and ended up with an invitation to spend the evening with his older brother. And just like he'd offered comfort to Makayla earlier, Gabe went, hoping Bennett would help him be able to make sense of everything.

MAYA GRIPPED THE WHEEL of her car tightly, determined to make it home before falling apart. It was taking everything within her to hold back the tears that were determined to spill over, much like the hurt that was building within her heart. She hadn't thought she could do it, but all day she'd known what she had to do, and somehow, she'd found the strength to follow through on that knowledge.

But she'd never forget the look on Gabe's face when she'd told him she couldn't be with him. Maya had known that he would offer to stop the adventure trips, but all she could picture was the day his zest for life would fade in much the way her mother's had. Or if she encouraged him to continue, the day would come when someone would knock on her door to let her know that one of those adventures he loved so much had killed him. Either way, she would lose him. Even just imagining that caused the pain to balloon within her.

Doing it this way meant that—if the worst happened—at least she would have moved past this depth of feeling for him. She would grieve his passing as a friend, but not have her heart ripped out by his death. Hopefully. But at the end of the day, he wouldn't have lost his zest for life, and he would have died doing something he loved.

When she reached the turn-off for the long winding driveway that led to the mansion, Maya felt a mixture of tension and relief. She wanted to get home, to the sanctuary of her room where she could finally fall apart. But there was still the possibility of running into her mom and having to explain her distraught state.

As she approached the security gate that was located halfway down the driveway, Maya pressed the remote on the visor to open it. She knew that would alert anyone paying attention that she was on her way home. All she could do was hope that her parents were out for the evening. She certainly didn't feel like sitting through a family dinner with the two of them. Her appetite was pretty much gone, lost in the emotional maelstrom present in her body.

Maya noticed right away that the Mercedes wasn't in its usual spot as she pulled into the garage. After quickly gathering up her purse and phone, she left the car and headed for the door leading into the house. Moving as quietly as possible, Maya stopped only long enough to tug off her boots in the mudroom through which she had to pass to get to the main part of the house.

There was no aroma of cooking food which she assumed meant that her parents had given Elisse the night off which was just fine with Maya. She made it up the stairs to her room without seeing anyone, and with a huge sense of relief, she closed the door behind her and locked it before allowing her emotions to have free rein.

Leaning back against the door, her legs finally gave out, and she slid down to sit on the floor, pain swamping her. Maya pulled her legs in, wrapping her shaking arms around them, squeezing herself into a tight ball as if to contain the hurt that she had inflicted upon herself. Though she'd known that moment with Gabe was coming, until she'd said the words, it hadn't been real. The pain she'd felt at knowing what was to come was nothing compared to the hurt she felt now that it was over.

Tears flowed, and silent sobs wracked her body as she mourned the loss of a love that was impossible for her to have. Why couldn't it have been Mitch that she'd fallen for? Someone dependable and present. Someone who had no desire to go out and tempt death at every turn. Instead, her heart had chosen a man who exuded life and excitement.

The memory of his arms around her, the press of his lips against hers, just about did her in. They'd only had such a short time together, and yet there were so many memories that assailed her on an endless loop. As each memory lit up her mind, another shaft of pain would pierce her heart.

She wanted him. Her heart cried for him. In that moment, awash in pain and hurt, Maya didn't think she could ever love another man the way she loved Gabe Callaghan.

Chapter Eighteen

June

"OKAY, WHO'S COMING WITH ME?" Matt hefted his keys into the air and then caught them again. "We need more snacks since Damon decided to eat more than his fair share already."

Gabe pushed himself up off the couch with a groan. "I'll go with you."

It wasn't that he wanted to go, but he would rather be with his friend than stay at the apartment where the rest of their group had gathered to celebrate Alex's birthday. The apartment in Denver was where he had come to stay when Winnipeg had just been too painful for him. It was just one place he'd called home over the years. Matt and Damon had been the ones who had rented it initially, but they had let Gabe pay them for the third bedroom in the apartment, so he'd have a place to stay when he needed it.

And boy, had he ever needed it over the past few months. Thankfully, his family had understood his need to escape when he'd left a couple days after his conversation with Maya even though he'd planned to stay a week. In the months since that day, he'd kept in contact with his family through Skype or FaceTime sessions like he had in the past, but they'd all been careful to not mention Maya or what was going on with her beyond letting him know that she still worked at C&M.

Her Facebook page had remained dead, with her not posting any sort of status updates or pictures. Though it would probably have been painful, he would have loved to have had a glimpse into her life. To see that she was doing okay.

The last communication they'd had was the text he'd received in response to the one he'd sent asking how her doctor's appointment had gone.

All clear for now. Thank you for caring.

Of course, he'd cared. He loved her. It would have killed him to hear that her cancer had returned. He'd wanted to try to convince her to give him a chance to prove how much he loved her, but he'd known that as long as he had his commitments hanging over his head, he couldn't ask that of her.

Maybe once he *showed* her that he was going to give it all up instead of just *telling* her that he planned to, she might give him another chance. He was willing to wait as long as it took for her to see that he was going to make Winnipeg his home. Permanently.

"Doritos, man," Damon called out. "Get lots of Doritos."

"M&Ms for me," Jill said from her spot on the couch.

She'd finally given up trying to get Gabe to realize that there should be something between them. Now she just gave him pitying looks, not at all sympathetic about the heartache he was dealing with. Thankfully, Matt was much more willing to listen to him and support him as he struggled to accept what had happened back in February.

Instead of celebrating their first Valentine's Day together, Gabe had gone off the grid for a week around the time of the dreaded holiday. Then he'd returned to carry out the trips and adventures that he'd been committed to.

"I think I can figure out what everyone wants more of," Matt said. "It's not as if we haven't had these get-togethers before. Be back in a bit."

Gabe slid his feet into the flip-flops he'd left by the door earlier and followed his friend out into the hallway of their three-story apartment building. They took the stairs instead of the elevator then headed out into the warmth of the evening as the sun was finally setting. The buildings around them cast long shadows as they walked toward Matt's car across the large parking lot.

They'd just about reached the car when Gabe heard the roar of an engine. He turned in time to see large headlights bearing down on them, their brightness blocking out his view of the vehicle they belonged to. But instead of slowing down, the lights swerved a few times then came straight for them.

Gabe heard Matt shouting something, but it was too late as the engine revved, and the vehicle reached Gabe. He'd tried to get out of the way, but it was as if the vehicle was focused on him. Matt's arms wrapped around him and together they tumbled away from the direction of the vehicle, but it wasn't far enough because it swerved one more time and hit them.

Pain exploded in Gabe's lower body as he felt the impact against him. He could hear Matt groaning in pain next to him, but he couldn't move to check on his friend. Gabe held as still as he could, hoping the pain would abate, but instead it seemed to be increasing, a tsunami of pain that slowly drowned out everything around him.

As he lay there, praying that God would spare his life, Gabe had a moment of clarity of what it truly meant to stare death in the face, and he was doing it right then. And he had no idea if he was going to win this battle like Maya had won her battles to live. As he fought to remain conscious, Gabe realized that this might well be a battle he lost. All the times he'd flirted with death—just like Maya had said—now meant nothing as he lay there in more pain than he'd ever felt before, wondering if his life was going to just fade away.

Blackness began to creep in as he felt hands touching him, and voices asking him questions that he couldn't understand. All he could do was whisper what he hoped weren't his last words.

"Tell my family I love them. Tell Maya I love her. Please. Tell them."

"Stay with me." A woman's voice managed to break through the pain, accompanied by a brush against his cheek. "What's your name? Can you tell me?"

"Gabe. Will you tell them?"

"Hang in there, Gabe. We're going to get you help," the woman said again, just before he felt jarring movement.

"Tell them I love them. Tell Maya I love her. Please." He was frantic to have someone promise to convey his messages. "Please. I need you to tell them how much I love them."

"I'll tell them, Gabe, but I need you to focus on staying with me so you can tell them yourself."

"Thank you," Gabe whispered, finally giving in to the blackness that was pulling him under. As long as his family and Maya received his messages of love, he could let go. The love he felt for them was like a warm blanket, a comfort in the midst of the pain that eclipsed everything else, even his desire to fight.

MAYA WAS SURPRISED to see only one car in the parking lot when she got to work. Usually, Bennett, Makayla, and Ethan all beat her in, but today, she only saw Bennett's truck there. Makayla hadn't mentioned anything about taking the day off, so the fact that she wasn't there gave Maya an uneasy feeling in her stomach.

She left the car and walked into the quiet of the office, hoping that she was just overreacting to things. After she had put her stuff away, Maya sat down at her desk as she had every work day since she'd started. The last few months had been difficult. She hadn't counted on how hard it would be to get over her heartache for Gabe when she saw his carbon copy almost every day. Though she could tell at a glance that it wasn't Gabe, there was still that moment when she'd see Mitch and hope…

For what?

She was the one who'd ended things without any hope of a future for them. She hadn't been willing to accept his offer to stop going on his dangerous adventures because she'd been so sure that he'd come to resent her eventually. The thought of being the reason someone else lost their joy in life was more than she could handle.

In the months since she'd ended things, there hadn't been a day when she hadn't shed a few tears for the loss of what she could have had with Gabe. Her mom asked her on an almost daily basis what was wrong. Maya couldn't bring herself to share her heartache, so she just brushed it aside, but she had a feeling that her mom wasn't fooled. She just hadn't figured out yet what was going on with Maya.

Because she apparently wasn't sad enough, Maya had continued to torture herself by watching any video Gabe put on his YouTube channel. When he'd look into the camera and talk, it was like he was talking right to her. She couldn't help but be captivated by his words and his appearance.

She'd also regularly checked Facebook to see what he was posting. At first, it had seemed like he was doing just fine, but then she'd begun to see that he wasn't as dynamic in his videos as she'd remembered him being. He still took selfies in various places, but his eyes didn't sparkle with excitement, and his smile wasn't as wide or engaging as it had once been.

He'd get over it—she was sure of that—it just might take a little more time. She wasn't so sure that was how it was going to work for her. In fact, each day it seemed to get harder and harder. Her love for him wasn't fading the way she'd hoped. The memories weren't dimming. The feeling of his arms around her was still as vivid as it had been the day he'd hugged her for the first time. And she didn't think she'd ever be able to forget their first kiss. *Her* first kiss.

"Maya." Bennett's voice held a weariness that was only reinforced when she got her first glimpse of him. He looked like he hadn't slept all night, and there was strain around his eyes.

"Is something wrong?" she asked him. "No one else is here."

"Yes. Unfortunately, we got some bad news last night."

"Did something happen with Makayla's pregnancy?" Maya felt sick at the thought. It wasn't until later that she'd discovered that on the same day she'd ended things with Gabe, Makayla had been in the midst of miscarrying. She'd only just announced earlier that week that she was pregnant again. It would be horrible if she lost a second baby.

Bennett shook his head. "It's not Makayla." He cleared his throat, glancing away from her, and suddenly, Maya knew. She *knew*.

"No. Not Gabe," she said, her voice barely above a whisper. The pain that seemed to always be present in her heart suddenly exploded to fill every part of her body. "No."

Bennett let out a long breath and sank down on the second chair at the reception desk. "We got word last night that Gabe had been in an accident."

"Is he...?" Maya couldn't say the word, couldn't bring herself to even think it.

"He's been in surgery for several hours. It's been touch and go."

Tremors began in Maya's stomach and spread to her extremities, making her clasp her hands together tightly to keep them from shaking. "What...what happened? His Twitter said he was in Denver for a bit. He wasn't supposed to be out doing anything dangerous."

"He wasn't." Bennett ran a hand down his face. "From what we've been told, Gabe and his roommate Matt had just left their apartment building to run to the store for some food when a truck went out of control in their parking lot and hit them both."

"What?" Maya stared at Bennett, sure that she'd misunderstood. "He was hit by a truck? In his parking lot?"

Though Bennett's eyes remained pain-filled, a corner of his mouth lifted in a half smile. "I know, right? We all had anticipated that if he ever got hurt, it would be falling off a cliff or jumping out of an airplane, so this was something of a surprise, over and above the fact that he was hurt at all."

Maya swallowed hard, her stomach churning and making her nauseous. Regret joined the fear and pain that were already resident within her as she realized that she'd been so worried about the dangerous stuff that she'd missed out on the fact that danger actually lurked around every corner. Putting life on hold because of fear of that danger would be ridiculous, and yet, that's what she'd done. She'd focused on the danger of his life choices instead of just enjoying the time they could have together.

"Is he going to be okay?"

Bennett shrugged. "He has fractures in his legs and pelvis, and they had to remove his spleen. He had internal bleeding which was what concerned them the most, but last we heard, they had gotten that under control. Mom and Dad managed to get a flight out early this morning. I'm heading back to the house now, then Mitch and I will be trying to get a flight out tonight, if possible." He sighed as his brow furrowed.

"We're going to close the office for the day. Can you change the answering machine to state that we've had a family emergency and for callers to leave a message or send an email? Hopefully, some of us can be back in the office tomorrow if Gabe is stabilized. We're going to try and get him back to Winnipeg as soon as it's medically safe to move him."

More than anything, Maya wanted to fly to Gabe's bedside and stay there until he opened his eyes so she could tell him how much she loved him. But she no longer had that right. Because of that, all Maya wanted to do was go home and crawl into bed, so that she could be alone in her pain. But she had a job to do, and if doing it would be a support for the family, then she would stay and do it.

"I'll stay for a bit, and I'll be in tomorrow."

"Thank you," Bennett said. "I'm going to go make a few phone calls, and then I'll head out to the house."

Maya watched as he got to his feet and walked to the hallway that led to his office. His movements looked slow and heavy. Once she was alone, she took a deep breath, willing her tears to stay away because she had things to do. She had the ability to help, and she needed to get the ball rolling.

With trembling hands, she pulled her phone out and tapped the screen to call her father.

"Maya?" Her dad's image filled the screen of her phone. "What's wrong, sweetheart?"

"I need your help," Maya said, trying her best to not start crying. "A...friend of mine has been hurt. I need your help to help his family."

Maya anticipated a flood of questions, but her dad surprised her.

"I will expect more details from you later, but for now, tell me what you need."

"Is the jet available to fly some people to Denver? And do you have someone who can arrange medical transport from Denver back to Winnipeg?"

"Yes. I'll have Brad contact the pilot to get the jet ready to go, and he can go with the plane to deal with things on that end for the medical transport. Do you need a doctor to consult?"

"I don't know. He's been in surgery for several hours."

"Okay. I'll let Brad analyze the situation when he gets there." He moved out of frame for a moment, and Maya could hear him talking to someone in his office.

She felt an immediate sense of relief knowing she was doing something to help, and hopefully soon Gabe would be back home with his family.

"The jet will be ready to go within the hour. It will be leaving from St. Andrews Airport," her dad said as he came back into the frame of the screen.

Maya's shoulders slumped. "Thank you, Daddy."

"Anything for you, baby girl, but you owe me the story behind this."

"I'll tell you everything. I promise."

"Good. I will hold you to that. Keep me updated, okay? I mean, Brad will, but I want to hear from you as well."

"I will. I'm going to go tell Bennett about the plane now."

"Talk with you later."

The screen went dark, and Maya sat there for a moment, bracing herself as she prepared to reveal one of her secrets. She got to her feet and headed to Bennett's office. As she stepped into the doorway, she could see him sitting with his elbows braced on his desk and his head in his hands. She stood there for a moment, hating to bother him.

Finally, she said his name softly, and he looked up at her. "Did you get more news?"

"He's out of surgery, and they seem optimistic, but he still has a long road ahead of him."

"Were you able to get tickets to Denver?"

"I was, but there was nothing available until tomorrow morning."

"I can help you get there sooner," Maya said, clenching her hands together.

Bennett's brow furrowed. "What do you mean?"

"My dad has a private jet, and he's made it available for you to use to fly to Denver."

"Are you serious?" Bennett asked. "Your dad has a private jet?"

Maya nodded. "He is also sending his personal assistant along with you to do what needs to be done to make things easier for you all. That means he can set up hotel rooms, car rentals and when needed, Brad will line up the medical transport to bring Gabe home."

Bennett's eyes widened more with each revelation of what she was offering. "Who *is* your dad? And why would he do this for us?"

"My dad is Maximilian Zevardi, and he's doing this for me. I'm doing this for you all."

"We can't accept this. It's too much."

"Please don't turn this down, Bennett," Maya begged. "What's the use of having money if we can't use it to help others?"

"I just...I'm having a hard time understanding all of this." Bennett got to his feet and began to gather up his things. "But honestly, I can't afford to turn you down. We need to get to Gabe."

"The plane will be ready to go in an hour from St. Andrews Airport. Brad Davis will meet you there and travel with you to Denver. If you need anything, just tell him, and he'll arrange it for you."

Bennett paused as he was slipping his phone into his pocket. "I can't believe this, really. Thank you."

"You're welcome. I'm glad that I can help you out a bit."

Bennett came to her side and slid an arm around her shoulder. "This is more than a bit, Maya. It means the world to us."

"Please tell Gabe that…I'm praying for him."

"I'll tell him. Hopefully, we'll have him home soon."

Together they walked to the front of the office. Bennett pulled on his coat then turned to Maya.

"You don't need to stay the whole day. Just put a sign on the door that we're closed today and will be open again tomorrow. I've sent you an email of people to call to postpone my appointments over the next few days, please. Makayla and Ethan will be calling their own appointments to rearrange as necessary."

"I'll take care of it." Maya paused. "Please keep me updated, if you can."

"I will. Thank you again." Bennett gave her another quick hug before leaving the building.

Once alone, Maya locked up and went to her computer to print out a sign to hang on the front door. After she'd done that, she made herself some tea and then opened the email from Bennett and began to make the calls, pushing all his appointments to the next week. She needed to keep herself busy because otherwise, it was too easy for her mind to wander and to begin to imagine the worst.

After the last appointment was rescheduled, Maya made another cup of tea and then took a few minutes to check social media to see if any of Gabe's friends were posting things. On his page, she read through postings by Jill and other members of his team. It was there she read about Matt's injuries, which had turned out to be less serious than Gabe's, but he was still facing surgeries of his own.

As she read through the comments, Maya came to realize that Gabe had a lot of supporters and people who followed his adventures on a regular basis. They were coming out in droves to post their support for him, and Maya knew that it would mean a lot to Gabe. She blinked back tears as she read posts from people who were sharing what Gabe's videos meant to them. The posts from people who, because of physical reasons or anxieties, weren't able to travel the world the way Gabe was, were the most touching.

That had been her not that long ago. Sometimes she forgot how it had been when she'd been trapped in a hospital room and, later, her own home. The people she'd watched on YouTube had taken her places she couldn't go as she'd undergone treatments. Places she'd wondered if she'd ever be able to go if the treatments were successful. So she understood where those viewers were coming from, and yet it was all compounded for her because of the fact that Gabe had come to mean more to her than any of the people she'd ever watched on YouTube.

Overcome with the thought, Maya laid her head on her arms on the desk and let the tears come. She was painfully crippled by the knowledge that she'd pushed him away out of fear that his adventures would hurt him, only to have him be hurt while doing something that everyone did on a daily basis. It was a horrible thought to realize that she had allowed fear to rob her of time with Gabe, just like her mom's fear had caused her to try to protect Maya from the world. Regret and worry drew more tears from her, knowing just what her fear had robbed her of.

When that wave of emotion had finally passed, she straightened and rubbed the palms of her hands across her cheeks. Deciding that she would take Bennett up on his offer to leave early, Maya went around and shut off lights, closing up the office for the day.

As she drove home, she realized that she needed to prepare herself for a conversation with her dad. Thankfully, it was easier to talk with her dad about something like this than her mom. Her mom would have a million questions, while her dad would probably only have half that many. She really wished, though, that she would hear an update on Gabe soon.

She had no idea how long it would take to fly to Denver and then get to the hospital. Maybe having a conversation with her dad would help to pass the time until the update came in. Hopefully, Bennett wouldn't forget to include her when he updated the others in his family.

"Maya," her dad called out as she walked into the house from the mudroom where she'd slipped off her boots. He'd obviously been watching the security monitor for her arrival and had come to meet her. "How are you doing, sweetheart?"

His concern brought her emotions to the surface again, and she stepped into his arms when he held them out to her. He held her as her tears fell once again, then guided her down the hallway to his office. "Your mom's not home at the moment. Would you rather wait until she got home to tell me about it?"

Maya shook her head. She didn't exactly want to tell her mom about it at all, let alone while her emotions were running so high. Instead of taking a seat behind his desk, her dad walked over to the couch he kept in his office and sat down there with her.

"Talk to me," he said, his usually steely gray eyes soft.

So Maya did. She told him about starting her job and meeting Mitch, and then how everything had changed when she'd met Gabe. How he'd opened up a world to her that she hadn't thought she'd ever have the chance to experience. Then, with growing emotion, she told him about her realization of what his life actually consisted of and her decision to cut things off with him.

"So he was injured on one of these adventures?"

Maya gave a laugh that ended on a sob. "No. He was crossing the parking lot of his apartment building in Denver when he and a friend were hit by a truck."

"Did you love him, sweetheart?" her dad asked in a gentle tone, one she doubted anyone but she and her mom heard. "Do you still love him?"

Chapter Nineteen

AYA LET OUT A BREATH, her shoulders slumping as she pressed a hand against the ache in her chest. "I do. I thought it would get easier if I ended things with Gabe, but it didn't. And all I can think about now was how useless what I did was. In the end, Gabe still got injured, and it was while doing something that shouldn't have been dangerous at all."

Her dad slipped an arm around her shoulders and pulled her close. "I know it's hard not to make decisions out of fear. It's something your mama has struggled with too."

Maya nodded. "Yes, I know. And you would think that I'd have learned my lesson from her, but obviously, I haven't."

"What do you want now?" her dad asked.

"What I want, and what I deserve are two different things." She drew a shuddering breath. "I turned Gabe away. I refused to consider any other option, convinced I was going to lose him or worse yet, he'd come to resent me because I forced him to change his life."

Silence fell between them for a couple of minutes. Maya wasn't surprised that her father had no response. After all, what could he say? She'd had a chance to grab onto life and love and hadn't taken it. There wasn't much more to it than that.

"If he felt about you the way you felt about him, then maybe hope isn't lost. Maybe you still have a chance."

She gave him an indulgent, teary smile. Only her dad would think that. "I have a feeling that me butting back into his life right now is probably the last thing Gabe needs."

"Don't be so sure about that." Her dad leaned back against the couch, crossing his arms. "Love can be a powerful motivator, and if he's in bad physical shape, Gabe may need that motivation."

Maya pulled her legs up, hooking her heels onto the edge of the couch, wrapping her arms around her knees. "I don't know, Daddy."

"I'm not saying that you need to rush to Denver to talk to him right now, but maybe when he comes back to Winnipeg, you two will have a chance to talk again."

Maya didn't want to get her hopes up. She'd rejected Gabe—that was the hard fact—so how could they get past that? Would Gabe even *want* to get past it?

THE DARKNESS SEEMED to weigh down on Gabe, and his eyelids refused to open. Fuzziness blanketed his mind, keeping it from being able to put together the pieces of memory that kept popping up. On the edge of the fuzziness was the awareness of pain. It wasn't overwhelming him, but Gabe couldn't figure out why it was there. And why he couldn't open his eyes.

"We're keeping him sedated for now," Gabe heard a female voice say. "His body has obviously gone through a severe trauma, and it will be best if he can just heal without moving around. Pain control will also be an issue when he wakes up. Hopefully, keeping him sedated for now will help him over the worst of the pain."

"So everything went okay during surgery?" His dad's voice.

"As well as can be expected. He's young and in good shape. Those are things that are definitely in his favor. The next twenty-four hours will be the most crucial in his recovery."

"When do you think we could have him transferred home to Winnipeg?" This time it was Bennett's voice.

"Again, we'll have to see how the next twenty-four hours go. I wouldn't recommend moving him until he's stable. He's going to have a challenging journey ahead of him considering the internal healing that needs to take place along with the injuries to his leg."

Gabe fought against the fuzziness. He needed to know what they were talking about. What had happened? He couldn't remember. Couldn't recall where he'd even been. But try as he might, he couldn't beat the fuzziness, and soon it covered him completely, forcing him back into oblivion.

THE NEXT TIME HE CAME TO, the pain that had been on the edge of his awareness had moved in further, overtaking him. Gabe had experienced pain in his life, but this…this was more than anything he'd ever faced before.

He groaned and managed to open his eyes a crack. There was only a dim light wherever he was, and he was thankful.

"Gabe?" He heard his mother's voice and then a gentle touch on his cheek. "Are you awake, sweetie?"

"Mom?" The word didn't even sound like it was his voice, but his throat hurt, the pain letting him know he'd actually said the word.

"Oh, Gabriel, honey." More soft touches on his cheeks. "Can you open your eyes?"

With effort, Gabe managed to lift his lids far enough to see his mother hovering over him. Her eyes looked damp with tears as she gazed down at him. "Mom?"

"It's okay, sweetie. You're going to be fine." The reassurance of her words was in direct contrast to the worry in her eyes.

"What. Happened?" Gabe asked then swallowed hard. "Thirsty."

"Hello, there, Gabe." A female in a white coat came to the bed opposite where her mom stood. "How are you feeling?"

"Thirsty. Pain."

A nurse appeared beside the doctor with a cup in hand. It turned out to be a cup of ice chips which his mom fed to him as the doctor continued to talk to him, asking him questions he could answer with one word. He still didn't know what had happened, and he needed someone to tell him. There had clearly been an accident, but where? And how?

The doctor told him what they were doing for pain control. Thankfully, they must have done something as soon as they'd realized he was awake and in pain because the intensity of it had begun to ease as the doctor talked. But at the same time, exhaustion began to pull at him once again.

The doctor finally left after giving him a reassuring smile and a squeeze on the shoulder. He looked up at his mom, fighting to keep his eyes open.

"What happened?" He was desperate to understand what had put him in the hospital. From what he did remember, it didn't make any sense. He had been in Denver, so he hadn't been off on an adventure unless he had decided to go somewhere that he didn't remember.

"You and Matt were hit by a truck in the parking lot outside your apartment," his mom said, her brow furrowing.

Gabe let his mom's words sink in. Hit by a truck? That made no sense to him. But then something else his mom had said registered. "Matt? Is Matt okay?"

She nodded. "He had surgery as well, but he's awake and stable. You were injured worse than he was."

He tried to take a deep breath but stopped when the pain in his rib cage increased. "A truck hit us?"

"Your friends said you'd gone out to get some food for a party you were having, then Matt told us that the truck headed straight for you. It appears, from what the police have said, that the driver had some sort of medical incident while he was driving."

"Is the driver okay?"

His mom nodded. "The guy wasn't injured at all, but he'll be a while recovering from his heart attack."

Gabe's eyelids dipped, but he managed to drag them up and fix his gaze on his mom. "Is Dad here?"

"Yes. He, Bennett and Mitch are all here. Your dad is with Matt right now." His mom frowned. "His family hasn't come."

That didn't surprise Gabe. "His family doesn't really have much to do with him."

"I'm so sorry to hear that."

Gabe wanted to tell her more, but he just couldn't keep fighting, so when his eyes closed again, he didn't bother to try and open them. He let the exhaustion win as sleep pulled him under yet again.

MAYA WAS INTO THE OFFICE early in hopes that Makayla had some news about Gabe. Last she'd heard, he was still sedated. He'd come through the surgery fine, though, and that was a relief to hear. Now it was just a matter of time for him to heal from his injuries.

"He woke up!" The words grabbed Maya's attention, and she swung her chair around to see Makayla coming toward her desk. "Mom just called to say Gabe woke up and talked to her. He doesn't remember the accident, but otherwise, his memory appears to be intact. She said he seems to be in a lot of pain, but they're working to control it."

"That is so good that he's awake." The relief Maya felt was immense. She didn't care that there was no future for the two of them as long as Gabe was okay. That mattered more than anything. "Did the doctor say if he'd be able to be airlifted back to Winnipeg?"

"He's not stable enough yet, but they're hoping that in a few days he might be." Makayla sat down in the chair next to Maya. "Bennett told me how you've helped out."

Maya couldn't think of what to say, so she just nodded.

"I hope it was okay that he told me," Makayla said as her brows drew together.

"It's fine. I assumed that he would."

"Why didn't you tell us?" she asked.

Maya paused for a moment before she told Makayla more of her story. More of the details that she hadn't given to Bennett.

"I hope you know that we wouldn't have treated you any differently," Makayla said.

"I know that now, but I didn't know that at the beginning. Plus, it wasn't really something that you could work into the conversation, you know. Hey, I've had cancer, not once, but twice. And oh yeah, my dad is one of the richest men in the world."

Makayla laughed, her expression losing the tension of the past few days for just a moment. "Yeah. I guess that's true."

"After spending so many years of my life protected and somewhat secluded, I just wanted to be…normal. You know?" Maya looked down at her hands. "My job here has helped a lot with that. You and your family. Gabe. It's all given me a glimpse into a type of life I've not had before. Not just because of my cancer, but because of the money I have and who my dad is."

"Right now, I'm extremely grateful for you and your dad. What you've done." Makayla paused, swallowing hard. "It's taken a lot of the pressure off, knowing that there is someone there to help smooth out the details. Plus, having a way to get Bennett and Mitch to Colorado quickly was an answer to prayer. When we realized they might not be able to fly out until the next morning, we began praying for a way to get them there sooner."

"I'm just glad that I had the ability to offer help."

"I know that things didn't work out with you and Gabe, so I'm especially grateful that you were still willing to help out."

Maya looked away from Makayla. "I didn't end things because I didn't care for Gabe. I did it because I cared too much for him." She explained her reasoning to Makayla, even though now, in the light of Gabe's accident, it didn't seem as important as before.

"I figured it was something like that, and I understand completely. I don't think I could have been with someone that lived like Gabe either." Makayla rested a hand on her stomach. "Life is something to be cherished. I'm hoping that maybe what's happened with Gabe will give him a different perspective on things."

Maya hoped that too, but if Gabe *did* have a different perspective, so did she. In some ways, given her past, it was a perspective she should have had already. *Life is so short.* Gabe was proof that a person could live an adventurous life and then get hit by a truck crossing a parking lot.

"Will you give Gabe another chance?" Makayla asked.

Maya shrugged. "I'm not sure he wants one. It seems like maybe he has other things he needs to focus on right now."

"Maybe. But maybe you should keep an open mind where he's concerned. He's going to need a lot of support over the next…whoever knows how long."

Maya wanted to be there every step of the way for Gabe, but for now—until she knew what he was thinking—she was just going to stay in the background, offering whatever support she could that way. "I will always be there for Gabe, whether or not there's ever anything between us."

Makayla stared at her for a moment then nodded. "Thank you for caring for him and for our whole family."

After Makayla had returned to her office, Maya tried to get right back to work, but she couldn't help thinking about Makayla's question. Of course, she would give Gabe another chance. The bigger question was whether Gabe would want one, and considering the way she'd ended things, she wasn't too sure that he would.

Chapter Twenty

*G*ABE STARED AT THE DOCTOR, willing her to say the words he'd been waiting a week to hear: that he could be transferred to the hospital in Winnipeg. As much as he loved Denver, he wanted to be home.

When he'd left for Denver in February, he'd felt like he was leaving home. Not just *a* home, which had been the case when he split his time between Winnipeg and Denver, but *his* home. There was no question that he'd left his heart in Winnipeg—even though the person he'd left it with hadn't wanted it.

But regardless of that, he wanted to be closer to his family. Thankfully, Matt was doing better, and Damon was more than capable of helping him through his recovery. The rest of the group would step up to help Matt as well. This turn of events, however, meant that neither of them would be traveling anytime soon. How that would impact the remaining commitments he had for the year, Gabe wouldn't know until he'd had the chance to heal a bit more.

And he wanted to do that healing at home.

"I think we can safely say you're good to travel," the doctor said, shoving her hands into the pockets of her white coat. "You've made good progress this week. Better than I would have anticipated, to be honest."

"It's because of all the people he has praying for him," his mom was quick to point out.

Gabe had expected a skeptical look from the doctor at his mom's words, but instead, she just nodded. "There is no denying the improvement. After all my years of doctoring, I've learned never to dismiss the role a patient's faith plays in their recovery."

"Thank you for all you've done for him," his dad said as he came to stand next to his mom. "You've made a difficult situation a lot easier."

"You're very welcome. Seeing a patient well enough to move on is the most gratifying part of this job." She gave Gabe a smile. "I've forwarded all your medical records to the doctor in Winnipeg as you requested, and we've had a couple of conversations as well, so you're good to go."

Gabe knew he had a bit of a journey ahead of him, but right now, all he was focused on was getting himself back home. Once he was there, he would deal with the difficult news he'd received the previous day with regards to his leg.

He looked over to where his mom and dad stood. "How soon can we get out of here?"

"All we gotta do is let Brad know we're ready to go, and the plane will be prepared."

Gabe nodded, still reeling from the news that the woman he'd dated ever so briefly was part of a super wealthy family. It certainly explained the mystery he had sensed about her, and her unwillingness to share too much about herself. Was that part of the reason she'd ended things with him? He supposed that regardless if it was, he was grateful that she had so generously stepped up and helped his family.

Though Gabe hadn't wanted to go to the hospital in Winnipeg, the doctor there and his doctor in Denver had insisted it was necessary. He had a feeling that even if the doctors had been willing to let him go home, his mother still would have insisted on hospitalization. So, instead of fighting them on that, Gabe insisted on something of his own.

He wanted to see Matt before he left.

Since Matt was in better shape, they brought him to Gabe's room in a wheelchair. Gabe's first look at his friend would have been alarming if he hadn't seen himself in the mirror already. Matt was sporting some of the same bruisings on his face though Gabe's was worse since he'd borne the brunt of the fall. His friend also had a cast on his arm from hand to shoulder. Though he wished they could have been spared the injuries they'd each received, he was glad that Matt wasn't any worse.

"Hey, buddy!" Matt exclaimed as the nurse wheeled him into place next to Gabe's bed. "You are looking a little worse for wear."

Gabe grinned, ignoring the pain the action caused. "You're one to talk. Looks like you got a little road burn on your face too."

Matt gave a shake of his head. "More like parking lot burn."

In the week since the accident, bits and pieces of the incident had come back to Gabe, but for the most part, he couldn't remember much of what had happened. After hearing accounts from others, it was probably just as well. He was dealing with some negative feelings toward the driver of the truck even though he was aware that it had been something beyond the man's control. If it had been drug or alcohol related, the anger would have been much more intense. Still, he couldn't allow his thoughts to linger too much on the accident or what lay ahead for him because he had already discovered that doing so brought an immediate flood of negativity into his mind.

He and Matt talked a bit about their upcoming commitments and the impact their present situation would have on them. Damon had already contacted the companies to let them know what had happened since he was supposed to have accompanied them on the scheduled trips. There weren't any firm plans yet if they would be rescheduled, but Gabe had a bad feeling that even if they were, he wasn't likely to be part of them.

"So I guess we'll be making use of Skype," Matt said, rubbing his hand up and down his cast as if his arm itched or something. "I need to know how you're doing on the daily, man."

Gabe nodded. "I'll do my best to keep you updated. It's not like I'm going to have much else to do for the next little while."

His dad's phone rang, and when he got off a couple of minutes later, it was with the news that the plane was ready to go. Given that Gabe's departure was imminent, Sammi had flown in on the plane the day before and would be monitoring him during the flight home. She'd met with the doctor to get instructions for the flight and was ready to put her nursing skills to good use to get him back safely to Winnipeg.

Matt didn't stay much longer, offering his uninjured hand for Gabe to grip before he let the nurse wheel him from the room. Gabe watched his friend go, wondering how long it would be before he'd see him again. Though he did want to get back to Winnipeg, it was hard to imagine leaving his friends behind. All of them had stopped by several times over the week to check on him. It made him appreciate their friendship even more.

"Well, are we ready to get this show on the road?" Brad asked as he entered the room. "We've got a private ambulance on standby whenever you're ready to go."

With his words, the doctor gave the go ahead to prep Gabe for the trip to the airport and then the flight home. Brad had been a godsend, a help that his family couldn't have even imagined. Any issues that had come up, Brad had—with his dad's permission—stepped in to handle. Whether it was rental cars or the ambulance to the airport, Brad had dealt with it all, allowing his parents and siblings to just concentrate on him. Gabe hoped that some day he'd be able to meet the man behind all this generosity so that he could thank him.

And hopefully, he'd be able to thank Maya too. If it hadn't been for her talking to her dad, the past week would have been even more stressful than it had been. And most likely he wouldn't have been heading home to Winnipeg.

The whole process of getting to the airport and then back to Winnipeg was long and exhausting for Gabe. By the time he made it to his room in the hospital—a private room once again arranged by Mr. Zevardi—Gabe was more than happy to sleep as per the nurse's suggestion.

"HE'S BACK IN WINNIPEG."

Maya smiled at Makayla's announcement. While it really didn't mean anything different for her—whether he was in Denver or Winnipeg, he was still out of her reach. So, while she knew it didn't mark a change for her, it was very important for his family. She knew that Makayla and Tristan had been able to Skype with Gabe, but it was nothing compared to actually being able to see him in person.

"Are you guys heading up to see him?" Maya asked, noting the purse slung over Makayla's shoulder.

"Yes. Are you okay to close up?" she asked as Ethan joined her.

"Sure thing." Maya wanted to tell them to say hi from her, but instead, she just smiled, ignoring the ache in her heart as best she could.

"I can't wait to see him," Makayla said. "Bennett might be in a bit later, but if not, just lock up at five."

Maya nodded. "I'll see you guys tomorrow."

She watched as they left the building, wishing she could go with them. There was a bit of a battle going on within her. She wanted to claim friendship so that she could go see Gabe, but in her heart, she knew that what she felt was so much beyond friendship. Maya didn't know how to be friends with Gabe when she still felt so much more for him.

Left alone, she tackled the project she'd been working on for Makayla. Phone calls and emails helped to keep her busy as well. When Bennett showed up around four, he had a broad smile on his face.

"Welcome home," Maya said. She'd been surprised that Bennett had spent the whole week in Denver, especially after Gabe had stabilized, but it was a testament to the Callaghan and McFadden family's closeness.

"Thank you," Bennett said with a nod of his head. "I'm glad to be back. I've just stopped by to check on a few things before heading home. Can't wait to see Grace and baby Olivia."

"I'm sure they've missed you," Maya observed.

"Not as much as I've missed them. This whole thing has been difficult. With it being just over a year since Franklin's death, this has been a hard week for Grace, especially with me being away. I just want to hold them both in my arms again."

Maya saw the love in Bennett's eyes, and it was an emotion that she had a sudden understanding for because it was what she felt for Gabe. She knew the journey Bennett and Grace had taken to get to this point, and she was happy for them. It was too bad that she hadn't been able to get a similar end to her own journey with Gabe.

"Does your dad happen to be in the city?" Bennett asked.

"Not at the moment," Maya said with a shake of her head. "He flew out to New York yesterday, and then he's heading on to Zurich. I think he said that he'd be back in a week."

Bennett's brow furrowed. "Did he need the jet?"

Maya shook her head. "He was able to rent another one to get to New York. Brad and the jet are probably already on their way to New York. He'll have it for travel to Zurich and then home."

"I'm sorry if he was inconvenienced by being so generous with his jet."

Maya laughed and shook her head. "You don't have to worry about that. My dad is rarely inconvenienced by anything. He has enough money to buy himself another jet if he wanted to, so don't worry at all about that."

"Well, when you talk to him next, can you let him know that we'd like to meet with him, if he has the time."

"I'll let him know," Maya said. She knew from conversations she'd had with her dad that he'd be happy to meet them. Brad had kept him updated as well as he had Maya. In the end, it had seemed her dad was as invested in what was going on in Denver as Maya had been. "I'm sure he'd be happy to meet you and your family."

"Great. I look forward to it." Bennett gave her another smile then moved down the hallway to his office.

He wasn't there very long before he left, briefcase in hand. Alone in the office again, Maya went through her end of the day ritual of checking email, switching the phone over to the answering service and shutting off lights throughout the building. The sun was still shining brightly as she left the office, the polar opposite of how things had been at the beginning of the year when leaving the office at five had meant it was dark outside already.

Once in her car, Maya sat for a moment, fighting the urge to turn her car toward the hospital where she knew Gabe had been taken. But she didn't know how to get past how she'd ended things with him. Sadness filled her as she thought of the mess she'd made of the situation. She would have liked to blame it on her inexperience, but the reality was that fear had driven her decision. Fear had taken her prisoner as much as it had held her mother in its grip. While her mom seemed to be escaping from it, Maya was still caught up in the consequences of allowing fear to govern her decisions.

Resolutely, she started her car and headed for home. Knowing that Gabe was so close and yet so far away seemed to deepen the sadness within her. She'd been battling this sadness ever since she had told Gabe things wouldn't work between them, but this... It was getting so much more difficult to deal with.

She swallowed hard, not wanting to be an emotional mess when she got home. Her mom was still unaware of what had happened that week. Thankfully, her dad had agreed to not tell her about it. Maya had no idea how her mother would react, so she just hadn't wanted to deal with it. The emotional stress she was already under was more than enough. She didn't need her mother trying to interfere in everything, telling her how she should be feeling.

Once home, she made it through dinner, talking with her mom about her dad's trip and the latest fundraising effort her mom was a part of.

"Your dad wants me to join him in Zurich," her mom said as they finished their meal.

"Are you going to?" Maya asked. Not that long ago, her mom would have said no, but now Maya was not sure what her response would be.

Since her mom had accepted the way Maya was spreading her wings, she'd begun to leave Maya alone for longer stretches of time, which was fine by Maya. She was thrilled that her parents were able to spend time together in a way that they hadn't been able to in recent years, since her mother had refused to leave her alone during the treatments or the times afterward, even once she'd been in remission for years, it was nothing short of a miracle that she was even considering a trip to Zurich.

"Will you be okay if I do?" her mom asked, lifting her mug to take a sip of her after supper tea.

"Of course, Mama. You've gone away a few times now, and I've been fine."

"As long as you're sure."

"I'm positive."

Her mother smiled, joy lighting up her face in a way that it hadn't for many years. The return of her mother's joy helped to ease a bit of the sadness in Maya's heart. More than anything, she wanted her mom to be happy again. To be able to live her life without the constant worry of what was to come for her daughter. It was somewhat ironic that while Maya's attempt to spread her wings had ended up bringing joy to her mother, she was left with heartache and sadness. If only it could have ended well for both of them.

"Are you okay, sweetheart?" her mom asked, concern replacing the joy on her face. "You've seemed kind of down lately. Is something going on?"

"I'm okay, Mama." Maya pulled her shoulders back and lifted her chin, smiling as she did. She didn't want to lie, so she stayed as close to the truth as possible without spilling her soul. "Just got some stuff on my mind. Nothing you have to worry about."

They had been so close for so long, she wasn't sure if her mom would accept what she said, but when she didn't press, Maya breathed a sigh of relief. She contemplated telling her mom everything, but the idea didn't feel any better than it had earlier. Though it was tempting to share, she had a feeling that her mom would have a more negative outlook on Gabe and his life choices, and Maya didn't want to hear that right then.

They reverted to small talk as they finished off their tea, then Maya helped Elisse clear the table before heading up to her room. Not too long ago, the sanctuary of her room—being alone there—had been a solace for her. Now, however, it was like the sadness that she managed to keep under control while outside her room, began to unfurl and seep into every part of her body the minute she stepped across the threshold.

So, like she did every other night, Maya ran herself a bath, brushing aside the tears that silently tracked down her cheeks. She hated how weak she was when it came to her emotions. She wanted to be able to accept what she'd done so she could get past the heartache, but it just didn't seem to be happening. Every day the sadness seemed to get worse, not better.

How was she supposed to get on with her life when she spent all day trying to seem like she was doing fine only to fall apart after she got to the safety of her bedroom? That wasn't moving on. That wasn't getting over things. The sadness dominated her life in a way she'd never thought possible.

How did someone get over a broken heart? Initially, Lainie assured her that the pain would pass, but Maya was beginning to think that her friend hadn't loved the previous men in her life the way Maya loved Gabe. She'd admitted as much when she'd talked about how she felt about Stewart in comparison to her ex-boyfriends.

On the previous Sunday, the pastor had preached about finding joy in whatever circumstances a person might be. Maya had questioned that at the time, and she questioned it again as she sank into the warm water in the tub and stared up through the skylight to the dark sky beyond, the stars blurry through her tears. She wasn't sure what joy she could find in her current circumstances…the ones she had created herself.

She didn't deserve a second chance with Gabe, so she wasn't about to ask for one. If there was one positive thing in all of this, it was that Gabe was still alive. That was something she would be eternally grateful for. The heartache, even with Gabe still alive, would be nothing compared to how she would have felt if he'd died. So maybe she needed to find joy in the fact that Gabe was still alive, even if she wasn't in his life anymore.

GABE GLARED AT THE CAST that ran from his foot to his hip. How was he supposed to live like this? He couldn't walk and—from what the doctors had said—when he managed to walk again, it would most likely be with a limp. And apparently, no one could tell him if he'd ever be able to climb again. Or ride his mountain bike. Or hike. Over half the adventures he loved to do might be things he couldn't do again. What kind of life was that going to be?

Discouragement threatened to overwhelm him, but Gabe tried his best to push it aside. He was alive. Over and above everything else, the fact that he and Matt were alive was something to rejoice about.

Also, something to rejoice about was that he was home. After five days in the Winnipeg hospital he'd been released. Now he was staying at his parents' place, relegated to a small guest bedroom on the main floor, but he at least had his own bathroom. And more than his fair share of "nurses."

Hearing voices coming down the hall, he quickly slid down the bed and leaned back against the pillow, closing his eyes. He'd been checked on less than fifteen minutes earlier. Surely he was due for some peace and quiet. If he'd still needed that type of care, he should have stayed in the hospital.

"You awake, bro?" He felt Mitch jostle the foot on his good leg.

Knowing he couldn't fool his twin, Gabe cracked one eye open and saw Mitch standing beside his bed, his hands full of…food. He had a large pizza box balanced on one hand with a two-litre of soda tucked under his arm.

"Hungry?" Mitch asked as he put the soda on the nightstand and reached out to pull a chair from the desk in the corner.

"Oh yes. Mom's food has been great the past few days, but I could really do with something a little less healthy."

"I'm actually here for double duty," Mitch said as he set the pizza box on the edge of the bed and opened it.

"Double duty? Please tell me you're not here to babysit me if Mom and Dad have to go out."

"If only. I could hook up a gaming console, and we could play games all evening. That would actually be fun."

Gabe pulled a piece of pizza out of the box, taking the napkin Mitch held out to him. He said a quick prayer for the food before pinning Mitch with a look. "What are you talking about?"

"Apparently Mom has decided you stink and that you need a shower, and since I'm your twin...I get the privilege of helping you out."

"Seriously?" Gabe took a bite of the pizza, not even bothering to hold back the moan of appreciation for the cheesy, tomatoey goodness.

Mitch nodded and finished chewing the bite he'd taken. "She even gave me a huge garbage bag and a roll of duct tape so we can protect your cast."

Gabe couldn't deny that the thought of a shower was appealing, and of all the people to help him with it, Mitch was top of the list. He would have done the same for his brother.

"Then maybe after that we can play some video games," Gabe said. "Goodness knows I could use some excitement in my life. And you could let me win so that I feel even better about myself."

Mitch grinned. "Not gonna happen."

They talked smack for a bit as they managed to eat their way through almost the whole pizza. Gabe knew he needed to watch what he was eating since he wouldn't be exercising to work off the excess calories, but right then, he didn't really care.

"Have you talked to Maya?"

Chapter Twenty-One

*M*ITCH'S QUESTION CAUGHT GABE off-guard. It was the first time anyone had brought her up since the accident, outside of letting him know it was her father that was helping them, and he was surprised—and a bit dismayed—at how his heart beat accelerated at the mention of Maya's name. "No, I haven't."

Mitch finished off his piece of pizza then wiped his hands on one of the napkins he'd brought into the room. "Do you want to?"

"She made it pretty clear that she didn't see things working out for us," Gabe reminded Mitch. "She had her reasons, and I respect them."

"So you didn't have strong feelings for her?" Mitch asked.

"I didn't say that." Gabe scowled as he tossed the crust of the piece he'd been eating into the pizza box. "I couldn't be who she needed then. And now…Well, I definitely can't be, now. Add into that who she is, and there's just no way I could be the right man for her."

Mitch scowled back at him. "Wait a minute. Are you seriously saying that you think Maya feels you're not in her league because of who her father is? Because if you are, I'm going to have to smack you on the head."

"Well, yeah, that's what I'm saying. I also can't believe that her father would think I'm the best guy for his daughter."

"And yet, her dad has done all this stuff for you."

"Dude, you're not that dumb," Gabe said with a shake of his head. "He did it because Maya asked him, not because he wanted to do it for me."

"And why would she want him to do it if she didn't feel anything for you?"

"For you guys? She no doubt could see how upset you all were and then did what she could to help ease that."

"You can claim to have the looks in this twinship, but clearly I have the brains." Mitch stretched out his legs and crossed his arms. "I think you're just scared, frankly."

"Well, everyone is entitled to their opinion." Gabe shrugged. "Doesn't mean they're right."

"True. Your opinion, in this particular instance, is definitely not right."

Gabe rolled his eyes but didn't rise to the bait. Truth be told, he didn't want to talk about Maya. He thought about her all the time, and that caused enough pain. Talking about her wouldn't make that any better. Even though she'd given a perfectly valid reason for ending things, with all the knowledge he had about her now, he couldn't help but wonder if there was more to her walking away.

He recalled the pain in her eyes when she'd ended things with him, so he knew that she'd felt something, but it hadn't been enough. When he'd been introduced to Brad and told who he was, Gabe had wondered if he'd still been under the influence of the pain medication.

Maya was Max Zevardi's daughter? The man was well known for being a real estate mogul in addition to owning companies who researched and produced advanced technologies. His companies were said to be preparing to release prototypes for everything from computers to cars far and above what was currently available.

There was no way a man of Max Zevardi's status would accept someone like him as a love interest for his only child. For all that the man had done for him, Gabe would be eternally grateful, and he wouldn't repay the man by pursuing his daughter. Especially when that daughter had ended things between them in the first place.

"I think you need to at least have a conversation with her," Mitch said. "I think she would be receptive to that."

Gabe squelched the hope that flared to life within him. It had been five months since that awful day when he'd found out about Makayla's miscarriage and Maya had let him know there was no future for them. He hated that he was still harboring any type of hope where she was concerned.

"I just can't understand you guys," Gabe groused to his brother. "First you all warn me off her, and now you're encouraging me to get back together with her." He gave Mitch a hard look. "So what changed your minds? The fact that her father is super wealthy? Or that I now have a gimp leg that will likely curtail my adventurous lifestyle? And what makes you think she'd even want to be with me now that I'm injured and will probably never walk properly again?"

Mitch shook his head. "You really are being ignorant right now. I have half a mind to let you wait another day for the shower."

"Sounds good to me. It wasn't like I asked you to come here and do it." Gabe knew he was being difficult, but the truth was that he really was frustrated. He had no doubt that it was partly the comments made by his siblings that had put doubt in Maya's mind about their lifestyles not meshing, so it really chafed at him to be faced with Mitch's observations now.

Maybe she was willing to talk with him. Maybe she wanted to be friends, but Gabe wasn't in that place just yet. Five months later and he was still trying to get his heart to move on.

Mitch let out a sigh and pulled in his legs, leaning forward to rest his elbows on his thighs. He met Gabe's gaze, and the two of them stared at each other in silence. Gabe knew that Mitch wouldn't leave the room without them getting past this, regardless of what he threatened. His twin was the one person who would understand more than anyone else how he was struggling with his injury and with thoughts of Maya.

"Let me go get that garbage bag and do this shower." Mitch got to his feet and left the room.

When he didn't return right away, Gabe wondered if perhaps he'd decided to abandon him after all. He leaned his head back and closed his eyes. The never-ending prayer that seemed to be continually whispered by his heart, of late, rose in volume within him.

Please, Heavenly Father, help me deal with all of this. Please heal my leg completely. Make my heart understand how things are with Maya. Gabe let out a long sigh. He wished he knew why this had happened to him. *Help me understand.*

"Ready to do this?"

Like earlier, Gabe opened his eyes to find Mitch standing by his bed, a black garbage bag in one hand and a roll of tape in the other. "I guess I am."

As he pushed up to a sitting position, Gabe knew that things between him and Mitch were fine. That didn't mean that Mitch wouldn't revisit something that they'd talked about at some point, but for that night, it was done, and he was just grateful that his brother was willing to help him out. Especially after he'd taken out some of his frustration on him.

"Thank you," Gabe said as Mitch peeled off the garbage bag a while later.

"I'm glad to be able to help you." Mitch dipped his head and focused on the tape he was trying to remove from the black plastic. "The alternate ending to that accident is not something I want to consider. So helping you?" Mitch looked up and met his gaze. "I'm grateful to be able to do it."

Maya frowned at Lainie's image on the screen, and when she didn't respond, her friend repeated herself.

"I think you need to go talk to him."

"And tell him what?" Maya asked, wanting an answer to the question that had been plaguing her since Gabe's accident. "That I've had second thoughts? That now that he's had an accident and will likely not be able to continue with his adventures, I'm happy to consider a relationship with him?"

Lainie shook her head. "How about telling him that you love him? That the accident made you realize that having him for only a little while each year is better than not having him at all."

Everything Lainie said was true, but Maya still wasn't sure.

"The truth is, your fear of rejection is going to rob you of something special." Lainie didn't mince words that time. "You rejected him once, I think it's time that you gave him the chance to reject you."

That didn't sound like a good idea to Maya. Rejection was the absolute last thing she wanted. Seriously, who went out of their way to put themselves in a position to be rejected?

"I don't think—" Maya began.

"Stop thinking," Lainie said with a slash of her hand. "Feel."

But *feeling* hurt, and she told Lainie as much.

"Only you can decide if the risk is worth it. And only you can decide if your fear is greater than the regret you'll feel at not having at least tried to see if you can have a future with Gabe."

Nerves warred with the sadness that had been consistently present within her since that day back in February. She knew that Lainie was right.

"Everything still going good with you and Stewart?" She wasn't just changing the subject, she really did care about how things were going with her friend.

Lainie hesitated before a smile lit up her face. "It's going great! His hours are pretty crazy since he's still a resident, but he makes time for me when he can. That's why I want you to take this chance with Gabe. When you talk about him, I understand the feelings behind your words because that's how I feel about Stewart."

Maya nodded, feeling the same way when Lainie talked about Stewart. She wanted to have what Lainie had, but she knew she wasn't going to have it without being vulnerable. "I…I will go talk to him."

"That's my sugar!" Lainie exclaimed with a clap of her hands. "And then I want you to tell me all about it."

The sadness and hurt she'd been feeling for months slowly gave way to a flame of hope. There were still nerves to deal with, though, and they would no doubt be present until she talked with Gabe and had a final answer.

THE NEXT MORNING, Maya got up and dressed with the thought that she was going to be seeing Gabe for the first time in months. So, once her hair and makeup were done, she slipped on the pair of black capris and lavender blouse she'd chosen to wear. After spritzing on a bit of perfume, Maya slid her feet into a pair of black sandals, glad that she'd taken the time to get a mani-pedi with her mom the previous week.

She knew that Gabe was back home at his parents' place, so Maya planned to head over there. It was a bit nerve-wracking to think about showing up uninvited, but she was afraid if she tried to contact him, he might turn her away before she even had a chance to talk to him.

"Heading out, sweetheart?" her mom asked as Maya went into the kitchen to grab a bottle of water. Her mom—who had returned home the previous evening with her dad—was seated at the breakfast nook, a mug and a laptop in front of her.

"Yeah. I'm going to the Callaghans' home." Through the night, as nervous thoughts had circled around in her head, Maya had come to the decision that after talking to Gabe she was going to talk to her mom.

Regardless of the outcome of her conversation with Gabe, Maya knew it was time to tell her mom everything. It seemed that lately, her mom's mindset about life, in general, was improving. And because of that, their relationship had been improving as well. She wanted to take advantage of that and see if they could build a relationship as parent and adult child instead of parent and sick child. It was her hope that her mom would be willing to have that type of relationship with her.

"Is there something going on?"

"Sort of. One of their kids was injured a little while ago, and I was going to go visit them."

Her mom nodded but, surprisingly, didn't ask any further questions. "Your dad and I are meeting Ian and Iliana for dinner."

Maya lowered the bottle she'd been about to take a sip from at the mention of her aunt and uncle. Her estranged aunt and uncle.

"Something come up?"

"Ian called last night and asked to meet with your dad. He decided we would have a social meeting first and go from there."

Maya knew that a lot of the conflict between her dad and his brother had come from her uncle feeling entitled to some of her dad's wealth simply because he was related to him. Her dad was willing to pay for education for any family member and would give jobs to any relative who was willing to work. However, he refused to give out money just so someone didn't have to work when he had worked hard to build his business and still continued to work hard to this day. Maya knew that was one of the main reasons her dad hadn't objected to her getting a job.

"Let me know how it goes," Maya said as she picked up her purse. "I definitely want the details."

Her mom smiled. "I'll take notes."

With a laugh, Maya crossed to where her mom sat and pressed a kiss to her proffered cheek. "Love you."

"Love you too."

Though her nerves had settled a bit during the conversation with her mom, they gradually resurfaced as she drove to the Callaghan home. The last time she'd been there had been on Boxing Day. That had been a day of ups and downs, but Maya hoped that this day would only have ups.

There were a few vehicles parked in the area in front of the house. Maya pulled in beside one of them and sat for a moment, praying that this was the right thing to do. Praying that God would give her the right words to say and then to be able to accept the outcome, even if it was bad. Her relationship with God had changed a lot since the beginning of the year. From not thinking about God much at all for a lot of years to finding a peace and joy she hadn't really experienced before.

And it was that peace she felt as she prayed that God would help her to accept His will for her and Gabe—whether it was for them to be together or apart.

The knock on her window made Maya jump and open her eyes. She turned to see Mitch standing there, a curious look on his face. As she lowered the window, Mitch dropped down into a squat beside the car.

He braced his folded arms on the open window. "Hey, Maya. What're you doing here?"

Maya hesitated. Nothing about Mitch's demeanor made it seem like he thought she shouldn't be there. "I came to see Gabe."

Chapter Twenty-Two

ITCH'S FACE LIT UP, and for a moment, she saw a flash of Gabe in his expression. "That's great."

He pushed to his feet and opened her door. Maya turned off the engine and grabbed her purse before unbuckling the seat belt and getting out. "Thank you."

Mitch closed the door then gestured to the house. "He hasn't been feeling so hot today. Maybe you can put a smile on his face."

Maya hesitated at the bottom of the steps. She didn't have Mitch's confidence that her visit would make Gabe happy. "Maybe I should visit when he's feeling better."

"No. I think today is perfect." He gave her another smile as he held the door open for her. "He's in the guest bedroom on the main floor." Mitch paused as they walked into the house. "Like I said Gabe's struggling a bit today. He hasn't gotten out of bed yet, which is unusual for him. So be prepared, but I think seeing you will help him a lot."

Clutching her purse strap, Maya followed Mitch down the hallway past the kitchen and living room. They heard voices as they drew closer to the bedroom, and once again she wondered if this was a good time.

"I'm fine, Mom," Gabe said, and even though she'd heard his voice on videos over the past few months, hearing it in real life caused her eyes to sting.

"You're not fine if you're still in bed," Emily Callaghan said, her concern evident in her words and her tone.

"Just wait here for a minute," Mitch said in a low voice then left her in the hallway while he went into the room.

Maya heard some murmured conversation before he reappeared with Emily right behind him. Her smile was warm and welcoming when she spotted Maya.

"You're here to see Gabe?" she asked softly as she came to Maya's side. When Maya nodded, she said, "I'm so glad to hear that. I think he needs to see you."

"Why don't you go on in?" Mitch suggested, then moved aside to let her pass. She glanced at him one last time before stepping into the room.

It was a small-ish room—although she realized that compared to her own room, most rooms seemed small—and decorated in shades of gray and yellow. There was a queen size bed flanked by two nightstands, and in the bed lay Gabe.

The covers were tossed to the opposite side of the bed so she could see he was dressed in a worn T-shirt and a pair of long gym shorts. On his left leg, she spotted the cast that almost fully encased his leg from foot to hip. He lay with his head on the pillow, his eyes closed.

On silent steps, she approached his bed and sat in the chair beside him. He suddenly took a sniff then his eyes popped open, his gaze immediately landing on her.

"Maya? I thought that was your perfume."

The idea that he recognized the scent she wore and associated it with her gave Maya a bit of encouragement. She smiled tentatively at him. "I hope it's okay that I've come to visit you."

"It's fine." He stared at her for a moment, his expression unreadable. "How have you been?"

Then it was her turn to stare. *How had she been*? "Worried."

"Worried?" Gabe asked as he struggled to push himself up to lean against the headboard. "About me?"

She supposed it was her own fault that he didn't realize what he meant to her. What he still meant to her. Or course, she had no idea what she meant to him either, so perhaps it was time for them both to let each other know. "Yes. I've been worried about you."

Gabe didn't reply right away, but then he said, "Thank you for what you had your father do for me and my family."

"He was happy to help, and I was glad he was able to."

"So I guess that kind of explains why you never wanted me to pick you up at your house. I imagine that would have been a pretty big giveaway."

Maya gave him a quick smile. "Yeah. Dad built a ridiculously huge house back before I was born. I think the plan was to fill it with lots of children, so it has some crazy things in it like a movie theatre. A pool. A single lane bowling alley. Stuff like that."

Gabe arched a brow. "Stuff like that? Sounds like a kid's dream house."

"It was for awhile even though I was an only child, but once I got sick, I didn't enjoy it much."

"I guess even having money doesn't guarantee good health."

"No, it doesn't." Maya gave him a rueful smile. "My dad had the best doctors he could find look at my case, and the treatment was pretty straightforward, but even so there was no guarantee of success. Sure, they said it was highly treatable cancer, but really, that didn't help the psychological issue of knowing that the treatment didn't *always* work. My dad's money couldn't guarantee that the treatment would cure me."

"I never would have guessed." Gabe frowned slightly. "About any of it."

"That was what I wanted," Maya told him. "I wanted to be treated like normal. Like just any other person. Not a cancer survivor. Not the daughter of a billionaire. Just Maya. A girl wanting to contribute to something in a positive way. So while I do have some involvement with charitable organizations, I also really enjoy working for C&M because it gives me a sense of purpose. A reason to get up in the morning."

Gabe looked away. "I don't really feel like I have much of a reason these days."

"What have the doctors said?" Maya asked.

"That my leg was basically crushed. I have pins and hardware in my leg that will probably get me stopped every time I have to go through security at the airport. But the bottom line is that I'm probably never going to be able to walk without a limp."

"But at least you're going to be able to walk, right?"

Gabe shrugged. "Probably. With a lot of work."

"Then it's a good thing you're not afraid of work. I've seen that."

He didn't say anything, just closed his eyes for a moment and let out a sigh. "I suppose."

"If I could fight to live, you can fight to walk." Maya waited until his gaze met hers. "I need you to fight, Gabe."

After a moment's hesitation, he asked, "Why?"

And that was her opportunity. The moment she needed to make herself vulnerable. "Because your accident was a wake-up call for me. I thought I would protect myself by ending things between us before they got too serious because even after just a few weeks, I…well, I felt a lot for you. I was scared of what that would mean if I lost you…and then I almost did. And you weren't even doing something dangerous but just walking across the parking lot." She took a deep breath. "I should have known better. I should have known that some time with you—even if it was just a few days here and there—was better than nothing at all. Because when you had that accident, I had a glimpse of what nothing at all would be like when we didn't know if you were going to make it."

"Are you just saying this now because you know I can't go back out and do that dangerous stuff anymore?"

Maya shook her head. "No, because the reality is that you can still do plenty of dangerous things. Believe me, I've watched all your dangerous adventure videos, and yes, while some might not be feasible anymore if you have limited mobility in your leg, plenty of them would still work. Especially the water ones." She gave a brief shudder. "Like your shark cage one."

Gabe's expression was still unchanged, looking the same as when he'd first opened his eyes and seen her. Maya wasn't sure what to make of that. Every time she'd seen Gabe, he'd been smiling or, as was the case with their last conversation, frowning in hurt and confusion. This stoic look was something Maya didn't know how to interpret. She'd just told him that she had feelings for him and wanted another chance, and he'd had hardly any reaction.

Maybe while she'd struggled to accept the decision she'd made and get over him, Gabe had been able to move on. And she could only blame herself if that was the case. It was hard to see him with fading bruises, lips in a tense line and a furrowed brow. He looked so unlike how he had during the weeks they'd spent together, but Maya found herself wanting to be there for him now more than ever.

Before, it was like he had been teaching her how to live, but now, she could teach him how to heal. She understood how discouraging it could be to have a body that wouldn't do what you wanted it to. To be held back by physical constraints.

Her heart longed to be part of his journey. To offer him a place where he could find someone to rejoice with him over his good days and to support him through the bad ones. But maybe that wasn't what he wanted. After all, it wasn't like he didn't already have a huge number of people in his corner. Between his family and his friends, he had a ton of support. Maybe he didn't need the woman who'd walked away from him because she was too scared to take the chance of loving him.

"There were still plenty of things I'd planned to do that will be impossible with a gimpy leg." Gabe rested his fist on his cast, rubbing it against the surface. "I'm finding it a bit difficult to be thankful for the adventures I've already had when all I can think about is what I won't be able to do from now on."

Maya gripped her purse with her hands, realizing that in spite of what Mitch had said, it might not have been a good time to visit with Gabe. There was a part of her that wanted to wish Gabe well and escape to cry her eyes out, but if she wanted to prove to him that she was there for him, she really had to be *there* for him.

Though she wanted him to look up and smile at her, to see that twinkle in his eyes that had first drawn her in, she realized that she was wanting him to make this easy for *her*. However, that wasn't what this was all about. It wasn't about making the situation more comfortable for her.

She remembered well the days during her first round of treatments when she hadn't wanted to smile for her mom. Hadn't wanted to pretend that she felt better than she did. But she'd done it anyway. All she'd wanted was to be able to feel what she was feeling and know that someone was there by her side. Once she'd hit rock bottom and hadn't had the strength to hide how she felt, her mother had realized what she'd been trying to do and had tried to be better about looking for other signs rather than just her words for how Maya was handling things.

Gabe was clearly having a bad day—whether it was physical or emotional really didn't matter. A physically bad day could create an emotional day and vice versa. Maya knew that, and she knew that if she wanted to stay in Gabe's life—as a friend, if nothing else—she needed to remember it. Always.

With that in mind, instead of reassuring him that everything would be okay, Maya reached out and covered his other hand that was fisted against the sheets. Though he didn't look up at her, she saw his head turn in the direction of their hands. When he didn't respond right away, she had to resist the urge to remove her hand. If he wanted to break the contact, he could move his.

After what felt like an eternity, his fist relaxed, and he opened his hand so their palms touched. She wrapped her fingers around the edge of his hand and felt him do the same with hers. Maya blinked back tears as he lifted her hand and pressed it to his lips, holding it there as he took in ragged breaths. It wasn't so much a kiss to her hand as it was a connection. A connection that had been severed for the months they'd been apart.

When Gabe lifted his head, Maya saw his blue eyes were swimming with tears and knew that the man she loved had—for whatever reason—hit rock bottom. Moving carefully, Maya sat on the bed beside his uninjured leg and then leaned forward to rest her forehead on his shoulder. Almost immediately, Gabe buried his face against her neck, tangling his hand in her hair.

"I love you," Maya whispered, knowing that with their proximity Gabe would hear her, regardless of how softly she spoke. "I want to be here for you. If you want me to be."

Gabe's nod came right away, and then he sat back, capturing her face between his hands. "I want you to be—more than anything—but I'm not the man I was back in February."

"But you are." The discouragement Maya saw in his eyes tugged painfully at her heart. She lifted her hands to cover his where they cupped her cheeks. "All the things that make you special are still there. Your leg being injured hasn't changed who you are. Maybe it has changed what you can do, but I know that your zest for life is still there. I know that once your leg has healed, you're going to find a way to feed that zest. It might look a bit different from how it has been up until your injury, but I have no doubt you're going to rise above it." She gave him a soft smile. "And you'll do it all while still maintaining your title as the better-looking twin."

For a moment, Gabe just stared at her and then—there it was—a smile. Not the biggest she'd ever seen from him, but it was genuine, and the worry that had wrapped tightly around her began to ease.

"And don't you forget it," he replied, his smile growing just a bit. The moisture that had been present in his eyes earlier was gone, but his expression grew serious again. "I love you, too, beautiful. I've missed you."

Leaning forward, Gabe drew her face toward his. He pressed several soft kisses to her lips before lingering.

His words and kisses were what finally released the last of the worry and fear that had taken residence in her heart. When he drew back from her a short time later, Maya said, "I've missed you too. I'm so sorry."

"I don't blame you at all. In your shoes and circumstances, I would have done the same thing."

Maya gave him a rueful smile. "Somehow, I doubt that, but thanks for trying to make me feel better."

"I feel better when you feel better, beautiful."

"Do you?" Maya asked. "Do you feel better now?" He opened his mouth to speak, but before he could say anything, Maya pressed her fingers to his lips. "Only honesty between us now, love."

Gabe let out a puff of air against her fingers then nodded. She moved her hand and asked again. "Do you feel better now?"

"Physically? No. Pain and itchiness have been tag teaming me since early this morning, and I couldn't sleep. I hate it. Absolutely hate it."

"The painkillers aren't helping?"

Gabe grimaced as he jammed his fingers through his hair. "I'm trying not to take them unless I absolutely have to."

"I think perhaps you might be in a *have to* situation, especially if you're dealing with something else like itching. Enduring pain when you don't have to doesn't make you a hero, it just makes you cranky. Trust me, I speak from experience."

"I guess if anyone would understand, it's going to be you." He lowered his hand to rub against his cast again. "I just wish the itching would stop. I can't seem to do anything about that."

It seemed that once Gabe began to talk, the words just spilled out of him as he shared what he'd been through over the past couple of weeks. Though she'd heard much of what the doctors had already told him about his break and recovery, hearing it again in Gabe's own words with his emotions mixed in made it more real for Maya. It hurt her to hear it, but when he began to talk about what lay ahead, she wondered if he realized that he was focusing on the future.

Because of her own experiences, Maya knew that one moment of focusing on the future and feeling positive didn't mean the road ahead was going to be smooth and trouble-free. But it would be the memory of these positive moments that would help get them through the rough spots ahead. The rough spots didn't scare Maya. She'd experienced them before and lived to tell the tale. This time around, she'd be doing it at the side of the man she loved, secure in the knowledge that he also loved her.

*G*ABE LOOKED OUT OVER the group that was gathered in the living room of the Airbnb they'd rented in Thailand. He and his friends had decided to take a two-week trip back, focusing on the southern part of the country where—among other things—they planned to go on another kayaking trip. This would be a bit longer kayaking trip since they were only visiting the southern city of Phuket and not all the other locations they'd hit the last time they'd been there.

This was Gabe's first major trip since his accident almost seven months earlier. His leg still pained him, but much less than it used to. This trip to the tropics was definitely a welcome break since the frigid cold weather back in Winnipeg this time of year caused his pain to intensify.

Most the people in the group had been present on his previous Thailand trip. Matt, who was part of their usual group, was there as well, having recovered from his injuries much as Gabe had. New faces in the group this time included Mitch and, more importantly, Maya. This was the first trip they'd taken together, and Gabe knew that Maya was a little nervous about it.

He hoped that this trip would be memorable for her and the first of many they'd take together. And if this trip went as planned, future ones they took together wouldn't require them to bring others along as chaperones.

During their time together that day when Maya had come to see him for the first time after his accident, she had revealed that she'd never told her mom about him, but that she planned to rectify that when she got home later. And she had. When she'd called him that night, it had been with the news that she'd talked with her mom and when Gabe felt ready, Yuka Zevardi wanted to meet him.

Since he'd already wanted to meet Maya's dad to thank him for all his help following the accident, it ended up being a dinner at the Zevardi home which had also included his parents. After that first meal together, the two families had shared many more times together in the months since. Whether it was a birthday barbecue at his folks' house or Christmas dinner at Maya's, their families had gotten along amazingly well.

While his dad and Max Zevardi had bonded over their roles as businessmen—even though his dad had retired—his mom and Yuka had bonded over their children. And while from appearances it seemed that his mom and Yuka would have little in common, somehow, they'd found things—even beyond their children—that drew them together.

Both he and Maya had been thrilled to see how their parents' friendship had blossomed. He and his siblings—especially the younger ones—had enjoyed spending time at the Zevardis' spacious home. They'd watched movies together, bowled numerous times and enjoyed swimming in the outdoor pool during the summer and then the indoor one as temperatures had plunged.

In the months following the accident, he'd come to realize how fortunate and blessed he was to have Maya in his life. His feelings had nothing to do with her money, but rather in her, he had found the strength to get through the rough days. She'd been his encourager when he'd wanted to just give up and walk with crutches for the rest of his life. When he'd lashed out in pain and frustration, she'd been there to soothe him and remind him of what he was fighting for.

She thought he was fighting to once again be able to walk so that he could travel, but Gabe fought every day to be the man who was worthy of the love Maya showered on him. There were days that he wondered if he'd ever be that, but he was too selfish to set her free so that she could find such a man. She was his world, and he would do everything he could to prove how much she meant to him.

He hadn't missed the dangerous side of his adventures at all, but he was glad that Maya had been willing to come on this trip with him. Although they both had responsibilities at home, they had agreed to fit in a few trips each year to places that Maya wanted to see. Gabe had a few ideas as well of destinations he'd been to that he thought she'd enjoy. But first up was this one. During his previous trip, he'd thought a lot about how he wished he could share the experience with Maya, and now he was doing just that.

"Are you ready to head out?" Gabe asked as Maya joined him on the small wicker couch.

She smiled at him, her dark eyes alight with excitement. "I can't wait. I cheated a bit and watched the video of your previous trip here again."

"The video was good, but it really didn't do it justice." Gabe slipped an arm around her shoulder and pulled her close, pressing a kiss to her temple. "I can't wait to experience it all again with you."

Just then, Damon let out a whistle to get everyone's attention. "We're ready to go, so grab your bags and head downstairs. We've got a small bus that will take us to the departure spot."

Gabe waited until everyone else had started down the stairs before he did. Carrying both his and Maya's bags, he moved more cautiously than he might once have. He was experiencing some stiffness in his leg that was most likely due to the inactivity during the long flight from Chicago to Bangkok. Max had tried to get them to take the jet, but both Gabe and Maya had agreed that for the time being, no one needed to be aware of her family's wealth.

Once on the bus, he settled into the seat beside Maya, their bags stowed at the back for the trip to the boat. She turned to look out the window as the bus jerked into motion, and for the duration of their ride, she chatted excitedly about what she was witnessing. Gabe felt a sense of satisfaction, knowing that the joy and excitement Maya was experiencing was more than enough for him. He didn't need the adrenalin rush any longer, and even though he could have done some of the dangerous things he'd done in the past now that his leg was more mobile, the desire was gone. His only desire now was to live his life with Maya and do whatever he could to keep a smile on her face.

ON THE SECOND DAY of their trip, they gathered on the escort boat for their dinner which was no doubt going to be another delicious spread of Thai food. It didn't seem that being on a boat had hampered the ability of the cooks to provide scrumptious fare, in any way.

Their first night on the boat, the sky had been cloudy, blocking their view of the sunset. But as they finished up their meal on the second night, the nearly clear sky gave them a front row seat to the sun sinking slowly toward the horizon. Shades of orange and yellow filled the sky, and Gabe knew that now was his moment.

Maya was in conversation with Sue to her right, so Gabe turned to Mitch. "It's time."

Mitch looked at him then smiled, knowing the role he had to play in this. With the sunset window closing quickly, Mitch got up and went to his bag. He pulled out the phone that Max had sent along with them. When Gabe had met with Max to ask for his permission to marry Maya, the older man had insisted they bring one of his company's prototype phones on their trip so that they could witness the proposal even if they weren't there. So now, using the satellite data the man had also paid for, Mitch got to work.

Gabe slipped his arm around the back of Maya's chair and leaned close. "Excuse me, love. Can I steal you away?"

She glanced at him then smiled. "Of course."

"The sunset is so beautiful tonight, I want to watch it with you."

Maya excused herself to Sue, then got to her feet. She took his offered hand and followed him toward the railing of the boat that faced to the west. Gabe put his arm around her shoulders as she leaned against him, her arm around his waist.

"It's gorgeous. All of this is. I can see now why you like to travel to places like this. Swimming in that cove today was one of my favorite experiences so far."

"Well, I hope to offer you the opportunity to have a new favorite experience."

At his words, Maya turned to look at him, her face awash in the colors of the sunset. "What are you talking about?"

With a glance over at Mitch, Gabe moved his arm in order to take her hands in his. "Maya, I never knew that the excitement I chased was an attempt to fill a void that I didn't even know was there. It was only after I had a taste of your presence in my life that I came to understand that you brought me more than any of those adventures ever could. I think my folks were praying hard for God to change my heart about the way I was living my life, but I'll bet they never imagined that it would happen this way. I always thought that the woman I fell in love with would join me as I chased the adrenalin highs, but once I met you, I knew that wasn't going to be the case. My heart was no longer chasing an elusive thrill, it had found its home with you."

Maya's fingers tightened on his, and her mouth dropped open slightly as he got slowly lowered himself to one knee. As he gazed up at her, he saw a tear escape and run down her cheek, dropping onto their joined hands.

"I love you with all my heart, beautiful, and want to spend the rest of my life at your side. If you'll have me." Gabe took a deep breath as he released her hand to pull the ring from his pocket where he'd placed it right before dinner. "Maya, will you marry me?"

"Yes." Her answer came without hesitation. "Always and forever…yes."

Gabe quickly slid the ring onto her finger so that he could stand and take her into his arms. "Thank you, love. You have made me the happiest man on earth. I can't wait to spend the rest of my life with you."

"I love you, Gabe," Maya said as she reached up to link her fingers behind his neck. "I thank God every day for bringing you into my life, and I ask Him every day to give us many, many years together. But just in case He doesn't, I plan to live each day to the fullest with you. Nothing would make me happier than to do that as your wife."

She went up onto her tiptoes, drawing him down so their lips could touch. They had kissed many times over the past few months, but this kiss, on the boat, in front of the setting sun with their friends and family watching—courtesy of a Skype call for the ones not in Thailand—felt like their very first one.

And while he had, at one time, loved the adrenalin rush that came with risking his life, he now loved Maya's life and the prospect of their life together too much to do the risky things he once had. With her acceptance of his proposal, Gabe now knew without a doubt that while he had been in search of something to give him excitement and a thrill, God had had something far better planned for him.

ABOUT THE AUTHOR

Kimberly Rae Jordan is a USA Today bestselling author of twenty-plus Christian romances. Many years ago, her love of reading Christian romance morphed into a desire to write stories of love, faith, and family, and thus began a journey that would lead her to places Kimberly never imagined she'd go.

In addition to being a writer, she is also a wife and mother, which means Kimberly spends her days straddling the line between real life in a house on the prairies of Canada and the imaginary world her characters live in. Though caring for her husband and four kids and working on her stories takes up a large portion of her day, Kimberly also enjoys reading and looking at craft ideas that she will likely never make.

As she continues to pen heartwarming stories of love, faith, and family, Kimberly hopes that readers of all ages will enjoy the journeys her characters take in each book. She has no plan to stop writing the stories God places on her heart and looks forward to where her journey will take her in the years to come.

Visit Kimberly Rae Jordan on the web:
    Website: www.KimberlyRaeJordan.com
    Facebook: https://www.facebook.com/AuthorKimberlyRaeJordan
    Twitter: @KimberlyRJordan

44114330R00136

Printed in Poland
by Amazon Fulfillment
Poland Sp. z o.o., Wrocław